The
SMUGGLER'S
GAMBIT

The Smuggler's Gambit

First Edition.
ISBN-13: 978-0-9863252-0-5
ISBN-10: 0-986-32520-1

Cover and interior design by the author.
Copy edited by Marcus Trower.

www.sarawhitford.com
www.adamfletcherseries.com

SEAPORT
PUBLISHING

Printed in the U.S.A

To Isaac

You are my greatest inspiration and my most enthusiastic encourager. I hope you enjoy this story.

Love,
Mom

The
SMUGGLER'S
GAMBIT

Sara Whitford

SEAPORT PUBLISHING
Carteret Co.

gam·bit noun \ˈgam-bət\

 —a planned series of moves at the beginning of a game of chess

 —something done or said in order to gain an advantage or to produce a desired result

Full Definition of GAMBIT

 1. a chess opening in which a player risks one or more pawns or a minor piece to gain an advantage in position

 2. a. a remark intended to start a conversation or make a telling point
    b. a calculated move

(From Merriam-Webster's Collegiate Dictionary)

Prologue

ADAM TWISTED UP his nose. He wiggled his cheeks. He contorted his face every way he could to scratch the left side of his nose just below his eye, but it was no use. A torn bit of fabric from the blindfold that was tied around his head was flapping loose in the wind and, irritatingly, brushing against his skin with every gust.

Of course it would've been easier if his hands weren't tightly bound behind his back. To make matters worse, there was that cord tied around his lower legs from his knees down to his ankles. In fact, he could feel that it was cutting off the blood flow to his feet.

Oh well, thought Adam, *at least I'm not vomiting.* That answered a question he'd always wondered about—whether or not he had sea legs. Then again, maybe it was just because the cutter on which he was being held captive was slicing through the water at top speeds, thanks to fair winds and following seas.

If only he could tell which way they were going. As it was, he had no idea. Everything had happened so fast. First, two ruffians forced him into their boat at the tip of a knife. Then, as soon as they had gotten him out of clear sight of the town, Lot, the oaf-like, stringy-haired one tied up Adam's limbs and blindfolded him while Ajax—the shorter goon, who had a heavily scarred face—sadistically dug the knife deeper into Adam's side.

He understandably had a hard time concentrating in the midst of all of the confusion. It was enough of a challenge trying to be compliant while contorting his spine so as not to accidentally end up with a blade in his back. Trying to get some sense of direction from the jerky movements of the boat at that same time would've been impossible. Adam could detect that the men had intentionally made the boat take some unnecessary turns so that he'd be thoroughly confused about their course.

After what felt like hours, he felt the bottom of the boat scraping along sand. They had come to land, but where were they?

Oh God, he thought. *Don't let them leave me in the middle of nowhere.* Adam's heart was pounding. He realized what they were about to do, and he knew why. He had said too much back at the warehouse. He should have never asked Rasquelle about those barrels in that locked room. Now Rasquelle was dealing with the threat of Adam's knowledge as quickly and quietly as possible.

The two men jerked Adam out of the boat and tossed him onto the shore. He was still blindfolded, and his hands and feet were still tied.

"What are you doing?" Adam shouted. "You can't just leave me here!"

"Just watch us!" Lot replied. "Oh, wait. You can't. You're

blindfolded." He cackled sadistically.

"We don't ask no questions," said Ajax. "We take our orders from the boss. He wanted us to get rid of you, and this seems like a right good way to do it."

Adam tried to work his way up to kneel, but one of them came over and kicked him hard so that he fell back down.

"If you're just going to leave me here, this is murder. You're committing murder!"

"No. I ain't stickin you with this knife," countered Ajax. "I'm just leavin you here. I ain't takin your life. God can save you if he feels like it."

"That's right, boy," said Lot. "We ain't murderers. The Almighty might save you, but if he don't, that'll be his decision, won't it? Guess that'll tell you what he thinks about you."

"I know why you're doing this!" said Adam. "But it's not necessary. I won't be a problem. I won't say anything. Please just take me back! Or drop me off at any port—I don't care!"

"We are dropping you off—right here," said Ajax.

"And don't start thinking you're going to ever make it back," said Lot. "If you could see where we were leavin you, you'd know there's nowhere for you to go."

"That's right," said Ajax. "We're hours from Beaufort. Speakin of which, we better be gettin back. And by the way, you'll want to try to wiggle back a bit. Looks like the tide's comin in."

Chapter One

A<small>LL EYES TURNED</small> to Adam Fletcher when he entered the dining area of the Topsail Tavern.

"My, my! Doesn't he look handsome?" Mary Fletcher exclaimed as her son held his arms out to the sides and gave a proud turnabout.

"It's amazing what a waistcoat, coat, and dress shoes can do," said Valentine. "You look like a proper gentleman."

Adam smiled broadly. His brown eyes glistened. He was even more handsome than usual, with his face clean-shaven and his dark, wavy hair pulled back.

"Go on and have a good time," said Mary. She started to walk Adam to the door before she abruptly stopped him. "Wait a minute!" She grabbed his coat sleeves one at a time and adjusted them. Adam was a bit taller than Valentine, whose dress clothes he had borrowed, so the sleeves were a little short. Because they were cuffed, it wasn't hard to bring their lengths down a bit by moving the folds.

As soon as she had him adjusted, he was out the door.

Adam met up with Jackson, a busboy who also worked at the tavern, in front of Jackson's house. They walked the mile to the estate of Richard Rasquelle, a young, successful shipping merchant who was hosting a party for the town, and were impressed before they had even set foot on the property.

The sound of harpsichord music drifted across the lawn. A footman stood at the front gate, instructing partygoers where they should go. The event was already fancier than anything the boys had ever attended.

As Adam and Jackson followed the long walking trail across the lawn and around the house, they were excitedly anticipating what the party would be like. They were not disappointed when they finally reached the back garden, where they found more people than they'd ever seen gathered in one place in their tiny seaport town.

Everyone was wearing their best. In some cases, that meant church clothes, but the wealthier citizens wore finery imported from London and Paris.

"Look at all these people," said Adam.

The boys studied the crowd.

"Ho there! Attendant!"

Someone had tapped on Adam's shoulder. He spun around to see his nemesis standing there before him. Francis Smythe was a spindly young man about his age. He was wearing a curled, blond wig with a tricorn hat and a fancy powder-blue suit.

"Fetch me a drink, would you? And some hors d'oeuvres," Smythe snidely demanded.

"Go get 'em yourself, Smythe," said Adam.

"We're not working here today," said Jackson in an attempt to smooth over his friend's coarse manners.

"Oh really?" chuckled Smythe. "With what you're wearing, I'd assumed you were the hired help. I mean, why else would you be here?"

Adam rolled his eyes. He wasn't going to dignify Smythe's comment with a response.

But apparently Jackson didn't mind answering his question. "The whole town was invited. I reckon near 'bout everybody's here."

"Ha ha. Of course," said Smythe. "You lads would never merit a proper invitation if this were a private party."

"Why are you here, Francis?" asked Adam. "On your daddy's business, I reckon."

"My father is traveling. I came in his stead."

Adam scoffed. "Really? I'd think it might be a conflict of interest, you coming to fraternize with a shipping merchant, what with your father being who he is and all."

Francis hesitated for a moment before he responded. "We like to keep an eye on things."

"Uh-huh," said Adam. "Whatever you say."

"Well, since you boys are probably bewildered at a social function, just watch me. Do as I do and maybe you won't embarrass yourselves too much." At that, Smythe tipped his hat and made his way into the crowd.

"What an ass!" said Adam under his breath.

"Just ignore him," said Jackson. "You know he's only trying to egg you on."

The two of them resumed looking around to see if there was anyone else they knew among the partygoers.

"Who is she?" Jackson exclaimed as he tilted his head in

the direction of an arbor that was covered in climbing roses.

Adam scanned the crowd in that general direction until his eyes fell upon a young lady with honey-blond hair. She was wearing an ivory gown embroidered with pink roses. An older man and woman were conversing with her, motioning at her dress and the arbor, probably commenting on the similarity between the blossoms on the arbor and those on her gown. Adam guessed the girl was about his age. He wondered if she was from out of town—at least he knew he had never seen her before. He would certainly have remembered if he had.

Her hair was put up in the most intricate style Adam had ever seen. It was something that must have been done with the help of one or more servants. Her eyes sparkled in the sun, and once he'd caught sight of her, he couldn't look away.

Suddenly the girl happened to glance over in his direction. She caught him gazing at her and quickly looked away. He, on the other hand, was not embarrassed and made no attempt to hide his interest.

One thing Adam Fletcher did not lack was confidence.

"I'm gonna go talk to her," he said to his friend.

Jackson's jaw dropped. "No, you're not! You can't go up to her! She doesn't even know you!"

"She's about to." Adam grinned, then slapped his buddy on the back and walked away.

He strode across the garden toward the young lady. As he neared the arbor where she was chatting with the elderly couple, he grabbed two glasses of punch from a silver tray that was being held by one of Rasquelle's servants.

Adam threw a quick glance back at Jackson, who stood with his mouth agape as he watched his friend approach this group of people, who were well above the two of them in social standing. Adam stopped short before he interrupted the trio.

"Pardon me, sir," he said to the old man. "I hope you don't mind, but the sun is so bright and these two ladies looked as if they could use a bit of refreshment. Do you mind if I offer them some punch?"

The gentleman, already cheerfully intoxicated, smiled and took a step back and said, "Certainly not, my boy! Very kind of you. Very kind."

Adam first offered a glass of punch to the old man's wife, then offered the young lady a glass, along with a little bow.

"My lady," he said.

The girl demurred as she smiled and accepted the glass.

"What a gentleman," remarked the old woman.

"Indeed," said her husband. "What is your name, boy?"

"Adam Fletcher, sir."

Although Adam was answering the old man's questions, his eyes kept coyly darting back to the young lady.

"I'm Reginald Farrington, Esquire, and this is my wife, Martha."

"How do you do, ma'am?" said Adam, bowing his head.

"Very well, thank you. Mr. Fletcher, you said it was?" said Martha.

"Yes, ma'am."

Mr. Farrington then motioned to the young woman. "And may I introduce you to Miss Rocksolanah Martin?"

"Miss Martin," Adam cooed as he bowed his head. "I'm delighted to meet you. How do you do, m'lady?"

"I'm quite well, thank you." She gave him the obligatory cordial smile and kept her eyes fixed on the crowd, careful to avoid his gaze.

The old man chuckled and said, "Yes, well, my wife and

I were just observing that the roses on this arbor are exactly like the ones—"

Just then a bell was rung from a little stage that had been fashioned on the other side of the garden, and a man at a podium called out to the crowd, "My dear ladies and gentlemen, may I have your attention, please?"

The crowd's murmuring died down, and all eyes turned toward the stage.

The man continued: "Ladies and gentlemen of Port Beaufort, I am delighted to be here with you today, at the request of Mr. Richard Rasquelle, to celebrate his successful start in this town and a promising future."

Some of the audience cheered and offered applause. Others just listened.

"You were all invited here today because Mr. Rasquelle attributes his success to the good people of this town, and on this occasion he wanted to express his gratitude with a bit of fine food and entertainment." The man motioned to the long table set up on the opposite side of the garden near the arbor and then to the musicians, who quickly played a few bars of an upbeat tune.

"Now, I'm assuming you all know me—at least, if you're from Beaufort—but if not, my name is Everett Bell, and my family has been here since we ventured down this way from the Pamlico more than a decade ago."

The Farringtons were speaking to each other in hushed tones. Mrs. Farrington mumbled something unintelligible, then Mr. Farrington said under his breath, "I've been here twice as long and I've never heard of him."

Adam smiled at the old couple. "Me neither," he whispered.

Miss Martin stifled a giggle and said, "Nor have I."

The man at the podium continued his speech. "And in all the time I've been here, I've never known a gentleman as kind, as generous, and as heroic as Richard Rasquelle. And while you may have heard about his greatest deed in the papers over a year ago, you may not know about the depth and breadth of his goodness."

The crowd was attentive as Mr. Bell continued his speech.

Just then, Francis Smythe came to stand on the other side of Rocksolanah. "Miss Martin," he said, bowing to the young lady. "Mr. and Mrs. Farrington."

Adam clenched his jaw and dug his fingertips into his palms in an effort to restrain himself from saying something ungentlemanly. He knew Smythe had only come over to antagonize him.

"Fletcher," whispered Smythe, "I had no idea you knew these fine people."

Adam furrowed his brow at Smythe, then looked back towards the stage in an effort to ignore him. Smythe gave him a cocky grin and then excused himself from their company. Adam, Miss Martin, and the Farringtons turned their attention back towards the man at the podium.

"This man," said Mr. Bell. He stopped speaking and motioned off the stage to where Rasquelle was standing. Rasquelle bowed his head and raised his hand in a reserved wave to the crowd. Mr. Bell continued: "This man is too humble to publicize his good deeds. Those of you who are newcomers to Port Beaufort, or perhaps visitors, may not have heard about this, but not too long after this honorable gentleman set up shop here, he put himself, his crew, and his cargo vessel, *Fortuna*, at great risk in order to rescue another ship that was sinking not far off our coast. That other vessel, the *Sea Sprite*, was carrying not only valuable merchandise from Europe but, more importantly, the most priceless cargo—nearly seventy souls, including several women and children, whose lives would have surely been lost had the aptly named *Fortuna* not been able to come to their rescue that day.

"While some of the cargo containers were lost to the tides, more of them were recovered and, most importantly, not a single life was lost. All thanks to the leadership and bravery of this man and his crew."

The crowd across the garden burst into thunderous applause.

"Ladies and gentlemen," said Mr. Bell, "I'd like to introduce our gracious host, Mr. Richard Rasquelle."

At that, Rasquelle stepped up onto the stage. He smiled self-assuredly and gazed out affectionately over his garden full of guests before he began to speak.

"Dear friends," he said, "I don't know that I can express the deep gratitude I have for all of you who decided to join me here today. And to be honest, we are here because of you. You all have made the success I have enjoyed these last couple of years possible, and I am humbled and most appreciative."

Everyone began to applaud. A few even whistled and cheered.

"Thank you. Thank you so much," he said as he gently raised up his hand to silence the crowd. "I do hope you all are enjoying the food, the music, and the fine company of your friends and neighbors. I hope we can have many more days like this in the future—celebrating our success together as a town."

More applause.

"I'd like to tell you my story, in hopes that for some of you younger fellows, I can perhaps offer a bit of encouragement as you contemplate your futures. I'll admit I haven't always lived in a home like this, or worn finery such as this, or been able to have parties like this one. I wasn't poor by any means, but my upbringing was a rather unremarkable one. Unfortunately, although my father worked hard, he never was able to achieve greatness. He was a follower. He didn't lead. He didn't determine to do whatever was necessary to be successful. One thing I've learned from watching his example—and, granted, he was a good, morally upright man and a kind father, may he rest in peace—is that if you always want to be average, to stay exactly where you are, just continue doing that which you have always done. In his case, it was working as a bookkeeper for a shipping merchant. He never thought he could *be* the shipping merchant, the man in charge. I've learned that if you want excellence—in fact, if you want anything in this life—you have to go after it. You mustn't let anything stand in your way of achieving all that you hope to achieve."

When Rasquelle finished his speech, the party guests began to clap and cheer once more. Adam noticed that his friend Jackson was now standing near him, but Miss Martin was not. He surveyed the crowd, trying to see where she'd gone, but she was nowhere to be found.

When Reginald Farrington noticed Adam looking around, he said, "If you're looking for Miss Martin, she left a little while ago."

"Oh?" said Adam. "I didn't even notice her leave."

"Indeed, she slipped away just as Mr. Rasquelle went up on the platform. Whispered that she had another appointment."

"What a pity. And we only just met," said Adam.

Mr. Farrington shook his head. "My wife and I have met her once before, and we were delighted to see her here today, but we didn't chat long before you arrived. I believe the young lady lives just northeast of here, over 'round Lennoxville Point."

Adam nodded. "I see. Well, I only regret that I was unable to bid her farewell. I'm very pleased to make your acquaintance, however, sir and ma'am."

"The pleasure is all ours," said Reginald. "I noticed you appear to know young Mr. Smythe."

Adam nodded and took a deep breath before he said, "I do, sir," through a forced smile.

"And do you know Mr. Rasquelle personally?" asked Reginald.

"No, sir. Unfortunately, I do not. Although he does occasionally visit our place of employment."

Adam noticed Reginald looking at Jackson when he realized he never bothered to introduce him. "Where are my manners? This is Jackson Willis, a friend and associate."

Jackson extended his hand to Reginald. "How do you do, sir?" He tipped his head slightly to Martha. "Ma'am?"

Martha smiled. Reginald shook hands with Jackson. "Pleased to meet you, young man. So where is it that you two fellows are employed?"

Jackson answered before Adam could say anything. "Oh, we work over at the Topsail Tavern. Well, I should say I work there. Adam and his mother actually live *and* work there."

"Oh, really? What a surprise," said Reginald. "I never would have thought—"

Adam chuckled nervously. "Well, sir, ma'am, we better be going. It was a pleasure to meet the two of you."

"Likewise," said Martha.

"Indeed," said Reginald. "Russell's Tavern is nearer to where we live, so that's where I normally go. But perhaps I'll see you there at the Topsail sometime if I'm over that way."

Adam smiled and nodded. "That would be nice, sir. Hope the two of you enjoy the rest of the party."

He bowed his head and excused himself, then grabbed Jackson firmly by the arm and led him away from the festivities.

"You idiot!"

"What did I do?" said Jackson.

"You had to say all that about the tavern?"

Adam walked ahead at a brisk pace.

Jackson hurried to catch up. "He asked. There's nothing wrong with that. We do work there!"

Adam stopped walking. Jackson did the same.

"But you told them my mother and I *live* there!"

Jackson scoffed. "Well, you do live there."

"They didn't need to know that!" said Adam. "I was trying to leave a good impression. That man is an attorney. You never know what sort of connections can be made through a man like that. What impression do you think he'll have knowing I live at a tavern with my mother—no mention of a father?"

"Well, uh. . ." Jackson stammered. "What would you have told him?"

"I simply would have told him that my family runs the Topsail. It's true, and it sure leaves a better impression than the scant details you chose to share."

Adam's eyes were big, and he cocked his head, waiting to see if Jackson would have a response.

Jackson started to speak but could think of nothing to say. He suddenly motioned over to a bench near the entrance. Miss Martin was standing there talking with Francis Smythe. Adam couldn't believe it. Sure, Smythe was wealthy and the son of a royal appointee—the port's customs agent—but still, Adam couldn't understand how a girl like that would have anything to talk about with someone like Smythe. He seemed so transparently slimy.

Apparently, Adam's gawking was a little too obvious, because Francis turned his pale blue eyes from the conversation just long enough to offer a smarmy smile and shoot daggers from his pupils at his adversary.

Adam and Jackson left Rasquelle's estate and returned to Front Street in silence.

Chapter Two

THE FRIDAY FOLLOWING Rasquelle's party, Adam was working at the Topsail Tavern, like always, when a group of upper-crust boys came in. And what a surprise. Francis Smythe was with them.

They took one of the tables near a window and sat chatting and laughing until Francis finally shouted in Adam's direction, "Boy! You there!"

Adam had just begun taking an order from another customer. He raised up his finger to Smythe, motioning "just a minute," but otherwise ignored him, determined to finish with his current customer. Then he would try to get somebody else to wait on Smythe's table.

Smythe turned to his buddies and whispered something, prompting them all to laugh before he spoke up again. "Hey, Fletcher, do you think you might wait on us anytime soon? We're dying of thirst."

Adam gave an embarrassed smile to his customer and said, "I apologize, sir. One moment please."

The customer nodded in understanding.

"I'll be with you as soon as I'm done helping this gentleman," said Adam, making every effort to not take Smythe's bait.

"Fine, fine," said Smythe. "What choice do we have?" He was quiet for a moment and then said loudly to his friends, "I didn't realize the Topsail Tavern had such slow help!"

Adam glanced over at the bar and tried to motion for Valentine to wait on Smythe's table, but he had no luck. The tavern keeper shook his head and pointed at Adam, then Smythe's table, before disappearing into the kitchen.

Adam shrugged and made his way over to the group of young men.

"What can I get you fellas?"

"We'll each have a pint. Go fetch that first, then we'll give you our orders."

Adam nodded. "Fine. I'll be right back with those."

Francis was trying to show off to his friends by needling Adam, but he was unsuccessful so far at getting him riled up. Adam was used to dealing with rude patrons, and when he returned with their drinks he verbally bobbed and weaved between all of Francis's efforts to provoke him.

But then it happened. Francis ventured into forbidden territory.

"So where's your mother today?" asked Smythe.

"Out making a delivery," Adam responded.

Smythe looked at his friends, raised his eyebrows, and then pressed his lips together, nodding knowingly. "Mm-hm. Is that what they call it nowadays?"

"She's taking food to a widow." Adam hated the fact that he even felt it necessary to qualify his earlier response.

"I see," said Smythe. He smiled and then looked at his friends and chuckled. Adam began to walk away when Francis turned his attention back to Adam, calling out, "Tell me, Fletcher, does the lovely Miss Martin know what your mother does for a living?"

Adam turned back to face Smythe. He wrinkled his brow. "What is that supposed to mean?"

At this point, other patrons in the tavern were beginning to point and whisper as the boys had their increasingly public exchange.

"Ah, Fletcher. I'm only asking if the young lady knows that your mother is a practitioner of, well, shall we say the old profession. I saw you attempting to talk to her the other day, you know. She's just a dream for you, Fletcher."

Adam rushed over to Smythe's table. "You listen to me, Smythe, and listen good. You can say whatever you want about me, about anybody, but you start running your mouth about my mother, and you're gonna find out you've bitten off more than you can chew."

"Oh really?" said Smythe. "Now you see, fellas"—he turned back towards his friends, who were now starting to look a little nervous—"this is what separates us from them. No class, no upbringing. Of course, what else would you expect from the little bastard son of a barmaid?"

One of Smythe's friends nudged him and tried to whisper something to him, but Smythe dismissed whatever he was saying.

"Maybe we should take this outside," said Adam.

"Am I embarrassing you?" said Smythe.

Adam shook his head. "Nope, but I'm about to embarrass

you."

Moments later, Adam and Francis had moved their argument to the docks outside the tavern, followed by a slowly growing crowd of tavern patrons turned spectators.

The boys were in a standoff, just feet apart, when Adam pointed his finger at Francis and said, "I'm going to give you one chance to apologize for what you said."

"Like hell I will," said Smythe. He suddenly ran at Adam, who was stunned by the boy's sudden aggression but was able to hold him off easily just the same.

The boys wrestled with each other. Adam hoped to tire the boy out when Francis attempted to swing at him. Adam's reflexes were too quick, though. He swerved in time to miss the punch and then almost instinctively threw his own, knocking Francis to the ground with a single blow.

"Now get on up and start running your mouth again!" said Adam. "I dare you. You do it and so help me, I'll knock your teeth right out on these docks!"

Francis Smythe tried to get up. Adam's adrenaline surged as he looked down at his opponent, who appeared to be so stunned he couldn't coordinate his limbs enough to pull himself upright. When he finally moved his hand away from his face, Adam could see Smythe's nose was bloody, probably broken, and he was clearly in searing pain. Meanwhile, Adam felt as though he'd broken his knuckles, but he wasn't about to let Francis know that.

Anyone who had just seen the boys, let alone knew them personally, would have placed their bets on Adam. He was a couple of inches shorter than Smythe, but he was muscular and sturdy, whereas Francis was a willowy young fellow, tall and thin, as if a good wind might blow him away.

As Adam saw blood drip down Smythe's face onto his clean, white shirt, he asked him, "What were you thinking? How did you think this would turn out? That I'd be on the ground with a bloody face and you'd be standing over me?"

Adam knew Francis had probably never been in a fist fight, and he couldn't imagine what made him want to start one today. He certainly never wanted to fight with Francis. There was no way it could have ended well, not with him being the son of Ellison Smythe, but now what was done was done, and there was no avoiding the repercussions that would certainly follow.

A mass of spectators had gathered on the docks around the brawling teenagers, including some of the friends who had accompanied Francis to the tavern. They were all pressing in, trying to get a closer view of the action, until the crowd parted to make way for Constable Squires, who was closely followed by one of Francis's friends, who had reported the altercation.

"Alright, boys," said the constable, "you've had your fun for the day."

He snapped his thick fingers and motioned for a couple of men in the crowd to help Francis Smythe get back on his feet.

"Now, what's this all about?" he asked them.

"That peon attacked me!" Francis grunted.

The constable turned to hear Adam's story. "And what do you say for yourself, young man?"

Adam was seething. "He started this! That arrogant ass wouldn't stop running that big mouth of his, and then he ran at me!"

The constable quickly glanced over at Francis, then responded to Adam. "Everybody knows Smythe has a big mouth, but what I want to know is, what caused the fight—and you better come up with something good, Fletcher, 'cause Smythe's here bleedin and you ain't got a scratch."

"He's lost his mind! He came into the tavern and just started talking about my mother," said Adam.

"Everybody talks about your mother," Francis smirked, even as he held a handkerchief over his nose.

"I've already busted your face once. What difference will it make if I do it again?" Adam lunged forward to have another go at Francis, but Constable Squires stepped between them and held him back. "Now just you calm down, Fletcher. You ain't gettin anywhere by fightin with this one."

Adam fumed as Francis cracked a mocking smile.

"You boys need to come with me," said the constable.

"Us boys?" asked Smythe. He looked incredulous. "You mean *he* needs to go with you. And in irons, I'd say."

Squires spun around and leveled his gaze at Francis. "*Both* of you are coming with me. And I don't care *who* your daddy is, Mr. Smythe."

"My father won't like this! He'll be back in town soon, and I can assure you he'll hear all about it."

"I don't care, boy," said Constable Squires.

He grabbed the young men by the backs of their shirts and marched them straight to the magistrate's office.

THERE WAS NOTHING ABOUT Port Beaufort Magistrate's Office that looked judicial. Instead, it just looked like a simple one-story house. The little cedar shingle-covered building was situated catty-cornered across Front Street from the same docks where the Topsail Tavern was located.

The local magistrate, Peter Robins, was only thirty-two-years-old, but he displayed the maturity and wisdom of a man twice his age.

When Squires entered the magistrate's office, he tipped his head and removed his hat before he spoke. "Excuse me, sir."

It was strange for Adam to see a middle-aged man as big and brawny as Constable Lawson Squires show such respect and deference to a man who was young enough to be his son.

"Good day, Constable," said Mr. Robins. "Come right in and state your business."

"Mr. Robins," said the constable, "these two boys were fighting on the docks down by the Topsail."

"I see." The magistrate observed both boys for a moment before asking, "Who started it?"

"Sir, must you really ask such a question?" said Francis.

Adam scoffed and looked at Francis. "You must be joking, Smythe!" He turned his attention back to Mr. Robins. "He started it with that mouth of his!"

Mr. Robins looked directly at Adam and asked, "But did you start the physical altercation, Mr. Fletcher?"

Adam sneered at Francis. "No, but I finished it."

"I want to know what happened. Why were you trying to kill each other?" asked Mr. Robins.

"Come on, sir! I'd never bother fighting with someone like him," said Adam. "I mean, look at him! But I had to. He got out of line. He insulted my mother's honor."

Francis looked at Adam with contempt. "What honor? Your mother's nothing but a harlot barmaid."

It took every bit of self-control that Adam had within him to keep from pouncing on Francis once more.

The magistrate looked as if he could sense Adam's percolating rage, so he motioned for him to settle down before he asked Francis, "Mr. Smythe, tell me, sir: Do you have personal knowledge as it relates to Ms. Fletcher's occupation?"

Francis gasped. "Sir, I am a gentleman! I have no personal knowledge of the local strumpets." He paused mischievously. "But one does hear things. And I heard that Fletcher's mother practices the old profession. And that's how she got him."

He looked over at Adam and sneered.

Mr. Robins walked around to the front of his desk and leaned against its edge. "So, Mr. Smythe, let me understand this correctly. You admit you have no *personal* knowledge about Adam's mother. You also admit your accusation against her character is based on hearsay. Is that a fair assessment?"

Francis wouldn't respond.

The magistrate continued: "So indulge me if you would, Mr. Smythe. If you did not have personal knowledge as to the character or profession of Mr. Fletcher's mother, nor proof, why would you make such an accusation?"

Francis's eyes grew wide. "Because everybody knows it! Adam Fletcher is the bastard son of a loose barmaid, and he's a hot-tempered brawler to boot. I want to know when you intend to lock him up!"

Constable Squires looked at Mr. Robins. Mr. Robins returned the constable's gaze and nodded. Adam said nothing. He knew he'd blown it this time. This wasn't just an ordinary street fight with another working-class boy like himself. This time he'd thrown a hard punch at someone who could effectively ruin his life.

The magistrate looked at Adam, then Francis. "Mr. Fletcher, Mr. Smythe."

The two boys both stood a little more upright and looked at the magistrate. Francis looked like he was fighting a smile that was trying to spread across his face. *He'd love to see me put away,* thought Adam.

The two had never liked each other. Adam always hated how pompous Francis acted, and Francis had needled Adam since the first time they met. Adam was pretty sure it all came down to jealousy for Francis. Adam—in spite of his lower social status—felt sure he had at least a few qualities Francis wished he could possess. He was handsome, strong, and confident. Adam probably also seemed to have a more adventurous life, living and working at the Topsail Tavern, than eighteen-year-old Smythe, who mostly found himself being kept at home under the watchful eye of his father's many servants.

"I'm either locking both of you up or neither of you up," said the magistrate.

Francis was dumbfounded. "You are *not* locking me up. How dare you even suggest such a thing—I'll have your job!"

Mr. Robins nodded. "You may certainly try, Mr. Smythe, but for now I am quite literally sitting in the judge's seat. And I say that regardless of who started the fight, if you had insulted my mother that way when I was Mr. Fletcher's age, I'd have probably done the same thing. What kind of a son wouldn't step up to defend his own mother, for goodness' sake?"

Adam couldn't believe it. He wasn't going to be locked up after all.

"And as for you, Mr. Fletcher, with age I pray you will grow in temperance. Fighting in the streets is hardly the way to build a successful life."

"He'll never be successful," taunted Francis. "He's a worthless urchin now, and fifty years from now he'll still be a worthless urchin. You can't turn lead into gold."

Robins said, "That'll be enough, Mr. Smythe. Keep up with your attacks and I may yet reconsider putting you behind bars."

Adam looked at his adversary and just grinned.

Francis was outraged. "I can assure you my father will hear about this episode today. May I leave now?"

Robins nodded his head and motioned for Constable Squires to show him out. Just as they were about to leave the office, the magistrate had one more thing to say to him.

"Mr. Smythe," he said. "You were born a little gentleman. Your father is a gentleman."

"Of course," agreed Francis.

"I would like to suggest that you not dishonor your father, nor that you bring embarrassment to your family, by creating for yourself the reputation of being a spoiled brat. Just as you say you hear people talk about Mr. Fletcher's mother, so too have I heard murmuring about you, sir. Your father is a good man. Do not make the mistake of bringing his good name down with your actions."

Francis glared at the magistrate, then stormed out of the office.

Once he was out of the building, Mr. Robins walked over to look out the window. When he saw Francis crossing the road, he returned to his desk and sat down.

"Mr. Fletcher," he said, "what do you think your greatest problem is?"

"Sir?"

"If one were to ask me, I'd say you have too much free time on your hands."

Adam remained silent.

"I think it's high time you find an apprenticeship so that you can develop your talents—make something of yourself."

"An apprenticeship, sir? You mean learn some trade?" The suggestion took Adam by surprise. "I'm working down at the tavern. I've grown up there—I like it there."

"Apparently it isn't keeping you busy enough if you have time to get into fisticuffs so frequently down at the docks, and with Francis Smythe no less."

"He came in and started that fight, sir. I asked him to step outside, and figured that would've been warning enough to get him to back up and apologize, but he didn't, and he kept at it, so I had to teach him a lesson."

"Mr. Fletcher, while I can appreciate your desire to defend your mother—and I really do believe that is an honorable thing to do on your part—I will say it's quite foolish of you to think you can go through life getting into fights whenever a man insults you."

"He didn't just insult me, though, Mr. Robins. If it had just been about me, I'd have ignored him. But he threw my mama's name in the mud, and I just won't have it."

Just as Mr. Robins was about to respond, Adam continued: "I know folks say those kinds of things about her, but they know better than to say 'em to my face. Francis Smythe wanted that fight."

"Perhaps he did," said the magistrate, "but are you normally in the business of giving Francis Smythe whatever he wants?"

Adam rolled his eyes.

"You're a clever boy, Mr. Fletcher. I wouldn't think you'd fall for his bait so easily."

"You mean when someone says something like that, I should just let it go?"

"That's precisely what I mean, Mr. Fletcher."

Adam shifted his weight from one foot to the other and said, "May I go now?"

Mr. Robins quickly shook his head. "No. You may go after we discuss the matter of your apprenticeship. Is there a particular trade that interests you, or should I choose something on your behalf?"

Adam thought for a moment before answering. "Do I have to decide right now?"

"I'm being quite generous by giving you this opportunity. You could face criminal charges for that attack on Mr. Smythe." Adam was about to interrupt, but Mr. Robins raised his hand to silence him. "I'm not going to charge you with the assault. However, I do need to tell the boy's father something if he asks about it when he returns—and mark my words, he will ask about it. I want to let him know that I've dealt with the matter, but more importantly, I want you to make something of yourself, Mr. Fletcher. I don't want you to waste your life cleaning tables in that tavern and brawling in the streets in your free time. Wouldn't you like to be a productive member of society?"

Adam leaned his back against the wall, but he was too frustrated to answer.

"Tell me, if you could learn any trade, what would it be?"

Adam shuffled his feet in place as he thought about the question. "I'd just as soon run a tavern, sir. Why can't I do that?"

"That's not an option," said the magistrate sternly.

Adam hesitated, then said, "Will you give me the weekend to think about it?"

Mr. Robins gave him a strict look. "Monday morning first thing I want you back in this office with your decision. Do you understand?"

"Yes, sir. May I go now?"

"You may. And do not forget. I expect you back here first thing Monday. If you're not, I'll be within my rights to impose a stricter punishment for your assault on Mr. Smythe."

Adam nodded. He hung his head and left the office.

Chapter Three

THE TOPSAIL TAVERN was packed, as it typically was on a Friday night. In colder months, diners were left to compete for tables closest to one of the hearths at each end of the establishment, but in the month of May the warmer weather outdoors began causing the air inside the place to feel thicker. Tables near windows were preferable because of the fresh breeze that would blow through.

Year round the air was layered with a bouquet of scents that included the more pungent briny odor of the old salts who came in to drink, the cloying perfumes of the women who occasionally came to sit with their sailors, the intoxicating fragrance of spilled rum and sweet tobacco smoke, and the yeasty aromas of strong ale and hot bread. Added to all of that was the melody of smells that emanated from whatever dishes were being brought out from the kitchen.

In spite of the high energy in the tavern, Adam struggled to put one foot in front of the other on this night. He confused several orders and had forgotten to wait on one group of men entirely. When one of them finally lost his patience, Valentine had to intervene and wait on their table himself—something the tavern keeper rarely did.

Valentine returned to his place behind the bar and began to pour ale for the men. Adam was there leaning against the bar, absentmindedly staring out into the dining area.

"Listen, I know you're upset, boy, but there's work to be done, and it ain't going to do itself." The sixty-something-year-old barkeeper grabbed the four mugs by their handles and quickly delivered them to the thirsty men before returning to the bar.

"Can't this day just hurry up and be done with?" said Adam.

"Ah, don't wish your time away, boy. You know what the Good Book says—that life is but a vapor; it appears for a little time and then vanishes away." Valentine waved his fingers in the air as he said that last part.

"I know. But if any day could vanish, I wish it would be this one."

"What are you whinin about? Don't seem too bad to me. Seems like things could've been a lot worse for you after what happened this afternoon."

Adam scoffed. "I don't see how."

"They coulda thrown you right into the gaol, boy—or the stocks. How would you feel about spending the night in there? Then you'd *really* be wishing the time would go faster. And can you imagine what Francis Smythe would do then? Huh!"

Just then Mary Fletcher joined her son and Valentine at the bar. "Hello, boys."

Adam gave his mother a weak wave but wouldn't speak.

Valentine said, "Finally back, eh? How's she doing? Must've talked your ear off."

"Oh, you know how the Widow Simpson is," said Mary. "Bless her sweet heart, she's just lonely."

"Course she is," declared Valentine. "You know that's the only reason for her standing order here. Yes indeed. The Widow Simpson has her servants. She don't need to order food from this tavern, but she sure does love having you sit and talk with her on Friday evenings. I reckon it's the best part of her week."

Mary smiled. Her youthful brown eyes sparkled. As young as she looked, one would never guess she had a seventeen-year-old son. The dark-haired beauty had given birth to Adam when she was only eighteen herself. Her son's coloring and features were so similar to her own, passing sailors who dined in the tavern frequently mistook them for brother and sister rather than mother and child.

She noticed Adam's downcast expression and put her hand on his back before asking, "What's wrong with you?"

Adam looked at her and said, "I've been waiting for you to get back all day."

"You know I go to the Widow Simpson's every Friday," she said.

"I know, but there's something I have to tell you."

"He got in a fight this afternoon," Valentine interjected. "With Francis Smythe of all people."

Adam rolled his eyes.

"Please tell me you're joking," she said.

Adam shook his head. "He's not joking. But that's not the worst of it."

Mary gave a nervous chuckle. "Well, it can't be that bad, can it? I mean, you're here. You're not in the gaol."

"It must be bad," said Valentine. "He's been useless all night. Wouldn't tell me what happened, though. Said he was waiting for you to get here."

Mary put her hands on her hips. "Well, I'm here now. So what is it?"

Adam took a deep breath. "Mr. Robins says he wants to put me in an apprenticeship. He told me to pick a trade and let him know what I've decided by Monday."

The color left Mary's face. "He can't make you do that. Can he?"

She looked at Valentine with desperation. The old man had been the closest thing Mary had to a father since she was a young girl. Valentine Hodges and his wife, Margaret, now deceased, had taken Mary in at the request of her father when he was on his deathbed with yellow fever. Mary's mother died in childbirth, so she and her father had lived in a rented house owned by the Hodges. Since Margaret and Valentine had never been able to have children, Margaret joyfully looked after Mary as though she were her own, and Adam was like their grandson.

Valentine stroked his stubbly chin. "I don't know, girl. Mr. Robins could've locked the boy up today. You should've seen Francis Smythe's face. Adam busted his nose up good-fashioned."

Mary shot a disappointed look at her son and struggled to speak past the lump that had formed in her throat. "What have I told you about fighting, Adam? Huh? What have I said? You just had to do it, didn't you? Why couldn't you just ignore the arrogant little toad?"

Adam inhaled sharply, then shrugged.

"Well, I guess they're finally getting what they wanted," she said.

"What's that supposed to mean?" said Adam.

Just then the men at the table where Valentine had delivered drinks a few moments earlier called out. "Oy! We want to order somefin to eat. Any chance of gettin served ova 'ere?"

"Be right there, fellas," said Valentine. He turned his attention back to Mary and Adam. "You two might as well go upstairs to discuss this. I can see ain't neither of you gonna be fit for work tonight. I'll take care of these boys."

THE TINY ONE-BEDROOM APARTMENT shared by Mary and Adam was sparsely furnished. In the center of the room was a small table with four chairs. Mary's bed was on one side of the room, Adam's bed on the other. The connecting wall had only one small dresser and a fireplace, which didn't get much use for cooking in warmer months.

The tavern had been the only home Adam had ever known. That, coupled with his assumption that he would end up spending his life working at the tavern, made the fact that he was now being forced into an apprenticeship all the more troubling.

"Sit down, Adam." Mary was fuming. She stood with her arms crossed, tapping her foot.

He paced back and forth across the room. He didn't feel like sitting.

"Adam Fletcher! I've told you, I'm not going to try to talk to you like this. Now I said *sit down*!"

Adam huffed as he pulled the other chair out from the table and sat in it. He rested his elbows on the table and thought a moment before asking his mother, "What did you mean downstairs just now when you said they'd finally gotten what they wanted?"

"We'll get to that in just a minute, but first, have I not

told you before that your fighting would get you into trouble? But you! You hardheaded child! You just don't listen!"

"I know."

"Where does this temper of yours come from? I don't understand it. I've never been a hothead like you. And for the short time I knew your father, he didn't have a hot temper, either. So tell me, what is your problem? Why do you let those stupid boys get to you?"

"Mama, would you please just answer my question? What did you mean by what you said downstairs?"

Mary sighed and sat down with him at the table before she answered him. "Well, if you have to know, this isn't the first time they've wanted to take you away from here and put you in an apprenticeship. They've been after me about it since you were just a little thing. I never would agree to it, though."

Adam wrinkled his brow. "Are you serious?"

She nodded. "Yes. And even Valentine had to step in and help me one time. They were going to take you away from me and place you with a mariner so you could learn the seafaring trade."

"And you wouldn't allow it," said Adam.

"Of course not! I'm your mother. I'd never give you to some stranger to raise. Much less a mariner—I know *exactly* how they can be."

Adam tried to refocus the conversation. "You said Valentine had to step in and help you. Why did he have to get involved?"

"Well, because I was raising you without a father. The town doesn't want to be responsible for the well-being of fatherless children. If we were wealthy, that would've been one thing, but we're not, so I needed to be able to assure them that I could care for you, so Valentine stepped in as surety for me."

"He did that?" Adam was surprised. "Why have you never told me about this before?"

"Why would I have?" said Mary. "We took care of things, protected you. Why worry you with it?"

"But you never even mentioned anything about an apprenticeship."

"No," said Mary. "It was never something I've ever wanted for you. You don't understand. Unless your master is a family member or a friend, you'll normally just end up being somebody's cheap labor, and I didn't want that. I certainly wasn't going to see you leave on a ship when you were just a little boy to serve some old salt. A white slave is what you'd have been. That's all."

"Hmph. Doesn't look like I have much of a choice now."

"Well, pat yourself on the back, son. For seventeen years I've kept you out of a mess like that, and it sounds like it took you about two minutes to mess things up for yourself."

The two remained silent for a couple of minutes, contemplating what all of this would mean.

Finally Mary spoke. "I'm not happy about this. But it all goes back to that temper of yours. And I've told you a thousand—"

"I know that! I know! But I wasn't going to let that little cretin talk about you like that."

Mary shook her head in frustration. "I don't know what Francis Smythe said today, but I can assure you I have heard it all before. The fact that you got into yet another fight, and this time the law had to get involved—well, now you're just going to have to pay the consequences. And Adam, I want you to know something: you having to be taken away from here and bound out—well, that hurts me more than any insult Smythe or anyone could ever invent."

The full gravity of the situation finally hit him and he

dropped his head in shame. "I'm so sorry, Mama."

"You do understand this means you have to leave here, right?" said Mary. Her voice was shaky. Adam could tell she was trying not to cry.

He dropped his head onto his arms, which were folded across the table. "I know," he said, his voice muffled.

"Listen," she said, "this isn't a good thing, but at least you get to pick a trade. This is such a small town, that's almost as good as you being able to pick your own master."

Adam raised his head. He said nothing for a moment, then spoke. "Maybe you're right, but who would I choose? I mean, I've always thought I would work here, live here."

"That'll have to be your decision, but at least you have the weekend to figure things out."

Adam nodded and took a deep breath.

Chapter Four

By Monday, Adam had decided on a trade and his master of choice.

He told Peter Robins, the local magistrate, that he wanted to apprentice with a shipping merchant. There were only two men practicing that trade in town—Richard Rasquelle and an older gentleman, Emmanuel Rogers, who everyone knew had never taken on anyone from outside his own close circle of friends—so Adam felt confident that he'd soon be bound in service to the impressive Mr. Rasquelle.

At least he hoped he would. Emmanuel Rogers was ancient—at least to Adam—and well into his seventies. He was a bit of a recluse and rarely seen in town. Some folks thought him to be an eccentric, insisting he had some secret past.

Emmanuel Rogers also was the complete opposite of Richard Rasquelle in many ways. He didn't dress as nicely as the young shipping merchant. He didn't sponsor big town events like Rasquelle. And he certainly didn't seem to have the bustling business that Rasquelle had—in fact, Adam figured that with Rogers practically having one foot in the grave, Rasquelle might be the only shipping merchant in town in just a few years.

All of those observations added up to one thing for Adam—an apprenticeship with Rasquelle would turn this "punishment" into a redeeming enterprise, whereas being stuck with Emmanuel Rogers could be like being chained to a sinking ship.

He was instructed to come back with his mother on Wednesday to finalize the papers, so when they arrived at Mr. Robins's office that day, Mary was a nervous wreck.

"I'm not sure I'm ready to do this." Her voice was unsteady.

Adam put his arm around her back and squeezed her shoulder. "It's alright, Mama. Let's just get this over with."

She gave him a tense nod. He opened the door to the magistrate's office and led her in.

Mr. Robins looked up from his desk and took off his spectacles. "Miss Fletcher! Adam! I'm delighted to see you both." He stood and walked around his desk to greet them.

"Hello, sir," said Adam. He shook hands with the magistrate.

"I think you've come at the perfect time. Your new master will be here in, oh, let's see"—he strained to see the time on his pocket watch—"about fifteen minutes. In the meantime, we can go over the document you'll sign. And Miss Fletcher, if you have any questions, please ask away. I'll do my best to answer them."

"I do have a question," said Mary.

Adam looked over at his mother and wondered what she would say. He just hoped she wouldn't embarrass him. She wasn't afraid to speak up to authority figures, and Mr. Robins would be no exception.

"Yes, ma'am?"

"Explain to me, if you would, exactly why my son has to be apprenticed elsewhere. Why can't he just be bound to Valentine?"

The magistrate went back around and sat at his desk. He motioned for Mary and Adam to sit in the chairs on the other side, which they did.

"Miss Fletcher, you and I have discussed this topic before. On more than one occasion, as I'm sure you recall."

Mary nodded. Her face was stern.

Mr. Robins continued: "You have done a remarkable job raising this child alone. You have my respect for all that you've done, but your boy, he's pugnacious. His temper gets him into trouble. You know that."

She wouldn't speak. Neither would Adam. He kept his gaze fixed on a stack of papers on the magistrate's desk. The whole situation felt like a bad dream. He couldn't believe it was really happening.

"He fights over you, Miss Fletcher. Your boy loves you. He can't stand to hear anyone speak ill of you."

"And that's a crime to you?" she said. His mother's outwardly tough demeanor was just a disguise and he knew it. It killed him inside knowing that he had done something that was hurting her so deeply.

"I think it's honorable that his desire is to defend you. Any son worth his salt would do the same. However, I think it's unwise that he allows himself to be pulled so easily into fisticuffs anytime someone offends him. Granted, most of the time his brawling ends without consequence because it's with boys of equal status, but this time he broke the nose of Francis Smythe, who just happens to be the son of His Majesty's Customs Agent Ellison Smythe."

"Francis baited Adam into that fight! He wanted to get him in trouble! Adam, tell the man."

"I already have, Mama," said Adam.

"Indeed he has," said Mr. Robins. "But nevertheless, Adam took the bait. And if a lesson is not learned in this circumstance, he will always take the bait. Not to mention, if Mr. Smythe returns and I have not punished the boy who broke his son's nose, he will rightly say that I have been derelict in my duties."

Mary thought for a moment. "Can't he just spend a few nights in the gaol?"

The magistrate cleared his throat. "He could, but are you not concerned with the reputation he'll carry with him if he is incarcerated? He'd forever have a criminal record. As it is, he's being given the opportunity for an apprenticeship. I have no plans to put his assault in the public record, provided he takes this opportunity and makes the best of it."

"Is there no other way he could pay his debt, Mr. Robins?"

"No. I'm going to be very blunt, Miss Fletcher, if you don't mind."

She shook her head. "No, I don't mind."

"The boy's been raised with no father—"

"But, Valentine—"

"Valentine Hodges has indeed been a father figure to you, Mary, but he is not Adam's father, nor has he raised him as though he were. Valentine runs a tavern. His standards of morality, while perhaps not abysmal, are far from being venerable. Fighting, foul language, drunkenness, occasionally even loose women—all of it—his tavern is full of it. Maybe not all the time, but nevertheless it's there, and he tolerates it. Your son has grown up around that long enough. It's only by God's good grace that you yourself have maintained any semblance of virtue. Many women would've surely lost their way living and working in such an establishment."

"Valentine and Margaret raised me with better standards than that, Mr. Robins."

"I have no argument with how they raised you, but nevertheless your son's at a critical age. If he's bloodying the face of the son of an appointed official today, what will he be doing tomorrow? He needs some strong guidance. He needs someone to keep him in line and teach him wisdom. And that is exactly why I have chosen for him the master that I have."

Just then the door of the magistrate's office opened and an elderly gentleman came in.

The magistrate said, "Speak of the devil." He stood to welcome the man. "Mr. Rogers! How do you do today, sir?"

The old man smiled and nodded. "Very well, thank you, Mr. Robins. And I suppose this lad is my new charge," he said as he placed his hand on Adam's shoulder.

"Yes, he is, sir. Adam, I'd like you to meet Emmanuel Rogers, your new master."

Adam stood and shook Mr. Rogers's hand. While his body was going through the motions of social formality, his mind was screaming *What the hell is happening here? Where's Mr. Rasquelle?*

Mary looked up at the old gentleman and offered a reserved smile. "How do you do, Mr. Rogers?"

"Please pull up one of those and take a seat." The magistrate motioned to some chairs along the wall near his desk.

The old man moved one of the chairs near Adam. The men all sat down.

Adam glanced at his mother, his face fallen. This wasn't

right, he thought. Emmanuel Rogers? The new master was *supposed* to be Richard Rasquelle.

"Just before you arrived, Mr. Rogers, I was answering a few questions for Miss Fletcher. I was explaining to her and her son that I believe Adam is at a critical age, one that will require a strong man to lead him in the right direction, along the right path. He needs to learn wisdom and temperance, as well as a set of skills that can benefit him for the rest of his life. I was about to explain that I think you are the ideal man for the job."

"Oh, well, I appreciate your kindness, Mr. Robins," said Emmanuel, flattered.

His accent hinted at his English birth. One could tell he had lived in the region a long time, but his manner of speech still reflected the formality and cadence of the language as it was spoken in the old country.

"I do hope that once you've had an opportunity to get to know me and the men in my company, you will feel very much at home, as if we were truly your second family."

It was becoming apparent to everyone that Mary's efforts to keep her emotions under control were beginning to waver. Her eyes were starting to look very watery, and she seemed unsteady in her chair. She held her cheeks tense and appeared to be biting the inside of her lip. Mr. Robins immediately intervened by moving the proceedings along.

"Well, now that we have the introductions out of the way, let's get down to business, shall we?"

Adam's stomach began to ache. He felt hot, like he might be sick.

What have I gotten myself into?

He had no choice now but to go through with the process.

Mr. Robins explained the document to Mary, Adam, and

Emmanuel.

Once the paperwork was completed, Mr. Rogers said, "Take a couple of days to get your things in order, son, then report to my warehouse first thing Friday. Do you know where it is?"

Adam's face was sullen. He nodded. "Yes, sir."

Emmanuel looked at Mary tenderly. "Please don't worry, love. I promise you I will take care of your boy as though he were my own. Please trust that he's in good hands."

Mary nodded weakly. She couldn't speak. Her eyes were watery.

"See you Friday, sir," said Adam.

Emmanuel nodded. "I'll look forward to it." He smiled.

Chapter Five

FRIDAY MORNING BEFORE seven, Adam had just one small bundle, tied up with cord, that held all of his earthly possessions. It consisted of two shirts and two pairs of breeches, an extra pair of socks, a jacket, a thin blanket, a small pillow, and a drawstring pouch with a few coins inside.

"You sure you don't want to walk downstairs with me, Mama?" he asked.

Mary shook her head quickly, her face tense. It looked to Adam like she was struggling to hold herself together.

Adam tucked his bundle under his arm and gave her a weak smile. "I guess this is it, then."

She finally managed to speak. "Come here." She grabbed him in a tight hug. "I love you, child. I always knew you'd leave home one day. I just never thought it would happen like this."

Adam nodded. "I know."

She reached up and kissed her son's cheek, then stepped back and held his hands in her own. He stood a few inches taller than her and she was gazing up at him, her eyes full of sadness. Adam knew her world had always revolved around him, and now he was leaving. It all happened so suddenly, and it felt strange. Knowing he had somehow caused things to turn out like this, he felt pangs of guilt strike at his heart. By being forced to leave in this way, he was hurting the one person who had always cared for and protected him. He wouldn't be around to look out for her anymore, to stop drunk tavern patrons from harassing her, or to put someone in their place if they disrespected her. Still, Adam was ready to go to Rogers's Shipping Company. What other choice did he have? Standing here looking at his mother in the terrible state that he'd put her in was more than he could bear.

"You've grown so much. You're a fine young man and I expect great things from you. I know you'll do me proud."

He nodded again.

Tears began to pool in her eyes and her voice trembled. "Just remember all I've taught you. Do good. Be respectful. Honesty always. And be brave."

"I know, Mama," he said. "And listen, don't forget—I won't be far. I'll just be right down the road."

She nodded.

"I reckon you can come see me there anytime, and hopefully Mr. Rogers will let me have time off to visit now and then, too."

"Maybe so." She gave him a weak smile, then urged him out the door.

Adam started to leave but turned back to give his mother one more hug and a quick kiss on the cheek. "I love you, Mama. I'm so sorry about this."

ADAM DIDN'T HAVE TO walk far to arrive at Emmanuel Rogers's warehouse. It was a huge two-story structure about a mile from the tavern on the waterfront.

As he approached the wide-open cargo doors from the street side, he called out, "Hello!"

"Come on in!" yelled a voice from deep inside the building.

The morning light pouring in from the open bay doors on the waterfront made the dust in the air glisten and cast everything inside into shadowy silhouettes. Adam squinted, trying to make out the voice's location in the shaded interior.

As he walked into the warehouse, he was hit by the warm fragrance of sawdust, tobacco, and rum. He saw rows of barrels and casks along the walls, stacked high in some places and lined up in a single row in others. Not too far inside the entrance, men were working on shaping barrel staves.

A swarthy, stubble-faced man stepped over to welcome him to the warehouse.

"I'm Boaz Brooks." His voice was gravelly. "You Adam Fletcher?"

Adam nodded and extended his hand in greeting. "Yes, sir. That's me." He looked around. "Is Mr. Rogers here?"

"Yeah," said Boaz. "I'll call him down."

The man bellowed in a loud voice to an upstairs office, "Hey! Emmaaanuel!"

"Coming! I'm coming!" a voice called back from an upstairs room beyond the balcony.

"The Fletcher boy is here. You coming down to see him?"

A sprightly old man finally appeared on the balcony and responded, "Oh, yes, yes, of course! Be right there."

He made his way down the staircase, which connected

the ground floor of the warehouse with the second-floor balcony, then excitedly scurried over and extended his hand to greet the boy.

"Welcome to the company, son. I'm glad you're here."

"Yes, sir," said Adam. He shook the old man's hand.

"Allow me to introduce you to everybody," said Emmanuel. "You already met Boaz Brooks, of course."

Adam nodded. "Yes, sir."

"Very good. Well, you should know he's my right hand. He does a little bit of everything here."

Boaz gave a half smile.

"And these men here are Elliot and Joe Salter—they're cousins—and Martin Smith," said Emmanuel, motioning to each of the other coopers in turn as Adam shook their hands.

"And then, of course, there's also the crew of my sloop, the *Carolina Gypsy*. You'll get to know them eventually, but as the *Gypsy* is leaving next Friday and will be gone for several months, those men aren't here today. For the most part we're really quite a cozy family here."

Adam was underwhelmed by this quiet little warehouse, where he'd be stuck spending the next four years of his life. This was not how his apprenticeship was supposed to turn out, and this old man was not who he had wanted for a master.

If only I was at Richard Rasquelle's company right now, he thought. *I'll bet things are hopping over there. I'm sure he has a bigger, more interesting crew than this dull-looking bunch.*

Emmanuel started back towards the stairs and motioned for Adam and Boaz to follow. "I'll make sure you get a tour of the rest of the place later, but right now I'd like you two to come upstairs with me."

The three of them walked up the stairs. As they neared

the top, Adam was taken by surprise. The sweet fragrance of dried tobacco and stacks of cedar shingles down on the shipping floor permeated the air. It was more noticeable here than it had been on the ground floor near the bay doors. And there was something about looking down on the shipping floor from above that made the place seem more impressive. The bird's-eye view allowed Adam to get a glimpse of not only the large variety of shipping containers housed inside, but also the expansive space that appeared to be waiting for a pending shipment.

The building always looked so plain and boring from the outside. It also never seemed particularly busy—at least not compared to Richard Rasquelle's company. Rasquelle was Emmanuel Rogers's only competitor in town, as well as the man to whom Adam had hoped he would be bound in his apprenticeship. Nevertheless, now Adam was beginning to see that his new master's company was much busier than he had realized.

"Come right on in here," said Emmanuel, leading the way from the balcony through a door on the left.

They entered a little hallway, which then connected to a whole different section of the building. Emmanuel's home was hidden within the second floor of the warehouse. The temperature was several degrees cooler in this part of the building than it was in the hallway or out on the balcony thanks to plenty of open windows, which allowed the ocean breeze to blow through from the north, south, and east.

Even more impressive to Adam than the surprising architecture was finding out there was actually a proper living area on the second floor rather than just the bare-bones servant's loft he had expected. He felt like he'd wandered into a world bazaar rather than an upstairs apartment in a shipping warehouse. Everywhere he looked he saw objets d'art, housewares, and furniture from every corner of the globe.

They had entered the sitting room, which had a large Persian rug in the middle of the floor. There were exotic cut-velvet settees on either side of the rug, and two silk-covered chairs, probably French, beside end tables at the opposite ends. To the side of the sitting area was a square table with chess pieces in suspended play on the board. Adam guessed the set was from the Orient, based on the style of the figures. A long, ornately carved mahogany table with six equally ornate chairs was tucked away at the far side of the room next to what Adam guessed was the kitchen area. The wall hangings around the room were reflective of what appeared to be a lifetime of traveling the world.

Nothing was new. In fact, everything looked quite old, some things even ancient. It was all very well cared for, though, and quite a stunning collection.

Adam noticed that there were other rooms connected to this one with their doors open so that the breeze could blow through. He could only catch a brief glimpse of what was inside them. He was curious to continue the tour, but for now he'd have to wait.

"Let's sit down, shall we?" said Emmanuel, motioning to the sitting area.

Adam and Boaz each took seats on the settees, while Emmanuel took his place in one of the velvet chairs.

"Now then," began Mr. Rogers, "let us talk about your future here, young man."

Adam nodded. "Yes, sir."

He had trouble focusing on his future considering he felt like he was sitting in a museum.

"There's one thing you should know. I don't take on apprentices," said Emmanuel. "In fact, I haven't taken on an apprentice in over thirty years. The last time I took on a boy here, he came when he was about your age but he never left."

Adam swallowed hard. He wondered what in the world that was supposed to mean.

"I have my reasons for why I don't bring new people into this company," said Emmanuel, "but for you, I am making an exception."

"Do you mind if I ask you a question, sir?"

"Not at all. Ask away."

"What happened to your last apprentice?"

"I beg your pardon?"

"You said he never left."

Adam was tense as he waited for an answer.

"What? Oh, good heavens!" Emmanuel chuckled. "The other apprentice? Nothing happened to him! He's sitting right there!" Emmanuel pointed at Boaz, who popped up his hand and gave a quick nod.

Adam let out a big sigh of relief.

"Well, I suppose I did say he never left. I can understand how that might have caused you some alarm." Emmanuel looked over at Boaz, who was trying not to laugh, then back to Adam. "I imagine you might've been wondering what you'd gotten yourself into here!"

The men laughed. Finally Adam smiled, too, and chuckled.

"Alright then," said Adam, "I'm relieved to hear that's what you meant."

"Not to worry, not to worry. You'll be fine here," said Emmanuel. "As I was saying, I don't bring on apprentices. I only bring into this company people I trust and, sadly, those are few in number." The old man paused for a moment before he continued.

"But when Mr. Robins informed me of your situation, I knew I had to give you a chance."

Adam nodded to show he was listening but didn't know what to say.

"I try to follow my instincts, young man. Do you?"

Adam thought for a moment. "I do, sir. At least I like to think so."

"Good! That's good." Emmanuel nodded with determination. "Always do that."

"Yes, sir."

"I'm glad I brought you here," said Emmanuel. His voice was sincere. "And I hope you will find that this is a good place for you to learn many things. I pray that by the time you reach the end of your apprenticeship, you will feel well prepared to earn a successful living, that you'll be able to—" Emmanuel interrupted himself. "Well, you tell me. What is it you'd most like to do?"

"How do you mean, sir?" said Adam.

"I mean, are you most interested in learning the bookkeeping, assisting with the imports and exports? Do you like to work with your hands—maybe you would prefer learning the cooper's trade? Or is it ship work that interests you? There are many different facets of this business, young man. It's all down to what you think you might like best. We can start you there."

"To be honest, sir, I'd be happy learning any of those things—all of them, actually."

"How wonderful! That's what I like to hear," said Emmanuel. "You have a willing spirit. That's a virtue."

Adam smiled. "Thank you, sir."

Emmanuel gave him a nod. "Now, on to the matter of your living situation."

"Right," said Adam. "Where will I stay?"

"You will live here," said Emmanuel, using both hands to motion to the room they were in. "This apartment, if you will, has three bedrooms, a kitchen, and this room that we're sitting in. I stay in the room on that side," he said, pointing northward to the room that had been on the left of the sitting room when they first entered. "The kitchen is back that way, as I'm sure you've already noticed," he said, turning and pointing behind him. "And beyond that are two other bedrooms. The first belongs to Boaz, and the other room has been empty for ages, except when we've had the occasional guest. Now it will be yours."

Adam was struck by the thought. He had never had his own room at the tavern. He and his mother had always shared a one-room apartment, if you could even call it that.

Although he was beginning to feel a little less hopeless about spending the next four years as Emmanuel Rogers's apprentice, he suddenly felt a horrible pang of homesickness, not knowing when he'd be free to return to the tavern or see his family. He knew it would be inappropriate to ask so soon, but he couldn't wait for an answer.

"Mr. Rogers," he said.

"Yes?"

"I was wondering." He paused, unsure of just how much he should say. "My mama—"

"Ah, yes! She lives and works there at Valentine Hodges's tavern, doesn't she?"

Adam nodded. "Yes, sir. And, well . . ."

"And you're wondering when you'll be able to see her. Am I right?" Emmanuel smiled warmly.

"Well, yes, sir. She's taking my leaving real hard, and—"

Emmanuel raised his hand to stop the boy from continuing. "No need to say another word. You can check in on her every day if you'd like. As long as you get your work done, you're free to go back to the tavern whenever you please, so long as you're back here each night before eleven."

Adam's eyes grew wide. "Really? Thank you, sir."

"Oh, certainly! I had a mother, too, once upon a time, so I understand. You're a good son to want to ensure her well-being."

A great sense of relief came over Adam.

Boaz, who had been sitting in silence throughout the conversation, said, "Boy, I think you'll find you have a good situation here. If you work hard and do as you're told, you can do well for yourself."

Emmanuel nodded in agreement. "Indeed, and Boaz here will be your primary supervisor during this first stage of your apprenticeship. As I said, he does a little bit of everything, and he is my most trusted associate." He looked over at Boaz and smiled. "He's more like a son to me, really. And considering his past experience in your same shoes, I think you'll find he might be someone who understands your circumstances."

AFTER IRONING OUT ALL of the details of his apprenticeship with Emmanuel, Adam spent the rest of the day down on the warehouse floor with Boaz and the other coopers, getting acquainted with the tools of the cask-maker's trade. Though everyone else finished up their work at the usual time, Boaz told Adam that the two of them would have to work a while longer to make up for the time they had spent up in the living quarters with Mr. Rogers.

"One thing you'll learn working here," said Boaz, "is that you have to take this job seriously. That doesn't mean we never cut up and have fun, but it does mean that when work needs to be done, we do it. Every morning we set out a plan to accomplish certain tasks, and then we don't leave until we've each done our lot."

"I understand," said Adam.

He worked alongside Boaz, learning to shape boards, which would soon become staves for casks that would hold turpentine and pitch.

"So how old were you when you were brought on here?" Adam asked.

"Oh, let's see . . . I reckon I was about your age," said Boaz. "Well, I might've been a couple years younger. How old did you say you were?"

"Seventeen. My birthday was in March."

"Yep, I reckon I was a couple years younger, then. Fifteen—well, fourteen—but I turned fifteen during my first week here." Boaz chuckled. "You know, Emmanuel actually gave me a party. I had never had a party before that day."

The man's deep voice was coarse with age, but it exhibited a hint of childlike exuberance when he recalled his earliest years in Emmanuel's company.

"Were you an orphan?"

"No. No, I wasn't," said Boaz. He finished shaping a stave and picked up another plank and began examining it. "I lived with my mother, like you, but they took me away from her. Said she didn't have the money to look after me anymore. My father died and left her with too many debts. He was terrible with money."

He rejected the plank he'd chosen, then pulled another and examined it quickly before he began drawing it against the jointer.

"Anyway," he continued, "they forced me into an apprenticeship so I wouldn't be a burden on the town. I was just a boy—twelve years old. They first had me bound to this man who lived here in town—an old cooper—but he was just keeping me like a servant. Wasn't teaching me anything."

Adam was listening intently, so much so that Boaz motioned to the stave he had been shaping. He had been distracted and hollowed it out too much.

"Watch it, boy!" Boaz snapped. "Pay attention to what you're doing. These planks ain't free, you know."

Adam grabbed another planed board and began to work on hollowing the inside as Boaz had shown him earlier. Meanwhile, Boaz continued his story.

"So anyway, Emmanuel set up his company here in town, and he had heard about how that old man—his name was Stafford—was keeping me, well, like a servant. My mother had told him. You see, he—I mean Emmanuel—and my father, they had been friends when they were young men. Anyway, she told him about it to see if he could help. Of course Emmanuel, he was glad to help the widow and son of his old friend, so he went to the magistrate and lodged a complaint on my behalf to see if he could take me on in his shop. And of course the court went along with it, since Stafford wasn't teaching me the trade."

"You've had quite a life, then," said Adam.

Boaz chuckled. "You ain't heard nothing yet, boy."

"I'll bet! So you say Mr. Rogers had just moved into town when he took you on here."

"Yep."

"Where did he live before?"

"New Bern. You ever been there?"

Adam let out a loud "Ha! Have I ever been to New Bern? I've never even left Carteret County."

"Well, working here, I reckon that'll probably change," said Boaz. "One of these days I reckon you'll end up on

Emmanuel's sloop, but that won't be anytime soon."

"I think I'd like that," said Adam.

Boaz grunted. "Oh yeah? Not me. Seasickness."

Adam raised his eyebrows, quizzical. "Hmph. Don't know if I'd get seasick. Never been far enough offshore."

"You'll find out eventually," said Boaz. "But anyway, Emmanuel used to run a shipping company over in New Bern. A pretty successful one, too, from what I heard. Said he came down here to try to bring more things to the region. Had a lot of other merchant contacts in far-off places. Beaufort never has been much of a port, you know."

Adam nodded.

"So anyway, he came here in spring of 1732, I think it was, and by January of '33 he had rescued me from Stafford and brought me into his company."

"Rescued you, huh?" Adam said with a little laugh. "Was it really all that bad?"

Boaz stopped working and looked squarely at Adam. "You try being a twelve-year-old boy whose debt-ridden father has just died and then being yanked away from your loving mother and made a slave to a drunk, abusive cooper. Yes, it was *that bad*. It was hell. There's no other way to describe it."

"Well, that does sound awful." Adam swallowed hard. He paused for a moment. He wanted to change the subject to something more innocuous. "You ever been married?"

As soon as he asked the question, he felt like an idiot. That was far too personal. Adam realized that if Boaz ever had been married, he obviously wasn't now, so it probably wasn't the best way to turn the conversation in a more cheerful direction.

"Almost. Things didn't work out, though."

"I'm sorry," said Adam.

After a couple of moments of neither of them saying anything, Adam had to say something. He could tell Boaz's mood had changed, and now he was uncomfortable in the silence.

"I heard Mr. Rogers say you're his right-hand man, like a son. Do you do other jobs here? Other than this, I mean."

"You know, you sure do talk a lot, boy," said Boaz. "Maybe you should work for *The Gazette*. You ask a lot of questions."

"So I've been told," said Adam.

Boaz gave a nod. "Hmph. Well, since you asked, Emmanuel was like a second father to me from the start. When he took me in, he showed me how to do everything. Took me everywhere. Eventually, I learned how to do everything in this business, but this coopering, this is the job that needs to be done now, so this is what I'm doing."

After a moment, Boaz added, "The one thing I *won't* do is go out to sea."

"Of course. Seasickness, right?" said Adam.

Boaz nodded. "Yep."

Another few minutes of awkward silence eventually prompted Adam to ask another question. "So whatever happened to your mother?"

"My mother? . . . Ah, dear sweet lady she was." Boaz sighed. His tone was uncharacteristically tender. "She went to be with the Lord year before last. Lived a good, long life, bless her, but age just got the better of her, I reckon."

"I'm sorry to hear that," said Adam. "I don't want to think about my mama passing. She's only thirty-five, though, so hopefully she's still got a good, long road ahead of her. She's the only real family I have."

"And you always lived at the tavern?" asked Boaz.

Adam nodded. "Mm-hm. In fact, I was born in the same

room where we've been living my whole life."

"And what about your father?"

Adam scoffed. "What about him? He took off before I was born."

"You don't know much about him, then," said Boaz.

"No. The only thing I know is that he was a sailor. Apparently, he and my mother got married in secret. A few months after they tied the knot he set sail. And as far as I know, she hasn't heard from him since."

"What a rake!" said Boaz. "So you don't even know if he's still alive?"

"No."

"You said they married in secret," Boaz mused.

"Yeah, well, Valentine—he was her guardian at the time, 'cause she was only seventeen—he thought she was too young to marry, so he wouldn't give his permission."

"I see." Boaz nodded. "What was your father's name?"

"I don't know. My mother has always refused to talk about him."

"She ever say why? I mean, from what you've told me, I can't say I blame her, but . . ."

"No, well, I think she just didn't want me to go looking for him. Said it would only lead to heartache. I've tried to get her to tell me, but I reckon she'll take that secret to the grave."

Boaz shook his head. "Well, if she refuses to tell you, there's probably a good reason for it. You prob'ly best just leave it alone. When things get buried, they aren't usually meant to be dug up again."

"I reckon so," said Adam. "But still, it's always bothered me not to know, and it's even worse with the way people are always running their mouths."

"How do you mean?" said Boaz.

"You know. People who don't really know her or what happened—they don't believe the two of them really were married, so they say all these terrible things and call her awful names."

"Why is that?"

"Well, because she and my father never had a proper wedding. They said their vows, just the two of them, and the only witnesses were supposedly some of the men from my father's crew. By the time she had me, my father was already long gone. Folks got the wrong impression. She'd been living and working in the tavern since she was thirteen, so folks started thinking she was a prostitute, mess like that."

Boaz just shook his head. "I'd want to knock someone's head off if they spoke that way about my mother."

"I almost did," said Adam. "That's how I ended up here."

Adam proceeded to tell Boaz all about his long-standing clash with Francis Smythe and how he had recently allowed himself to be provoked into busting the arrogant little aristocrat in the face.

"And he's Ellison Smythe's son, no less!" Boaz guffawed. "Boy, sounds like you really picked a good one to get into a fight with."

Adam nodded sheepishly.

"Well, what's done is done," said Boaz. "Hot tempers and wagging tongues can do right much damage."

Adam nodded in agreement. "Yeah. You got that right."

"So your mother—she never remarried, then?"

"Nope."

"You've been the man of the house, then," Boaz observed.

"I guess."

"And you're seventeen, you said?" asked Boaz.

"Yeah."

"So let's see." Judging by the expression on his face, Boaz was trying to do the calculations in his head. "That would mean you were born back in '47."

"May of '48, actually."

"Forty-eight, huh? I remember those days. They were some rough times. Especially '47. That was a bad year. That's when the Spanish took the town. You ever heard about that before? Three different times those rascals attacked our town, then finally, late that summer, they just came in and took possession. We ran 'em out, though."

"Yeah, I know a little bit about that," said Adam. "I hear 'em talking about it down in the tavern from time to time—some of the men who fought those Spaniards off. Mostly just when they're drunk, though. They're always down there bragging about their old fighting days."

Boaz chuckled.

"Yeah. It's always either that, or the French and Indian War. Or some kind of war story," said Adam.

"Well, at least that last one's behind us now," said Boaz. "But I'm not sure how long the peace will last—not with all these damned new taxes and regulations."

Adam was uninterested. "Taxes are so boring. I always hear 'em going on and on about that down at the tavern, but it doesn't have anything to do with me, so I never pay much attention to it."

"Foolish boy! What do you know?" Boaz laughed and stopped his work to stretch his back. "Of course it has to do with you. It has plenty to do with you—you just don't know it yet. Any time a government starts *collecting revenue*, as they call it, it affects everybody."

"If you say so."

"Just think about it—that Sugar Act they passed last year, for example. When molasses and sugar gets taxed, and wine and coffee—well, that hits everybody. In fact, just think about that tavern of yours. Y'all use all that stuff, so you pay more for it when it gets taxed. Then your customers have to pay more. And when prices get too high, who can afford it?"

Adam shrugged. "I guess I understand."

"Well, you better. I hate to have to tell you this, but right now you're on the frontlines in the battle against those taxes. This is a shipping company. We import things from all over the place, and we export things, too, so when that pebble of taxation gets dropped into the big ol' pond of the economy, we're the first to feel the ripples."

Adam stopped working for a moment and held up the plank he had been hollowing. "How does this look?"

"Let me see," said Boaz. He examined the boy's work, turning the stave from end to end, back and front, and then compared it in length and width to the original that he had given Adam to use as a reference. "Not bad. Looks like you finally got one right. You're a pretty quick learner, boy."

Adam smiled. "Thank you."

"It's close to suppertime, and I'd say we've done our lot for today. You hungry?"

"Yeah, I am."

"You eating upstairs with us, or you goin back to the tavern?"

"If it's alright, I think I'd like to run down to the tavern for a while," said Adam. "You know, just to check on everything."

"Alright then."

Adam nodded and started for the bay doors.

"Listen!" Boaz called after him. "You need to be back by eleven. We start first thing in the morning."

Adam nodded. "Alright. See you later, then."

Chapter Six

ADAM WAS HAPPY to see Valentine Hodges in his usual spot behind the counter when he entered the Topsail Tavern. The ruddy-faced tavern keeper was sitting on a stool, sleeves rolled up and spectacles on, studying over the ledger. Adam could tell he didn't immediately notice the boy, but when Valentine looked up and saw him, he said, "Well, well . . . They fire you already, huh?"

"Ha-ha! Very funny." Adam gave a sarcastic laugh. "No, they didn't fire me already. Actually, Mr. Rogers said he doesn't mind if I come down here, so long as I've got my work done."

"Oh really? Well, I know your mama'll be glad to hear it. She just got back from the Widow Simpson's." He tipped his head back towards the kitchen. "Go on back there. I reckon she's fixin herself something to eat. Prob'ly talkin to Aunt Franny."

Adam smiled and slapped the counter as he darted past it

on his way to the kitchen. He gently pushed open the door and saw his mother on the opposite side of the room, her back to him, doing just as Valentine had said. She was fixing a plate of food and talking to the elderly black woman who was the main cook for the Topsail Tavern. Adam didn't know what her full name was. She'd always just been Aunt Franny to him. The short, plump, mahogany-complected woman was working at the Topsail long before Adam was born—even before Valentine had been made guardian to Adam's mother. Everyone called her Aunt Franny.

Franny saw Adam come in, but he put his finger to his lips and silently mouthed, "Shh . . ."

He grinned mischievously at her before sneaking up behind his mother and grabbing her at her sides.

Mary jumped and spun around, nearly dumping the plate she held in her hand. When she realized who it was, she gasped. "Adam! It's you! What in the world are you doing here?"

"What does it look like?" he said. "I'm back, Mama. They fired me."

Mary took a deep breath, then exhaled sharply. "Adam! What did you do now?"

Aunt Franny smiled at him. "You a little rascal," she said to him under her breath.

She gave him a wink as she walked past him and excused herself to go check on some pastries that were in the oven.

Adam laughed. He couldn't keep up the ruse.

"I'm just teasing you! Mr. Rogers told me I can come back here anytime, so long as I get done with my work first and get back to the warehouse by eleven."

Mary's eyes grew wide and she smiled broadly. "Did he really say that?"

Adam nodded. "Sure did."

"Thank God! That's such good news. You know, you're lucky. A lot of apprentices aren't allowed to go home to see their families very often."

She hugged her son with her free arm, carefully holding her plate in her other hand.

"Look, I was just fixing myself a plate." She motioned to the two huge iron pots that were suspended from hooks over the fire. "Let me fix you something to eat."

Adam was thankful he could eat in the tavern with his family. He chose Aunt Franny's beef stew with potatoes, onions, and carrots, and grabbed a couple of rolls from a basket near the oven. He and his mother went back out into the tavern and sat at the bar to eat their meal. Adam told his mother and Valentine all about his first day as an apprentice as they enjoyed their supper.

Adam ate ravenously. Mary observed him and then asked, "Didn't they feed you today?"

"Yeah, they did. But I just didn't have much of an appetite. So did I miss anything interesting today?"

"Nah," said Valentine. "Just like any other day."

"Actually, Mr. Rasquelle was here today," said Mary.

"He was?"

"Yep. I had his table. Told him you'd just started your first day as an apprentice in his trade."

"Really? What'd he say."

"Well, I might not should tell you this, but he said had he known you were looking for an apprenticeship, he'd have gladly taken you under his wing."

Adam dropped his spoon and wrinkled his brow. "You're joking. That means Mr. Robins never even bothered to tell him about me! He knew that Mr. Rasquelle is the whole reason I chose that trade!"

"Well, maybe Mr. Robins thought you'd be better off with someone more experienced," said Valentine. "Emmanuel Rogers has been supplying the tavern for decades now. He's got a good, steady business."

"But I never even met Mr. Rogers until today. I had wanted to be bound to Mr. Rasquelle. That's the whole reason I wanted to be a shipping merchant in the first place. Mr. Rasquelle is an impressive businessman, and he goes after what he wants. He's determined to be successful. And, well, learning under someone like him—I think it could help me be successful, too."

"Well," said Mary, "he did mention that if you wanted to come by sometime and see him, that he'd be interested in talking to you. Says he may still be able to help you out."

"Really?" said Adam. "How? I mean, the papers have already been signed."

Mary shrugged. "I don't know what he has in mind. But it might be worth your while to go see him—see what he wants."

"Yeah, maybe." Adam thought for a moment. "Mmm . . . Actually, I don't know. I mean, Mr. Rogers seems like a decent man. Boaz . . . he's alright. He'll be tough to work for, but I think I can learn from him."

Mary shook her head. "You do what you want, son. I don't know what to tell you. It's going to have to be your decision."

"I know. I'll need to think about it. I mean, on one hand, Mr. Rogers doesn't mind me coming back here whenever I want. It might not be like that with Mr. Rasquelle."

"That's true," said Mary.

"But then again, Mr. Rasquelle is—"

"Mr. Smythe!" Valentine said. "Good evening, sir!"

Adam whipped around to see Ellison Smythe, the father of the boy whose nose he had broken. Dressed in his customary powdered wig and a well-tailored dark blue suit, the man cut an intimidating figure, reflective of his social standing and power.

Mary and Adam both stood from their stools.

"Mr. Smythe, what a surprise!" said Mary.

"You're back, sir."

As soon as the words had left Adam's mouth, he felt like a fool for saying them. He didn't know what else to say, though. The town's customs agent was so formal, he made nearly everyone around him nervous.

"Mr. Hodges, Miss Fletcher, Adam, I am quite certain you can surmise why I am here this evening."

None of the three responded.

"Fact is, I heard from Peter Robins earlier today that you had been bound apprentice to Emmanuel Rogers as a gracious compromise to a stricter punishment for what you did to my son."

Adam opened his mouth to speak, but Mr. Smythe raised his hand to silence him.

"I had my coachman take me there to Rogers's warehouse just a little while ago, but I was told you had come back here for the evening."

"Yes, sir," said Adam. "Mr. Rogers said he didn't mind if I—"

"I just wanted to be very clear with you, young man. I was quite angry to arrive from my travels and learn about your vicious assault on Francis. Of all people, I know he can behave atrociously at times, but that is no excuse for you to attack him bodily. I have no tolerance for brutish behavior. That said, I think Mr. Robins exhibited his characteristic wisdom by offering you the opportunity of an apprenticeship rather than earning a criminal record at your young age. I was once a young man, too, of course, so I realize what a boy your age needs most is direction and guidance. Unfortunately, it does not appear that you have had enough of that here at this tavern."

"Now you wait just a damned minute—" said Valentine.

Mr. Smythe ignored Valentine and continued speaking. "Because clearly, if you had proper direction and guidance, you wouldn't have been allowed to get yourself into the situation that has led to your current circumstances."

Valentine fumed. "First of all, Mr. Smythe, Mary wasn't here when the boys got into their scuffle. Secondly, your boy was running his mouth about her. She is Adam's mama. Do you really think I ought to have told Adam he shouldn't defend her good name? If it'd been me, I'd have knocked that brat of yours out cold."

"And you prove my point," said Mr. Smythe. "You prove it perfectly. If you were wise, you'd have known that as proprietor of this establishment, considering Francis was apparently being loud and disruptive, it would've been entirely within your rights to ask my son to silence his insults or to leave. And if he refused your request, you'd have also been within your rights to have him physically removed from the premises. Instead, you thought it reasonable to allow Adam to take the argument outside. And so here we are."

"Forgive me for saying so, sir, but I think your son wanted to fight," said Adam.

"I have little doubt of that," said Mr. Smythe. "Boredom will drive a young man to seek diversion in many foolish ways. That said, my son is no brawler. In fact, I would reckon that was his first fight. Had you taken the high road and not given in to his taunting, you'd not be in the situation you're in. I believe your apprenticeship with Emmanuel Rogers will serve you well. I've known him for many years and I believe him to be a good, temperate man. If you commit yourself to learning as much as you are able under his tutelage, you will go far. If, however, you look for shortcuts or give less than your best effort in your training, you will compound your problems."

"What are you saying, sir?" Adam asked.

"I'm saying that I believe once a man has made amends for a crime such as yours, he should be given a fresh start—his slate wiped clean. Once you complete your apprenticeship with Mr. Rogers, it might surprise you to know that I will be one of your most enthusiastic supporters in this town. On the other hand, if for some reason you do not complete your apprenticeship with him, I will see to it that Mr. Robins issues to you the harshest punishment allowable by law."

At that, Adam was left speechless, but he nodded to acknowledge that he'd heard what Mr. Smythe had said. It appeared his decision about whether or not he should go see Richard Rasquelle may have just been made for him.

Chapter Seven

AFTER SEVERAL DAYS at Rogers's warehouse, Adam was starting to feel more familiar with the cask-making process. He hadn't learned all of the skills yet, but he was beginning to develop a familiarity with most of the tools and had a basic understanding of the different tasks.

On Wednesday morning, almost a week after Adam began his apprenticeship, he, Boaz, Elliot, and Joe were working outside the warehouse, heating and shaping barrels over a group of short chimneys. Things were uncomfortably quiet. Adam could tell there was some kind of unspoken tension, but he decided rather than trying to make conversation he'd best stay focused—especially since Boaz seemed even grouchier than usual.

Finally, Boaz broke the silence.

"Damnit! Where's Martin?"

"I told you. He's gone to pick up the hoop irons. He

weren't goin no place else, so I reckon he'll back anytime," said Elliot.

"Right. Well, he better be back soon. We're behind as it is. We're going to run out of hoops soon, and then we'll just be sitting around wasting time until he decides to show up."

"Stop worryin," said Elliot. "He'll be back. Maybe the irons weren't ready yet."

Boaz rolled his eyes and waved his hand, dismissing Elliot's attempt at making excuses for Martin. "He should have been back over an hour ago. We all know he's prob'ly just wasting time running his mouth. He could make conversation with a mute, and God help us if he's chatting with a young lady. The little Lothario might not make it back here until sundown!"

Adam gave a quizzical look at Elliot.

Elliot said, "Mr. Wiggins needs to be able to fill these with the turpentine and pitch before the *Gypsy* sets sail next week. We might have to work some late days to get all of these done by the end of the week since we're behind, and Martin not being back yet ain't helping matters none."

"No, it's not." Boaz made an impatient wave towards Adam. "And having to train this pup while we're under the gun isn't making things any easier."

Adam glanced over at Elliot, who dismissively shook his head and said, "Don't pay him no mind."

"If Martin isn't back soon," said Boaz, "I'm leaving to go look for him."

There was one worker in Rogers's company who almost never spoke—Elliot's cousin, Joe. He was a wispy little man who passed the time working by watching everybody else carrying on. Occasionally, he'd laugh and nod, but otherwise he stayed quiet. So when he pointed his finger and said, "Lookathere!," Boaz and

Elliot both turned their heads towards the street just in time to see a horse and cart driving into view. It was Martin.

"It's about damn time!" said Boaz.

Martin stopped in front of the warehouse and hopped out of the cart, grabbing a bundle of hoop iron to bring into the warehouse.

"Go give him a hand, Fletcher," said Elliot.

"Glad to," said Adam. He ran over and grabbed another stack of hoop irons and brought them over into the cooper's work area.

Boaz and Elliot followed Martin and Adam inside. They would need to get started making hoops out of the strips of iron right away if they were going to stay on schedule. Joe stayed outside, tending to the casks that were being heated and shaped over the makeshift chimneys.

"I ran into the rat today," said Martin as he brought the last stack of hoop irons over to the bench where they would be shaped.

"Oh, really? Is that what took you so long?" said Boaz.

"Don't start with me, Bo." Martin strode back over to the cart to grab a sack full of odds and ends from his visit in town.

"Where'd you see him?" said Elliot.

"Over at Moore's Mercantile."

"What was he doing there?"

"What do you think he was doing there?" said Martin. "Trying to steal our cheese."

"You must be joking," said Boaz. His voice reflected his disgust. "Moore didn't take the bait, did he?"

"Don't think so," said Martin, "but it's hard to say for sure."

"Who's the rat? What cheese?" said Adam. He couldn't

stand not knowing who the conversation was about, and it hadn't occurred to him that it might not be any of his business.

Boaz, Martin, and Elliot looked at one another.

"Oh," said Elliot, "he's no one, really. Just someone we don't like all that much."

Boaz let out a sarcastic laugh.

"Do I know him?" said Adam.

"Doubt it," said Boaz.

Adam was frustrated but intrigued.

"Did you hear them talking?" asked Elliot, resurrecting the conversation that Adam could tell Boaz had hoped to put to rest.

Martin shook his head. "No, I didn't." Adam noticed him look back over at Boaz and roll his eyes.

He was dying to find out what everybody was trying to hide. It aggravated him to be in the dark about something that everyone else knew. It made it even worse that they were obviously trying to conceal it from him. Naturally, that made him want to discover it all the more.

Unfortunately for his curiosity, however, the subject was not brought up again.

WHEN IT WAS FINALLY time for their midday meal, Adam and Boaz went upstairs to eat the fatback-seasoned butter beans that had been cooking in a Dutch oven over the fire in the kitchen's hearth since before dawn, along with some leftover cornbread. Adam was glad to have an opportunity to talk to Boaz alone. For what it was worth, in spite of his brusque demeanor, he seemed like an honest man and a straight shooter.

When Boaz made the comment about how having to spend time training him as an apprentice was slowing things down, Adam wondered if perhaps he should go see Mr. Rasquelle, after all. He hadn't thought a whole lot about it since his mother mentioned it the previous week—especially after Ellison Smythe's demand that he follow through on his apprenticeship with Emmanuel Rogers—but now he was wondering if it might be an idea that would be mutually beneficial for all parties involved.

Adam hoped the right opportunity would present itself to bring the conversation up, but it never seemed to happen. Finally, he decided he better speak up before he lost his chance.

"You know I went back to the tavern again last night," said Adam.

"How's your mother?" said Boaz, shoveling a spoonful of beans into his mouth.

"Great. She was great." Adam was quiet for a moment.

"Bet she was glad to see you," said Boaz.

"Mm-hm. She sure is glad that y'all don't mind me going over there to see her. Said I'm real lucky to have such a kind boss."

"You are," said Boaz, mouth full of cornbread. "My first master never let me go home."

"Are most masters really like that?"

"Can't say for sure, but I imagine so. But then right many apprentices are orphans, so who'd they go home to, even if they could?"

"That's true," said Adam.

He paused for a moment. "Boaz?"

"Yes?"

"Do you mind if I ask you something?"

"Go ahead."

Boaz was polishing off his bowl of beans quickly and wouldn't wait around to chat once it was done. Adam knew he better get to the point.

"You know anything about Richard Rasquelle?"

Boaz nearly choked on his cornbread. He coughed to clear his throat. "Yeah, I do." He coughed a bit more and then said, "Do you know him?"

Adam shook his head. "No, it's just my mother was telling me last night that he was in the tavern yesterday. He was last week, too. She waited on his table. He comes in there sometimes, you know."

"Hmph. Well, everybody's gotta eat."

Adam suspected that Boaz wasn't fond of Mr. Rasquelle, considering the mere mention of his name caused him to choke on his food.

"She had told him about my new apprenticeship here. And he told her that Mr. Robins never even mentioned me to him."

"Oh, well," said Boaz. "If you ask me, you ought to count yourself lucky for not getting mixed up with him." He sopped up some gravy from the beans with his cornbread and popped it into his mouth.

"Maybe so," said Adam, "But I gotta tell you, when I first was told I'd be apprenticed, I had hoped that I'd be working for him."

Boaz inhaled sharply but said nothing. He just took another bite of cornbread.

"Don't misunderstand me," said Adam. "I like it here. I do. But I had never known much about Mr. Rogers—or this company—before I started working here."

"Yeah. I can understand why. You already heard that Emmanuel never takes on anyone new. In fact, I'm still not sure why he decided to bring you here."

Adam was caught off guard by that last statement. He still

wasn't used to Boaz's blunt manner of speaking. Finally, he managed to say, "Me neither."

Adam thought for a moment. Maybe Boaz wished he hadn't been brought on as an apprentice. Maybe he resented him.

"I can tell you this, though," said Boaz. He pointed his spoon at Adam. "Emmanuel is a wise man. I might not always understand why he does some of the things he does, and a lot of times I might not agree with him, but in the end I trust him. Him taking you on here? If he did it, he must have had a good reason."

"Is him taking me on here one of those decisions you didn't agree with?"

Boaz cocked his head to the side and raised his eyebrows, but he said nothing. Instead, he just kept eating.

"I could leave, you know?" said Adam. "You don't like me here. I can go. Mr. Rasquelle wanted me to stop by and talk to him sometime. Said he may have something for me."

Boaz wouldn't respond.

Adam was getting impatient. "What do you think about that?"

Still nothing.

"Look, I know Rasquelle is a competitor and all, but if you don't really want me here, and since you're the one who's been burdened with having to train me, maybe I should try to find another situation—relieve you of this chore."

"You want me to be honest with you?" said Boaz. He dropped his spoon in his bowl.

Adam nodded. "Of course."

"If it were up to me, I would say that I don't give a damn what you do. You have no history here, no sense of . . . loyalty. But like I said, Emmanuel doesn't hire anybody new. He doesn't take on apprentices. Everybody in this company is related to him or connected to him somehow. For the life of me I don't know why he brought you here, but he did, so he must have had a reason. Go on and talk to that jackass Rasquelle if you want, but regardless of how fancy he dresses, regardless of how much folks think he's some kind of hero, regardless of how much he tries to impress everybody with his business, underneath it all I know he's a fraud."

"A fraud?" said Adam. "How?"

"You wouldn't believe me if I told you what I know, but I'll say this. Richard Rasquelle is not who he seems to be."

"In what way?"

Boaz pushed himself away from the table, grabbed his empty bowl and spoon, and dropped them into the dish basin and scrubbed them before rinsing them in a basin of clear water.

"I've said all I'm gonna say. You wanna know about Rasquelle? Just watch him. I'm telling you—he ain't what he seems. But I'll tell you this." Boaz pointed his finger at Adam. "You do anything to betray Emmanuel's kindness to you in any way—anything—and you best not show your face in this warehouse again."

He abruptly left to go back downstairs. When Adam was done eating, he went back downstairs as well. Just then Emmanuel came into the warehouse.

"Alright, lads, it seems we're getting close to the time when the *Elizabeth Ella* should be arriving. She was leaving Liverpool on April the eighth, so by my calendar she should be due here any day now."

"Will we be taking it in here at the warehouse?" said Martin.

"This shipment we will, yes," said Emmanuel. "But there's another shipment that should be arriving a week or two after the

Elizabeth Ella. We'll receive that one at the other dock."

"When would you like us to go over there and get everything in order?" said Boaz.

"I should think it might be wise to do it before the week's end. You know how these things are. We can never be certain when a ship will arrive," said Emmanuel.

"We can go on Saturday as soon as we're done delivering these," said Boaz as he motioned to several finished casks, as well as the casks-in-progress.

"Very well," said Emmanuel. He started back up the stairs, then stopped and said, "Wait! On second thought, I think it'd be better for Martin to go."

Martin waved in acknowledgment of his suggestion.

Emmanuel continued: "Boaz, I'm going to need your help here for another task on Saturday."

"Good enough, sir," said Martin. "Elliot and I will take care of it."

"You know what? Take Adam with you, if you don't mind. Leave Elliot here so he can help Boaz on that other task I mentioned. Adam is a part of this company now, so he needs to learn about the second dock, how we do things, and so forth," said Emmanuel.

Boaz gave a worried look to Emmanuel but said nothing. Emmanuel subtly shook his head at Boaz in response, as if to say, *Don't worry—I know what I'm doing.*

Chapter Eight

AT THE END of work, Adam went back to the tavern to eat, enjoy a pint, and visit with his mother and Valentine for a while. He felt a little awkward about skipping dinner at the warehouse again, but for now at least he knew Boaz wasn't too keen on him, so he wanted to stay out of his way.

It wasn't long after Adam finished his supper that Mary suddenly got up from the stool at the bar beside him.

"Excuse me, boys," she said. "I think I have a customer." She quickly grabbed an apron to tie around her waist.

"But you're not working tonight," said Adam.

Mary flashed him a smile and went over to a table where some customers had just sat down. Richard Rasquelle was there. She had gone over to take his order.

"What in the world was that about?" Adam asked Valentine.

The old man shrugged. "I don't know. He was already in here once today—at lunch. She had his table then." He narrowed his eyes and scratched his chin. "He's awfully chatty, that one. And he's been in here right regular lately."

Adam repositioned himself on his bar stool so he could look in the direction of Rasquelle's table. It was strange to see how his mother had virtually flown over to wait on him. Was she flirting with him? Adam wasn't sure—he hadn't seen his mother engage in that sort of behavior before.

Adam used to appreciate it when men like Richard Rasquelle came into the tavern. He would feel proud that wealthy and important men like him thought it worth their time and money to dine in his family's establishment. Rasquelle especially cut an impressive figure. He was lean, slightly tall, and exceedingly handsome, with dark hair and piercing blue eyes. Rasquelle was an impeccably dressed gentleman, and his clothing ensemble was neatly tailored, but then he'd never be seen in anything less than the very best. In fact, his outfit likely cost more than the average Beaufort resident earned in a year. He also seemed unusually gracious for someone in the shipping business. Even though they had never actually conversed, Adam had always wondered what it might be like to work for someone like him. Not necessarily in shipping, but someone classy, refined.

Just then Mary waved to Adam from across the room.

"Come over here for a minute, son!" she said.

Adam looked at Valentine, who in turn just shrugged his shoulders. The boy reluctantly made his way through the maze of noisy drinkers and diners to join his mother beside Richard Rasquelle's table.

"Sweetheart," she said, "Mr. Rasquelle said he wanted to meet you. Mr. Rasquelle, this is my son, Adam."

"How do you do, sir?" said Adam.

"Very well, thank you," said Mr. Rasquelle. "Your mother tells me you've recently started an apprenticeship to learn my trade."

"Yes, sir. Started nearly a week ago, as a matter of fact."

"Ah, how wonderful! Well, I wanted to tell you that had I known you were seeking such an opportunity, I'd have surely extended an offer to bring you under my wing."

"Oh, well, thank you, sir. I appreciate the sentiment. It's alright, though. Things are going fine at Mr. Rogers's warehouse."

"That's delightful to hear!" said Rasquelle. "However, I may still have something for you. A little work on the side, if you're interested."

Adam wrinkled his eyebrows. "Sir?"

"Listen, I'll be away tomorrow, but if you'd like to come by my warehouse and see me in my office on Saturday, I'd like to talk to you about a little opportunity. I'll make it worth your while. And don't worry. It shouldn't interfere with your duties for your master."

"I'll see what I can do," said Adam.

"Wonderful," said Mr. Rasquelle.

At that, Adam looked at his mother and smiled before returning to the bar to finish his pint and his conversation with Valentine.

When Rasquelle finally left, Adam was relieved. His mother rejoined him and Valentine over by the bar.

"What in the world was all of that about?" he asked her.

"Well, Mr. Rasquelle was in here earlier today. He asked me if I had mentioned to you about going by to see him."

"What did you tell him?" said Adam.

"I told him the truth. I told him that you weren't sure

whether you should. I also told him about what Mr. Smythe said."

"So why is he here again tonight?"

"I told him you've been coming by for supper—that Mr. Rogers doesn't mind you visiting. I reckon he wanted to speak to you himself."

"I appreciate all of that, Mama, but I'm not sure about working for him."

Adam couldn't believe what he had just said, especially after what had happened with Boaz earlier.

"Why not?" she prodded. "Sounds like he might have some extra work you can do. You aren't getting paid at Emmanuel Rogers's place. Maybe you can do little jobs for Mr. Rasquelle and earn some pocket money. Who knows? You might like working for him. You don't have anything to lose, do you?"

"I don't know. Something just seems strange about this. I mean, what kind of man tries to employ someone apprenticed to his competitor? Second, I've been asking around, and I've heard some things about him. They're not very good."

"Who have you been checking around with, Adam? The men down at Rogers's Shipping? You don't think they might be influenced by the fact that he's their competition?"

"They may be," said Adam, "but regardless, something in my gut just doesn't feel right about this. I can't tell you exactly what it is, but you have always told me to trust my instincts."

"I know, son, but don't let those boys over at the warehouse influence you just because they're jealous. You know as well as I do that Mr. Rasquelle's business has been growing these last couple of years—he's made quite a name for himself around town. And even more so after that big ol' party of his a couple of weeks ago."

"Well, he ain't got my business," said Valentine.

"Oh, Valentine," said Mary, "of course he doesn't. You've had the same standing order now with Emmanuel Rogers since before I came here! And that was a hundred years ago!"

"That's not true," said Valentine. "I did try Rasquelle once. Ended up going back to Emmanuel, though."

"Well, you two stay here and talk about it," said Mary. "I'm going on up to get some sleep. I've got to be up before the sun tomorrow. Gimme some sugar, son." She tapped her cheek.

Adam gave his mother a quick peck on the cheek before she went upstairs.

After Mary was out of sight, Valentine poured another pint for himself and Adam. "So you're wantin to find out more about that Richard Rasquelle?"

Adam nodded.

"Listen, your mama don't know nothing about this . . ." said Valentine.

He stroked the fading reddish stubble on his face and looked to be thinking hard about what he was about to say.

"It may be nothing at all, but I'm gonna mention it. The reason I only got that one shipment from Rasquelle was because he came up short. That never happened with Emmanuel Rogers."

"What do you mean, he came up short?"

"I mean, I think Rasquelle shorted me on what I had ordered. Oh, he insisted that I was mistaken, but I ain't no spring chicken. I know how long my supplies are supposed to last, and I know what a cask of molasses looks like, and his delivery just plain came up short."

"Do you think he did it on purpose?" Adam asked.

"I won't go so far as to say that, but I didn't want to risk coming up short again, so I switched my accounts back over to Emmanuel Rogers. I've always gotten my supplies from him.

Don't know why I ever switched. I guess when Richard Rasquelle came to town a couple years ago, he promised he'd sell things cheaper. And he said he'd be bringing in more merchandise than Emmanuel Rogers."

"More merchandise? Like what?"

"Well, I was mostly just interested in seeing if he'd have some different things from Europe and the Orient—spices and such."

"Did you buy anything like that from him?" said Adam.

"No. That first shipment, he didn't have no more than what Emmanuel has. I think one of the things he meant as 'more merchandise' was, well, laborers. And I ain't got no use for that."

"You mean slaves?" said Adam in a shocked whisper.

Valentine nodded.

"Rasquelle is a slave trader?" Adam was stunned.

"Shh!" Valentine motioned for the boy to lower his voice. "No, he ain't really a slave trader, but I know at least one time he done it. He may still do it, but it ain't something he really advertises, you know."

"No," said Adam. "At least I've never heard about it."

"Emmanuel Rogers, on the other hand—well, what he imports and what he sells is good quality. It is what he says it is. I trust him."

"You said my mama didn't know about that experience with Rasquelle."

"Oh, yeah. Well, that don't mean nothin, though. She's just never been involved in the books—you know, who we buy from. And all the shipments are received in the back anyway, so she wouldn't even know the men making deliveries."

"I see," said Adam.

"Yep. I reckon you ought to think long and hard before

you go see that man. In fact, I'm gonna give you some advice. I think I'd just leave it alone if I were you. Be happy with where you are. Otherwise, you might end up with more trouble than what you got already."

◇◇◇

AS ADAM WALKED ALONG the winding, lantern-lit road by the waterfront back to Rogers's warehouse, he had plenty of time to think. In spite of what Valentine had told him, he couldn't stop wondering about Mr. Rasquelle's offer.

It didn't help that some rowdy sailors were making music on the docks, and one of the songs they were playing on their penny whistles and fiddles was a popular tune that had been played at Richard Rasquelle's big party. Adam's thoughts drifted back to that day. He remembered Rasquelle's speech from that party. Then he thought about the dull routine he knew he'd face when he started another day's work in Emmanuel Rogers's warehouse the next morning. He started thinking that maybe he should take Rasquelle's advice—"if you want anything in this life, you have to go after it."

Chapter Nine

ADAM SPENT ALL of Thursday and Friday contemplating Richard Rasquelle's offer. By Saturday, he had decided he would go talk to Mr. Rasquelle and find out what kind of opportunity he wanted to offer. He was nagged briefly by some second thoughts, but he silenced them by calculating that if nothing else came from the meeting, it would at least give him a chance to observe the man, as Boaz had suggested.

As he approached Rasquelle's building, which was at the opposite end of the town from Rogers's warehouse, he felt his pulse quicken. He was conflicted. Part of him wanted to forget the whole idea, but another part of him felt compelled to go through with it. When he finally arrived, he approached the street entrance, which, unlike his master's warehouse, was just a regular door rather than a large set of cargo doors.

Once he was inside, Adam noticed how much bigger

his master's warehouse was than Rasquelle's. It wasn't surprising, though, considering Emmanuel Rogers had been in town for decades, whereas Richard Rasquelle had only been around a couple of years. The building was positioned longways facing the water, while Rogers's property was on a deep lot that extended from Taylor Creek back several acres to a roadway.

The waterfront thoroughfare in Beaufort wasn't straight. It was a winding path, and there was a big curve just before Mr. Rogers's property began. It gave his parcel of land a much greater depth than the shallow, wide lot owned by Rasquelle. On the other hand, Rasquelle's warehouse was newer and right in the heart of town. The two factors, combined with the bustling activity around the building, lent the impression that Rasquelle's company was much busier.

Adam asked a couple of men working inside where Mr. Rasquelle was. Just as one of them was about to motion to the opposite side of the building, Mr. Rasquelle came through the waterfront cargo doors and spotted Adam, then crossed the warehouse to greet him.

"Mr. Fletcher! So glad you decided to come by today. I wasn't sure if the old man would let you get away."

"It's alright. I'm on a break."

Mr. Rasquelle smiled. "Very good then. Why don't you follow me to my office?"

Adam nodded and followed him to the other side of the building, where there was a cluster of little rooms side by side. The floor of the warehouse was barer than that of Emmanuel Rogers's warehouse, and the mood of the place was different. While the men at Rogers's company worked hard, the atmosphere was friendlier—even with grouchy Boaz. Richard Rasquelle's workers, on the other hand, didn't exude that same sense of camaraderie.

Even the coopers went about their tasks in silence.

As they neared Mr. Rasquelle's office, Adam noticed a door that was different than the others. It was made of thick wood, had a little window with bars over it, and was secured with two padlocks. As they walked past it, Adam craned his head to see if he could glimpse into the little window, but Mr. Rasquelle turned and spoke before he was able to see anything.

"Right in here," he said.

Adam stepped into his office, glancing quickly back into the warehouse.

"What are the bars for?" he asked as he motioned to the room next door.

Mr. Rasquelle smiled and cocked his head in the direction of the room. "That one over there, you mean?"

Adam nodded. "Yes, sir." He didn't care if he seemed nosy.

Mr. Rasquelle sat down at his desk and motioned for Adam to have a seat as well.

"That's where we store the most valuable cargo items until they can be delivered."

"Oh, I see," said Adam.

"We have all sorts of shipments that come and go through this warehouse, Mr. Fletcher. I doubt you would have seen the likes of some of the items you would find here over at Rogers's Shipping."

"Is that so? Interesting."

"So tell me, young man. How do you like working for Mr. Rogers?"

Adam shrugged. "It's not bad. I like it just fine, actually. Don't see Mr. Rogers all that much, though, so I can't really say how it is to work directly for him."

"Are you enjoying your job? Your apprenticeship, I mean.

Is it what you expected it would be?"

"Well, I've only been at it for about a week, so it's hard to say."

"I would expect you're not getting paid, being that it is an apprenticeship."

"No, sir. I do have room and board, though."

"Ah, yes. But you already had that before you went to work for him."

Adam smiled and tipped his head in consent. "That is true."

"Well, maybe we can change your financial circumstances a bit. I was wondering if you might be interested in an opportunity—one that I imagine would certainly be to your benefit. I know it would be to mine."

"What's that, sir?"

"I'm glad you asked. I'm sure you're aware of my commitment to the growth of this little seaport," said Mr. Rasquelle as he stood from his desk and walked over to gaze out the window overlooking the creek. "I have invested a great deal by setting up my company here when I could have just as easily set up my business in New Bern or Charleston—anywhere, really. Why do you think I did this, Mr. Fletcher?"

"I don't know, sir. Why?"

"Because I believed my talents and my connections could help bring life to this little village. I felt I could bring in a greater variety of merchandise and commodities, and help the people here find eager customers for the fruits of their labor—naval stores, shingles, livestock, tobacco, whatever it may be."

"That's good of you, sir," said Adam.

Mr. Rasquelle smiled. "I'd like to think the people know my heart is set first and foremost upon the well-being and growth of this town."

He sat back down at his desk. "I also believe in doing everything aboveboard."

Mr. Rasquelle waited for a moment. Adam wondered if he was waiting for him to agree with his statement. When he did not, the merchant continued.

"Let me be very plain. I do not condone smuggling, as much as a burden as tariffs can be. I think we cannot expect to see this town rewarded for its hard work if we do not abide by the rules."

"I understand," said Adam.

"But in the last two years since I came here, I have uncovered a problem."

"What's that, sir?"

"What I'm about to discuss with you requires your complete confidence. I need to be assured that you will not breathe a word of this to another living soul."

Adam nodded. "My word is as good as yours, I can assure you."

Rasquelle smiled. "Very good." He leaned back in his chair and pressed his fingertips together. "I believe there is someone in this town who has been, shall we say, duplicitous in his dealings—not only with those good souls bringing much-needed merchandise into our port, but also with the Crown's customs authorities, as well as the very citizens of Port Beaufort."

"Who is this man, sir?"

Rasquelle hesitated before he said, "Emmanuel Rogers."

"Emmanuel Rogers? My master?" said Adam. He shouldn't have been surprised. There was only one other merchant in town, but duplicitous? Surely Mr. Rasquelle must've been talking about somebody else.

"I have heard things," said Rasquelle, "but I have no way to investigate them. You know how Emmanuel Rogers isolates himself and his company. He never brings anyone new in to work for him, and I believe it's because he is afraid they will uncover his wrongdoing."

Though typically quick on his feet, Adam was unsure of how to respond, so he decided to stay quiet.

"I think he may have agreed to bring you on as an apprentice because he believed you were young, naïve, and that you could be easily tricked into thinking the way he does business is perfectly normal. I'll admit that smuggling behavior may be normal in the colonies these days, but it is my intent to set a higher standard, not only for my own company but for Port Beaufort, and even this colony."

Adam wrinkled his brow. "Why are you telling me all of this, sir?"

"Because I believe you are much smarter than this man takes you for. Your mother has told me about you, about your aspirations for the future, and I share your desire to see you become successful. I think because of your new job there you may be able to play a vital role in helping bring Emmanuel Rogers to justice once and for all."

"Sir?"

"I would like you to consider working for me—as a matter of public service—to help me gather the evidence necessary to prove what I have suspected about your master since I arrived in this town."

"But how?"

"Your task would be an easy one. I simply want you to continue working for him—for now—but report to me anything and everything you see happening over there. If you hear about any shipments coming or going, let me know. If you learn of any contacts abroad, let me know. And I promise you I will make it worth your while."

"Wait a minute. You want me to spy on Mr. Rogers?" Adam was stunned.

Mr. Rasquelle hesitated before he responded. "Call it whatever you like. I believe you would be doing this as a loyal subject of King George, and I am willing to pay your wages for this great public service."

He reached in his pocket and pulled out three silver coins. "Consider this as a down payment." He slid the money across the desk.

Adam suddenly felt sick. He didn't know how to respond. He didn't want his loyalty to the Crown to be questioned, but at the same time he had no desire to spy on Emmanuel Rogers. Regardless of what Mr. Rasquelle was telling him, he didn't believe his master was cheating people.

His mind worked quickly, but finally he said, "Sir, if things are as you say they are, I can't possibly take payment from you. My reward will be in seeing that justice is done. You can keep your money."

Rasquelle studied Adam. After a moment he took the coins and put them back into his pocket.

"Very well. I can see I made the right decision by asking you to come here today."

"How would you want me to go about doing this?" said Adam. "I mean, wouldn't it look a bit suspicious if I was running down to see you every few days while I'm apprenticed to your competitor?"

"You are very perceptive, Mr. Fletcher, which is why I think we should meet down at the tavern. I'm sure your mother won't mind. And I doubt Valentine Hodges would say anything, either."

Adam did not like this one bit. It was one thing for Mr. Rasquelle to ask him to spy on his master, but it was quite another thing to try to involve his mother and Valentine and the tavern.

"I'm not sure if that's the best idea, sir. I'd rather leave my family out of this. No need to bring something like this to their doorstep."

Mr. Rasquelle's face turned very serious. "I will make it worth their while if they will facilitate our meetings at the tavern. However, I can assure you they will face far more serious troubles if we are not able to come to some sort of agreement. To put it another way, I'm not sure Mr. Hodge's record is spotless either, considering he's a longtime client of Mr. Rogers."

Adam again found himself speechless.

Mr. Rasquelle continued: "Now listen. You help me with this problem, and I won't report Mr. Hodges."

Adam felt hot. Richard Rasquelle had just crossed the line. Adam wanted to dive across the desk and grab the man's throat, but he resisted the temptation.

Mr. Rasquelle took no note of Adam's change in expression. "If Emmanuel Rogers is conducting the sort of business that I *think* he's conducting, it needs to be stopped, or the very future growth of Port Beaufort may hang in the balance."

"Now just wait a minute, sir. Let's be clear. Are you threatening me? My family?"

"Oh, I'm not threatening anybody." Rasquelle chuckled. "I'm simply trying to help you understand what's at stake here. Maybe Mr. Hodges is complicit in Emmanuel Rogers's illegal dealings, maybe not. That remains to be seen, but one thing I can tell you is this: if Rogers is not stopped, all of the people of this town will suffer. The Crown wants to see Port Beaufort a success—just as they do all of their colonial outposts—but if they believe that it is a haven for smugglers and tax dodgers, you can be sure that tight restrictions will be put in place, and it wouldn't surprise me if there weren't more government officials posted here to enforce the duties. As it is, I'm certain the people of this town enjoy the, shall we say, liberties of having so few officials watching over them."

Adam's jaw tightened. He was trapped and he knew it.

"Fine. I'll do it, sir. When would you like to meet with me again?"

"Good boy. You go back to the tavern to dine and visit every evening, do you not?"

"I try to."

Mr. Rasquelle thought for a moment. "I see no need to decide on a fixed time for our next meeting right now. I'll just find you there in a few days."

"How will I know when you're coming?" asked Adam.

"Don't worry about that. I'll find you."

Adam stood and said, "I better be going."

Mr. Rasquelle extended his hand to shake Adam's. "Indeed. Remember to keep your eyes open, but do not breathe a word of this. Don't forget what I told you."

Adam felt like he was going to be sick. He managed to get out a "yessir" before excusing himself to leave the man's office and the premises.

As ADAM MADE THE long trek back to his master's warehouse, he couldn't help but think back on the day he was bound to Emmanuel Rogers and something the old man had said to his mother—"*I promise you I will take care of your boy as though he were my own. Please trust that he's in good hands."*

Emmanuel had actually said that. He had said he'd take care of Adam as if he were his own son, and so far he'd treated him well. Why didn't that mean anything to Adam before? He had only been thinking of his disappointment at not having Richard Rasquelle as his master, and now Mr. Rasquelle was threatening Adam's family if he didn't comply with his demands to spy on the old man.

He knew he wouldn't be able to do it, but he had no idea how he'd evade Mr. Rasquelle's request.

Chapter Ten

WHEN ADAM GOT back to the warehouse, Martin was waiting for him so they could go to the second dock to make things ready for the pending arrival of *La Dama del Caribe.*

Adam climbed into the horse cart and looked around, wondering which way they would travel. "So where is this place?" he asked.

"It's a secret," said Martin. He smiled mischievously at Adam, then clicked his teeth and snapped the reins in his hand.

"A secret?"

"We're going to my cousin's place," said the handsome young cooper.

After a little while Adam said, "Where's that?"

"The Martin estate. Where else?"

Adam laughed. "I guess it's named after you then, right?"

"Mm-hm. Can you blame them?" said Martin, his tone cocksure as usual. Then he laughed. "I'm only joking. It *is* called the Martin estate, but it's because it belonged to my uncle, William Martin. He was my mom's brother. Anyway, he passed away, but now it's being held for my cousin, who got it from my uncle's estate but was too young to take ownership."

Nothing was said for a few more minutes, and Adam couldn't stand the silence. He asked, "So the second dock is there?"

Martin nodded and smiled. "Mm-hm."

"And it's a secret," Adam observed.

A few more seconds of silence.

"Why is it a secret?"

"You'll see."

Martin wasn't many years older than Adam—only twenty-five to his seventeen—so it aggravated Adam a little that Martin seemed like he was trying to play some kind of game with him.

They were finally approaching the Martin estate. The brick waterfront house was not especially ornate. Its architectural design was simple. There were no fancy architectural details, no elaborate cornice work. The only exception was a columned porch that wrapped around the house. On the waterfront, a modest dock jutted out into the North River.

They parked the horse and cart beside the house. Martin led Adam around to the waterfront. They went up on the porch, where Martin pulled a thin cord hanging by the door and waited. Within moments a black man with very dark skin and a shock of white hair upon his head came to the door.

"Mr. Smith. Good day, sir."

The man was very formal.

"Hello there, Charles!" said Martin. "Laney here?"

Charles nodded. "Yes, sir. One moment please."

As Martin and Adam waited, Adam said, "I assume Lane is your cousin?"

"Not Lane. Laney. And yes, she is," said Martin.

"She?"

"Yes, she. Laney's her nickname."

While they waited, Adam walked the length of the porch and leaned over the balcony to admire the water view from the house. Just then Adam could hear a young woman's voice inside the doorway.

"Well, hello, cousin," she said.

"Hello, sweet girl," said Martin. "I reckon the ol' warden's not here today, huh?"

"No. Thankfully, Absalom is traveling. Only six more months now, you know. I can hardly wait."

"You'll have him out on his ear then, won't ya, girl?" Martin laughed.

"Well, he'll no longer be my warden—I mean guardian." She grinned. "Getting him off the estate might be a problem if my brother has anything to do with it, though."

"Ain't much Will can say once you're of age, is there?"

"I don't know. We'll have to wait and see, won't we?"

"Laney, this is Adam Fletcher," said Martin. "Adam, come on over here."

Adam scurried back down the porch to where Martin stood. He was stunned when he saw the woman standing inside the doorway. It was the beautiful girl from Richard Rasquelle's party.

"This is my cousin, Laney," said Martin.

Adam smiled broadly. "Well, how do you do, ma'am?"

"I'm fine, thank you, sir." Her demeanor was

understandably more reserved and formal than it had been when she was talking to her cousin.

Martin put his hand on Adam's shoulder and said, "I've brought this fella here because we need to get the second dock ready for a shipment. Prob'ly be here in about a week's time."

"That's fine. Here you go." She reached into her apron pocket and handed Martin a ring with three keys. "Y'all shouldn't need any help, should you? Most of my workers are out fishing today. I gave them the day off."

"No," said Martin. "There isn't much to do. We just need to make sure the basement is clear and ready for everything. And I need to explain to Adam how this whole thing works."

"Alright then. Well, just holler at me before you leave, alright?"

"Will do."

Martin looked at Adam. "We better get to it."

"It was a pleasure to meet you, ma'am," said Adam. He bowed his head, then stood and smiled at the girl. She nodded and raised one eyebrow and gave a half smile before closing the door.

Martin grabbed him by the sleeve and said, "Come on, Fletcher. Let's get to work."

They went about their tasks, making sure the basement was clear and that the ramp leading in was still sound. Then Martin explained to Adam the assembly line–type protocol they would use when the shipment arrived. It didn't take long to do everything—not more than a half hour. When they finished, Martin let Laney know they were leaving, and then he and Adam climbed into the horse cart and headed back to the warehouse.

Once they had gotten a good distance down the lane from the estate, Martin looked at Adam and said, "What is it?

You act like you been burstin at the seams to say something since you met my cousin."

Adam was trying hard not to grin. He nervously scratched his temple, thinking about whether or not he should answer.

"I might not should say this, but your cousin is really something else. She's beautiful!"

At first Martin gave him a stern look, and then he laughed.

"I know she's a pretty girl. Good looks come with the territory in this family, but you need to just go on and get that out of your mind. Ain't nothing happenin between you and Laney."

"Why? Because she's wealthy and I'm not? Or because she's your cousin?"

"Both. Of course. But things are more complicated than that."

"Complicated? How are they complicated?"

"They're just complicated. Leave it at that."

"I saw her before, you know," said Adam.

"You mean in town?"

"No. Actually, I saw her at Richard Rasquelle's house. He had that party there a couple weeks ago. In fact, it was the weekend I decided on a trade for my apprenticeship."

"Rasquelle's house? And you're telling me Laney was there? Nah. I don't think so. You must be mistaken."

Adam laughed. "Martin, you've seen your cousin. Do you honestly think I could be mistaken about having seen a girl like that?"

Martin narrowed his eyes and tipped his head in deference. "I guess not, but it don't really make sense. Can't imagine why she'd have been there of all places."

"I don't know, but she was. There was this older couple there talking to her, too. But I don't think they knew each other well—the Farringtons."

Martin shrugged. "I don't know. Doesn't make sense to me. Richard Rasquelle is a crook. Laney knows that. I can't imagine why she'd go to a party at his house. In fact, I can't imagine why he'd invite her."

"The whole town was invited."

"Even still. Why would she set foot on that man's property? I sure as hell wouldn't."

Adam just shrugged. He wasn't going to tell Martin exactly how things happened that day at Richard Rasquelle's party, nor how forward he had been in his attempt to meet Laney.

"You know, come to think of it, I also saw her talking to Francis Smythe that day," said Adam.

"Really?" said Martin. "Ellison Smythe's son, Francis?"

"Mm-hm."

Martin wrinkled his eyebrows. "Well, if she was at Rasquelle's party, I guess I ought not be surprised if she caught Smythe's eye."

"Maybe," said Adam, "but he acted like he already knew her somehow."

"Aw, well that ain't too surprisin," said Martin. "They probably move in the same circles. She might know him from when her daddy was still alive. He was friends with all of the important folks in a three-county radius."

Of course, thought Adam, she certainly hadn't been moving in the same circles he did.

"And it's not a problem? With Mr. Rogers's second dock being at her place and her being friends with the son of the local customs agent?"

Martin shook his head. "Nah."

"Hmph." Adam thought for a moment, then said, "What

would happen if he ever popped in to pay her a visit at the same time one of Mr. Rogers's shipments was being delivered?"

"Aw, that wouldn't happen. First of all, before a ship even approaches the dock at Laney's place we send someone over there to let her know that one is coming. Then her servants secure the gate at the end of the lane that leads onto the estate so that no one—except us—can enter."

"I see," said Adam. "That's pretty clever."

Thinking about the day of Rasquelle's party and how he met Laney had him thinking again about the party's host.

Since they still had a ways to go before they got back to the warehouse, Adam debated filling Martin in on what had happened earlier with Rasquelle, but he couldn't bring himself to say anything about it—at least not yet—so instead he opted to push for more information about Laney.

"So you said the situation with your cousin was complicated. Is she already engaged or something?"

"Oh, it's a long story," said Martin.

"We've still got a good little ride ahead of us. I doubt it'll take longer than that. And anyway, you ought to know I'll just keep asking if you don't tell me."

Martin rolled his eyes. "My gracious, you sure ask a lot of questions!"

Adam grinned.

"Fine," said Martin. "Laney's mama died about five years ago, and her daddy—my uncle—died three years ago. When he did, he put it in his will that whoever she marries will have to meet the approval of her brother, Will—he's a lawyer in New Bern—and her guardian, Absolom Reading."

"Ah, well there's nothing complicated about that. Sounds like her father was wanting to look out for her interests is all—make sure that no one comes along and takes advantage of her."

"Yeah. You'd think that," said Martin, "but there's more to it. If she marries without the joint consent of her brother and Mr. Reading, she loses her inheritance—the estate and everything in it, except for her personal items."

"You're joking."

"I'm not."

"What would happen to it? I mean, would it all just go to her brother?"

"Yep. That's exactly what would happen."

"That doesn't really seem fair," said Adam. "I mean, wouldn't that tempt her brother to not approve of anyone she'd want to marry?"

"Will? Nah. He loves his sister. He wants to see her married and happy, and he sure don't want to come back to Beaufort."

"Well, even still . . . Can you really do that? Write a will that cuts a person off from their rightful inheritance just for marrying someone you don't approve of?"

"Apparently. Her daddy thought that by putting that little bit in there it would discourage anyone who might be after her for her inheritance from coming in and trying to marry her just so they could get their hands on the property. Uncle William was no fool, and he knew if there ever was a man that both Absalom Reading and her brother could agree upon, he'd have to be someone really impressive."

"Her father was just trying to protect her. Nothing wrong with that. I'd probably do the same thing if I were in his shoes."

"Well, there's another problem. The complicated part is that I don't think Absalom Reading will approve of anyone, because everyone knows he's had an eye on her since not long before her father died."

"Her guardian?" Adam found this disturbing. "How old is he?"

"About forty, I think. He's right much older than her, anyway."

"Did her father know that this Mr. Reading had an eye for his daughter?"

"Nah. I think Uncle William always just thought that Absalom Reading doted on her like he was family. My uncle was really bad off for a long time before he died, so he didn't see what the rest of us saw."

"So that's why Laney made that comment about only six more months, huh?" said Adam.

Martin nodded. "Mm-hm. She'll be twenty-one. Then she gets the house—tentatively. If she marries, so long as Will and Mr. Reading approve of her husband, then the transfer of the property becomes final—to her and her husband. Of course her husband would hold the title. I think she will have Reading out as soon as she can legally arrange it. Laney is a strong-willed girl. I reckon she'd happily live the rest of her life as a spinster if it meant that Reading doesn't get any more say about her life. There is no way she'd go to him for approval of a suitor—I can tell you that."

"So she'd really keep right on living on her own, then?" asked Adam.

"Well, yes and no. She'd be the lady of the house without a doubt, but as long as Charles and Aunt Celie are living, she won't be alone. Old Charles and Aunt Celie have been owned by the Martin family since they were children and have always looked out for Laney and her brother. Aunt Celie was Laney's nursemaid as a baby, and Charles—well, he's just a good old fellow. They have a grown son, but he's gone with Laney's brother and his wife in New Bern. The two of them were almost like brothers growing up, and now he's the overseer on William's estate."

"And you said your cousin is a lawyer."

"Yep," said Martin. "Uncle William was a lawyer before he died, and his father—my maternal grandfather—was also a lawyer, too."

"With all those lawyers in your family, why in the world are you working as a cooper?"

"Because my father was a cooper," said Martin. He smiled. "My mother didn't marry for status, she married for love."

Adam chuckled. "Well, it's good to know that does happen—especially for fellas like me."

"Me too," said Martin. "I sure ain't cut out to work behind a desk. Hey, I've been meaning to ask you. How is it you ended up at the warehouse, anyway?"

Adam recounted exactly how he came to be apprenticed to Emmanuel Rogers, including how he had originally hoped he would've been bound to Richard Rasquelle.

After hearing Adam's story, Martin said, "Emmanuel Rogers is a great man. You're lucky he was willing to take you on. Richard Rasquelle? Well, I ain't got nothin good to say about him. He's just a damned crook."

The warehouse was coming into view. Adam felt sick thinking about what had happened with Rasquelle earlier.

"I know that now. Boy, do I ever know that."

He sighed, then looked away from Martin and gazed out into the distance at the warehouse, which appeared bigger and was getting closer with each clip-clop of the horse's hooves.

"What's that supposed to mean?" asked Martin.

Adam took a deep breath, then proceeded to explain everything that had happened with Richard Rasquelle earlier in the day.

Martin was aghast. "Well, you have really made a fine mess out of things, my friend."

Adam nodded. "Yeah. I know."

"I mean, I can't say that I blame you for going by there to talk to him. If I were in your shoes, I'd have prob'ly done the same thing. It ain't like you really know Richard Rasquelle . . . what a crook he is. But then again, you know what they say? 'Curiosity killed the cat.' Well, I'd say you done killed that cat."

Just then they pulled up to the warehouse and parked the horse cart. Before they got out, Adam asked, "What do you think I should do?"

Martin shrugged. "I'm not sure, but for now I wouldn't tell Emmanuel or Boaz about this. You ain't planning to go through with it, are you? I mean, being Rasquelle's spy?"

"No! Of course not! Would I be telling you about this if I were planning on actually doing it?"

"No. No, I don't reckon you would. Well, just let me think about it some. Maybe we can figure out how you can handle this without everything going to hell in a handbasket."

They climbed out of the cart, and Martin tied the horse to the hitching post.

"Alright," said Adam. "I'm gonna go talk to Valentine about it. See if he has any ideas."

"You do that," said Martin. "Go on. We're done here for today. Go on and talk to him, and if I ain't here when you get back tonight, we'll just talk about this some other time."

Adam nodded in acknowledgment. He popped into the warehouse just long enough to get approval from Boaz so he could leave for the tavern.

Chapter Eleven

ADAM SAT ANXIOUSLY as he watched Valentine pace the floor of his sitting room. He knew his surrogate grandfather needed to be working at the bar right now, but Adam had begged him to talk in private for just a couple of minutes, so they had gone to his house, which was right behind the tavern. But after Adam told him about his conversation with Richard Rasquelle, it quickly became apparent that this subject was far too big and important to discuss fully in the limited time Valentine had available.

"Remember what I told you?" said Valentine. "What did I say? Huh?" He was livid.

Adam didn't reply. He hung his head in shame.

"I told you to leave it alone, didn't I?" Valentine scolded. "But did you listen? No, you didn't. I told you not to fight with that Smythe boy, but you didn't listen to me about that, either. Where did that get you? Not to mention, where did it get me? Here I am with one less worker, and everyone thinks I was happy for you to fight that boy."

"I know! I know," said Adam. He sank back into the settee and sighed.

"When you didn't listen about fighting with that little brat, that got you into the whole mess with that apprenticeship. And now this whole thing with Richard Rasquelle wanting you to spy for him? Well, now you really done it! You have just really done it!"

"Yes! I know! I've really done it! But what do I do now? How can I fix this?"

"I don't know that you can fix this. You have just really messed up this time."

A painful silence filled the room as they both contemplated the gravity of the situation.

"There has to be something I can do," Adam pleaded.

Valentine shook his head. "I don't know. I just don't know. But I'll tell you one thing you damned well better do. You better let Emmanuel Rogers know about the mess you've made. Don't you leave that poor old man to find out about this the hard way."

Chapter Twelve

ADAM AVOIDED RETURNING to the warehouse right away. He wasn't ready to face Emmanuel, and he certainly didn't want to risk running into Martin if he was still hanging around.

He didn't stay in the tavern, since he knew Valentine was angry with him, and he didn't want to get into a discussion about it there. He certainly didn't want his mother to find out about it. Instead, he spent several hours just killing time down near the fishing boats.

When it turned dark, he finally started the long walk back towards the warehouse. All of his thoughts were centered on how he could break the news to Emmanuel.

Adam had barely made it into the warehouse when Boaz, who had been waiting for him on the main floor, said, "Get on upstairs. Emmanuel wants to see you."

He started up the stairs, then turned back to ask, "Is everything alright?"

"That's a stupid question, boy," said Boaz. "Martin told us what happened. You best get on up there right now and tell him everything."

Adam swallowed hard and then ran up the rest of the stairs to the apartment.

The living quarters were especially cool on this late-spring evening. Adam still hadn't gotten so used to the world bazaar–like atmosphere inside that he took it for granted. Every time he stepped through the door, it made a part of him long to jump on the next ship and set sail for distant lands to see what exotic places he might discover.

One part of the room was well lit with the flickering glow of strategically placed lanterns. Emmanuel was sitting in his favorite armchair with a cup of tea, reading.

"Good evening, sir," said Adam. He entered the room with his head lowered. "Boaz said you wanted to speak to me."

Emmanuel looked up and smiled. "Adam. Come over here. Sit down, boy." He motioned to the settee beside his armchair.

Adam went over and sat down. He noticed the book in his master's hand.

"What is it you're reading?"

Emmanuel closed the book with his finger holding his place inside and glanced at the cover before holding it up to show Adam. "It's a book about chess. It was written by a Frenchman named Philidor."

Adam raised his eyebrows and pressed his lips together. "Hmm . . . Sounds interesting. I like chess alright, but I'm not very good at it. Would a book like that help me play better?"

Emmanuel studied the cover again, opened the book just long enough to put a ribbon inside to hold his place, then put the book down next to the lantern on the table beside him. Adam had noticed that there were always two books on that table—a Bible and whatever other book Emmanuel was currently studying.

"It very well might. Monsieur Philidor talks about how important pawns are in the game of chess. Says they are the very 'soul of the game.'"

"Pawns? I would think they'd be the least important pieces. I mean, you've got 'em all out in front and they're the first to go before your more important pieces advance."

Emmanuel gave a slight smile. "Don't you think it would follow, then, that the pawns are the most important pieces? After all, your success in the game often hinges on your opening, which sets the tone for all the play that follows. If you make wise moves from the outset, it will give you a much better chance of winning. Many of the most strategic moves in a game will be made by the humble pawns."

"I see. Guess I hadn't thought about it all that much."

The weary old man removed his spectacles and rubbed his eyes before setting his gaze upon the boy.

"I'd love to tell you everything you'd like to know about chess, but right now . . . right now, son, we need to talk."

"Yes, sir," said Adam. "I think we do."

Adam had been reluctant to have the conversation that he understood was inevitable. Now he knew he'd be glad to get it behind him.

Emmanuel began: "Let me start out by reminding you that I don't bring new people into this company. The only people who've ever worked here these many years are like my family, because they are the children or close relatives of my oldest and dearest friends. I told you that even Mr. Robins is the son of another old friend. Do you remember?"

Adam nodded.

"And do you know what he told me when he asked me to take you on as an apprentice?"

"No, sir. What did he say?"

"He said that he knew a bright young man—a good boy with great potential—but that this young man was getting himself into trouble for his lack of direction, not to mention a quick temper. That young man was you, of course."

Adam smiled.

"You've been here over a week now, Adam, and I have no reason to doubt what Mr. Robins said of you—that bit about you being a bright boy and having great potential—but we're going to have to get some things straight."

Adam nodded.

"First of all, there is something I haven't yet told you, but now I think I must."

"Sir?" said Adam.

"You should know that I did not bring you into this company only because of my old connection with Mr. Robins's father, but also because there is someone else to whom I once made a vow—a promise you might say—and I intend to keep it."

Adam's eyes grew wide. "Who? What was the promise?"

"I will not divulge the particulars. I swore my discretion, but I will tell you this: the promise was made long before you were ever born."

Adam furrowed his brow. "Then how can the promise be about me?"

"I cannot tell you that. You will simply have to trust that it was."

"Mr. Rogers, how can you tell me something like this and then not tell me at least who it is?"

"Because, dear boy, one's word is proof of one's character. A man who cannot keep a promise is a man who cannot be trusted. To tell you more than I already have could potentially begin pushing the boundaries of the promise—and the secret—which I swore I would keep."

"You're really not going to tell me who this was?"

"I'm afraid not, young man. I have intentionally been vague in what I have said here. And no amount of guessing on your part would result in me offering you any further details. This pact was made many decades ago, and I can assure you if I have kept it this long—and in spite of circumstances you couldn't even begin to imagine—you won't be able to convince me to break it now."

When Emmanuel said he had made the pact decades ago, that ruled out Adam's father. The boy had wondered if he might be who the old man was talking about, but since Adam himself was only seventeen years old, it couldn't have been him. His mother, Mary, had only known his father a few months before she married him and became pregnant.

"If you weren't going to tell me more than that, why did you say anything at all about there being another reason why you took me on as your apprentice?"

"That is a fair question," said Emmanuel. "I will tell you. It is because I wanted to preface the next part of what I'm going to say inasmuch as I want you to know that I am committed to helping you, Adam. I am committed to your success. It is of the utmost importance to me. In spite of mistakes you might have made or that you might make in the future, I want you to know that I will not turn my back on you."

Adam was unable to speak. Knowing he'd spent time in Richard Rasquelle's office earlier in the day made Emmanuel's words feel to him like a knife in the gut.

"You have gotten us all into a bit of a mess, wouldn't you say?"

The boy looked down. His stomach was in knots as waves of guilt washed over him. "I never wanted any of this."

"Perhaps not," said Emmanuel, "but here we are, and even though you are not the architect of this scheme, you have become the centerpiece of it, haven't you? I gave you an opportunity to come work for me, to become part of the family here, and I don't know if it was curiosity or the old 'grass is always greener on the other side' bit, but something made you go and see my competitor earlier today. And were it not for that, we'd not be sitting here tonight discussing the quandary we have before us, now would we?"

Adam felt awful. It was all true.

"I'm not angry with you, Adam. And I may be old but I'm no fool. If I were a boy your age and in your circumstances, I'd have very probably done the same exact thing. We'd still be in a fine mess, but nevertheless I'm sure I'd have done it. Now we just need to be honest with one another—because that's how I run my business, and that's how I live my life—and I think we'll figure out how to handle this, you and I."

The lump in Adam's throat made it difficult to talk. "You don't know how sorry I am, sir. I just want to tell you—"

Emmanuel patted the air in front of him with his hand in a calming motion. "Hush now. I need you to listen to me, Adam. I don't want you sitting there feeling sorry for yourself or me or your mother or anybody, because we need to sort out this whole business."

"Do you have any ideas, sir?"

The old man nodded. "I do. But first, may I ask you a question?"

"Of course, sir."

"Do you want to work here? For me?"

"I do, sir. I really do, especially now."

Emmanuel said nothing but nodded once and then listened attentively so that Adam could continue.

"When I found out I had to be apprenticed and I had to choose a trade, I chose what I did because I had gone to Mr. Rasquelle's party. He was impressive. I always thought he seemed so successful and that everyone thought so well of him for his good deeds and—"

"Not everyone," said Emmanuel. "You must admit you only know a limited number of people in this town, but I do realize that Richard Rasquelle has cultivated quite a reputation, although I'm afraid it's a bit of a Trojan horse."

"How do you mean, sir?"

"But of course you know the story of how the Greeks hid themselves inside that great wooden horse—the very symbol of the Trojan empire—and how they used the impressive subterfuge to be ushered right into the city of Troy. Once they were inside the gates and the townspeople were feeling quite secure in their beds at night, out sprang those cunning Greeks to attack the Trojans."

"Yes, sir," said Adam. "I do know that story. So you're saying Rasquelle is like the Greeks."

"Well, yes and no. You see, Rasquelle doesn't plan to wage war on this town, of course, but he has fooled the townspeople into thinking he's their great savior with his shipping business, as well as with his so-called acts of benevolence. His intention is to wage war on me. You see, I know he's been cheating his customers since he arrived here, so I'm not fooled by it, but many are."

"Forgive me for saying so, sir, but why haven't you spoken up? Seems to me that's the problem. And since you never let anyone new into your company, a lot of people don't know you. I know I sure didn't before I came here. You always just seemed like some kind of hermit to me."

Emmanuel chuckled at Adam's forthrightness.

"Let me tell you something, son. I like you—I really do—and I appreciate your honesty, but you mustn't always say everything that springs to mind. I recognize that quality, because it's one I used to suffer myself, but I promise you that your tongue will get you in trouble if you do not learn to filter the words that leap forth from it with wisdom."

"I didn't mean to offend you, sir."

"I'm not offended, Adam, but others would be. I've observed you since you've been here. Far too often you speak when you should be listening. Many times you offer commentary when you should be observing. And many times you ask questions when it might better serve you to remain quiet and study a situation to discover your answers."

Adam wanted to speak up to offer a defense but he restrained himself.

"Now, to answer your question. Why haven't I spoken up? Tell me what good that would do. Wouldn't I just look like a bitter old fool who's afraid he's losing business?"

Emmanuel paused as if he was waiting for Adam's response, but Adam remained quiet.

The old man continued: "I would look exactly like that, and that is not who I am, nor is that what I want. I am not worried about my business. My longtime customers know me, and they know what they can expect when they do business with me and my men. I've not cheated a customer in these thirty years that I've had my business here, and I don't plan to start now."

"So what do you think Rasquelle hopes to accomplish by asking me to spy on you?"

"Well, I can only imagine he hopes that you might give him some small bit of information that would allow him to go to the customs authorities and report me as a smuggler."

Adam looked at Emmanuel. He desperately wanted to ask a question, but he held his tongue.

"You want to know if I smuggle, of course."

Adam shrugged. "I reckon everyone smuggles—at least that's what I've heard."

"Then you've heard correctly. But do you understand why that is the case?"

"Not exactly."

"I'll explain it to you, then. Not long after I came here, Parliament passed a law called the Molasses Act. Have you heard of that?"

"I have. Didn't that law enforce taxes on molasses from anywhere but the British West Indies?"

"There was quite a bit more to it, but yes, it was something like that. In those days it was much cheaper to buy molasses from the French West Indies, but England wanted to ensure her colonies engaged in business profitable to the mother country, so she insisted we buy our molasses from the British West Indies, which unfortunately cost a great deal more. If we did not, we had to pay high tariffs on the molasses from the French islands. Now, as you well know, molasses is needed for many things, not the least of which is the production of that wonderfully popular libation we call rum."

Adam grinned and nodded.

"Well, what do you think people will do if they want to buy something and it costs too much from this fellow over here?" he said as he motioned to one side of the table. "I'll tell you what they'll do. They'll find another fellow from whom to obtain it over here." He motioned to the other side of the table. "It's always been that way, for thousands of years, and I imagine it always will be."

"And there's always a businessman willing to find a way to sell the people what they want," said Adam.

"Precisely! And so even England knew that we were bypassing the proper channels to bring in the supplies that the good people here in the colonies needed, and up until the last couple of years they've looked the other way. But you see, since the Crown spent so much money fighting France during that last war, King George is determined to recover some of those expenses, so he's decided to start enforcing these laws, which have been mostly ignored for the last several decades."

"I see," said Adam.

"And last year, if you recall, they passed the Sugar Act, which did away with the Molasses Act but added in some new regulations."

"I remember Boaz telling me about that."

"Yes, well, to answer your question, there are a great many old friends in distant ports with whom I correspond and do business. My relationships with them, both as friends and as business partners, reach far back into years past—long before His Majesty decided to change the rules of the game on us. And I intend, Lord willing, to continue doing business with them. Their families' livelihoods depend on their business with the colonies, and our families here in Beaufort depend on having customers in those same distant ports. Now don't misunderstand me. We do plenty of business with Great Britain, of course, but we simply could not survive on that alone. No one could. And the Crown had always understood that, but now the King has resolved to generate revenues, as they call them, regardless of the cost to the colonies or Great Britain."

"So you think Richard Rasquelle is smuggling too, then?"

Emmanuel scoffed and narrowed his eyes at Adam, making the boy feel naïve for even asking the question.

"I'm not foolish enough to risk committing slander by swearing to it, but I suspect he does a great deal of business *under the table*, as we might say."

"You know," said Adam, "I've even heard recently that he's been involved in some slave trading."

"Now *that*, that is something I would never do. It's not illegal for him to deal in slaves, but I do detest the slave trade. Had one experience with the business nearly a half century ago, and I swore I'd never do it again."

"Do you not agree with slavery, sir?" said Adam.

"I have my opinions about the institution of slavery. Man was made in God's image, so I believe freedom is the ideal circumstance for any man—white, Negro, Indian, it matters not—but it's not as simple of a matter as you might think. First of all, I have known some slaves who are likely much better off, and much happier, with their masters than they would be fighting to survive in the wilds of Africa. They've got warm houses, clothes to wear, and food in their bellies, and their families are able to stay together. A great many more of them, however, are a pitiable lot. There are slave masters who are wicked, evil men who beat their slaves mercilessly. They abuse the women and think nothing of selling the children off as though they are nothing more than livestock."

"I've heard about that kind of thing," Adam said solemnly.

"And the slave traders—they are the worst of all men. It takes a cold, hard spirit to be able to do what they do. And those cruel savages in Africa who round up their own people for the traders are no better."

"You said you had an experience with it once?" said Adam.

"I did." Emmanuel took a deep breath and folded his hands on his lap. "I'm not proud of it at all, but it seemed like an ugly necessity at the time."

"What happened?"

"My goodness! You're an inquisitive child—do you know that?"

"Well, you are the one who brought it up, sir."

Emmanuel offered a reserved smile and nodded. "Indeed. I suppose I did." He looked down for a moment before turning his gaze back to Adam. "I'm sure you heard about the Tuscarora War, haven't you?"

Adam nodded. "I know a little bit about it."

"Long story there, but at the end of it, the colony was just devastated—really hanging by a thread. I was living in Barbados with my family—hadn't arrived in America yet—when it happened, but I heard all about it, of course. When the Indians fell upon the settlers along the Neuse and Pamlico Rivers, the people across the territory found themselves thrust into a hard, long war with the Tuscarora Indians and their allies. It was a terrible time. And to make matters worse, there were all of these plantation owners with no help to work their land, build their barns, or clear their roads, much less rebuild what was lost in the war."

"So what happened? Is that how you got involved with the slave trade, I mean?"

"Just wait. I'm getting to that." Emmanuel smiled. "I

mentioned my family lived in Barbados—we were there by way of England, of course—so after my father died, my mother married again. Her new husband was a detestable fellow. I couldn't stand him. Unfortunately, I was not yet quite old enough to receive my inheritance, but to keep peace in the home, my mother gave me a good sum of money, and I took my father's sloop and went to sea, moving from port to port for a time. After a couple of years of living like a gypsy, I lost my sloop in a storm. I had already blown most of my money on wild living, so it seemed I was at quite a loss. As destiny would have it, another young captain offered me a chance to sail with his crew, and I took it."

Adam was riveted listening to Emmanuel's account.

"The young captain had come from Bath—not Bath, England, mind you, but Bath right here in North Carolina—and he had brought a few lads from his hometown with him. A driven man was he, determined to see what we could scavenge from Spanish fleets that might be of benefit to the Carolina colony, and of course we figured we might change our fortunes a bit as well."

"Are you saying that—?"

"Would you just listen, boy?" said Emmanuel. "I'm sure you'll have your questions answered if you would only be patient *and listen!*"

Adam nodded eagerly. He knew a fair bit about the colony's history, so he suspected he knew where this story was going.

"As I was saying, there we were, sailing round in paradise, and we had all sorts of adventures—more than most boys could hope to have in a dozen lifetimes. But you asked about my experience with that ugly business of the slave trade, so I guess I ought to jump to that part of the story."

Adam sat with rapt attention.

"One of the things in shortest supply in this colony—even

before the war—was men who could work the land. It's a gargantuan effort, building a country from scratch. It happened here, of course, but it wouldn't have been possible—or at least we wouldn't be where we are today—were it not for bringing in the Africans to help get the work done. Indentured servants from Europe can only get you so far, and their indentures do eventually expire. And the Indians always made the worst slaves!"

"They didn't work hard?"

"Oh, goodness! Not because of that, but because they were always so clever and knew the land—with all its creeks and pocosins—better than anyone, so they could escape quite easily, laughing the whole way home. You'd really have to treat them exceptionally well if you wanted them to stay on your land."

Adam nodded.

"So, it turns out that when we were off the coast of St. Vincent—this was late November of 1717—our captain, the young fellow from Bath, determined to capture this great French cargo vessel we had spotted. It was quite a show, but we overcame the French captain and his crew and took the ship."

"This all *really* happened?" said Adam. He never imagined his master had such an exciting history.

Emmanuel nodded. "It did. And do you know what the cargo was on that French vessel?"

Adam raised his eyebrows as he waited to hear the answer.

"Slaves. It was a French Guineaman called *La Concorde*, but our captain, he gave her a new name, *Queen Anne's Revenge*."

"Ha! I knew it! You're talking about Blackbeard! So it was Blackbeard! You sailed with Blackbeard! This is incredible!"

Emmanuel just nodded. He wasn't surprised the boy reacted with such enthusiasm. The notorious pirate's exploits had been published the world over since the Golden Age, and everyone had heard of that most famous sea rogue, though most of what was printed in the papers and literature contained far more sensational fiction than fact.

"But wait a minute," said Adam. "I'd always heard that the men who sailed with him—the ones who weren't killed in that final battle with Lieutenant Maynard—were hanged in Virginia by the governor."

"Ah, sure. Everyone has heard that, but you must remember, first of all, not all of us were in that last battle at Ocracoke. It was only our shipmates who fought alongside the captain against Maynard and his men who were dragged off to Hampton and hanged."

Adam gave Emmanuel a confused look.

The old man continued, "There were several of us back in Bath who had sailed with him, and we were arrested and taken to Virginia, but thank God, we escaped the gallows. Quite mercifully, before we'd ever even made it up there to face charges, in fact, word arrived from England that His Majesty King George I had granted us his pardon. Remember, those of us in Bath had never taken up arms against the Royal Navy. So it was that Lieutenant Governor Spotswood had no choice but to let us go, but they did tell us to leave Virginia immediately, and that if we ever engaged in acts of piracy again they'd hang us without delay."

"Goodness gracious," said Adam. "I reckon you were relieved about that!"

"Indeed, I was," said Emmanuel, "and yet I still felt very sorry for my old shipmates."

"You said the experience with the slave trade is what turned you against it. What happened?" Adam inquired.

"Oh, yes! Of course! You had gotten me so carried away with remembering those days that I forgot how I ended up back there remembering it all in the first place!"

Adam smiled.

Emmanuel continued: "We kept a few dozen of those slaves from La Concorde and brought them back to Bath. The rest we left with the French slave ship captain on an island in the Caribbean."

"Why didn't you keep them all?" asked Adam.

Emmanuel twisted up his face at the recollection. "That ship was the most vile, disgusting thing you've ever seen. Those poor Africans—hundreds of them—plucked up out of their homeland, naked, terrified, unable to understand a word we said, nor us them. It was a floating hell. And the filth down in the ship's hold was unimaginable. Consider most vessels carry casks, crates, and the like. Casks and crates aren't bothered by the call of nature. A vessel full of terrified slaves, on the other hand—well, let's just say the stench was unimaginable. The captain, like the rest of us, was disgusted with the whole business. He decided we wouldn't take all of the slaves, so we chose about sixty of the strongest, healthiest of the lot and brought them with us. The rest we deposited on an island, along with the ship's previous captain, then we set sail for Bath."

"You brought the slaves all this way, then?"

Emmanuel nodded. "We did. Everyone has their opinions about Blackbeard's treasure, but they don't know that the cargo we unloaded there on the edge of the Pamlico River that night was the most valuable we ever carried."

"I'm fascinated at all this," said Adam. "In fact, I can't even believe I work for you, sir! I've heard all about the pirate Blackbeard, but I never imagined I'd meet a real pirate myself!"

"Ah, well, thankfully those days are long behind me now. But to speak of you working for me, I suppose we need to turn our attention back to the matter that brought us together at this table tonight."

Adam lowered his head. "Your life story was so exciting, I'd forgotten all about that."

"My life story . . . Ah, well, you've only just learned about a few days in this old man's life," said Emmanuel. "So much more I could tell you, so many adventures, but now I've already told you so much that they could run me out of this little port if they wanted to. Young lads such as yourself may be excited to hear pirate stories, but there are a great many more who think us to be devils."

"I'll never betray your trust, sir. I pray you will believe me on that."

"I do, I do . . ." Emmanuel nodded. "So, on the matter of Richard Rasquelle—"

"I won't tell him anything!" said Adam. "I'll tell him I'm not spying or doing any other sort of work for him—that I don't want to be a part of this."

"And what? Land yourself into trouble for being suspected of aiding and abetting a smuggler? Don't be foolish, boy. Use your head. Go along with his ruse for a while. Tell him what you want. Enough people in this town know me. I'm not worried about what he might say. It'd be his word against mine, anyway."

"I'm not telling him anything, sir. I was thinking that maybe I can give him useless information. Maybe he'll grow tired of me and turn me loose."

"Well, we'll just have to see if he does, but for now, let's pray that nothing comes of it. We'll soon find out what sort of game he's playing."

Adam nodded.

"And son," he said, "I would never ask you to spy on

Richard Rasquelle for me, but I would encourage you to keep your eyes open. No need to report anything back to me. Just observe what you can. You never know. It may be helpful."

Chapter Thirteen

ALTHOUGH THE SUN was just now appearing over the horizon, the dock in front of the warehouse was already bustling with excitement. It was busier than Adam had ever imagined it could be.

The crisp, cool air of the spring night was beginning to warm as the morning that had been eagerly anticipated by all the men in the company finally arrived. Emmanuel Rogers's sloop, the *Carolina Gypsy*, was about to set sail.

A few local farmers had brought livestock—pigs, cows, and chickens—which had already been lowered down into the ship's hold and placed in their respective stalls. Adam watched the dock workers roll the last of the casks up the ramp.

The men who would crew the vessel were enjoying tender last moments with their wives and children before departing for their nearly four-month-long voyage. They promised their families they would return before autumn.

When the ship's captain, Carl Phillips, lifted up each of his small children in turn to embrace them once more before the voyage and then kissed his wife, Adam could tell that the time had come for the vessel's departure. His stomach felt nervous as he thought about what these men were about to do. On the one hand, he knew any such journey had its potential dangers, but on the other hand, a part of him deeply desired to be able to make such a voyage one day.

Finally, Captain Phillips and Emmanuel went up the ramp of the ship, where the old merchant stood and beckoned the rest of the crew to come on board so he could offer a prayer for their safe journey. Tears were shed, final hugs and kisses were given, and then the men all made their way up the ramp in single file.

"Good morning, family," Emmanuel called out in a loud voice. "I would like to first thank you dear ladies and your children for lending us your husbands and fathers for a time so they can make this journey. Of course you all know that I'd never allow men to leave my dock for a voyage such as this without asking for the Lord's protection over the *Gypsy*—her captain and crew. If you all would, please bow your heads as we pray."

The crowd fell silent, and everyone bowed their heads.

Emmanuel prayed, "Heavenly Father, we are gathered here today to see this vessel, the *Carolina Gypsy*, make her voyage to the West Indies, with Captain Carl Phillips at the helm. Father, we know it is only by your good grace that I have this company— and this vessel—and a capable crew to sail her. I pray that you would show traveling mercies to these men. Grant them fair winds and following seas. Keep them safe under your watchful eye. Grant them wisdom to respond rightly to every situation, and bring them home again to us safely when their work is done. In Jesus's most precious and holy name we pray, amen."

As soon as he was finished praying, Emmanuel shook the hands of the captain and every member of the ship's crew, then came down the ramp and joined Adam, Boaz, Martin, Elliot, and Joe on the dock. They, along with the company's dock workers, the families of the ship's crew, and the farmers who had stayed to see the vessel depart, all watched and waved as the crew of the *Gypsy* bade them farewell.

Once the ship drifted out of sight and the crowd began to disperse, Emmanuel called his warehouse crew to attention.

"Men, thank you for all your hard work these last several weeks. As you know, we've been expecting the arrival of the *Elizabeth Ella* from Liverpool any day now. The seas can be unpredictable, so she could be here as soon as today, or not for several more days. No matter when she arrives, I want you all to be ready. Be on constant standby."

Emmanuel turned his attention to the group of idlers. "You lot—since you all work all over the place, I expect you to keep an ear to the ground and be here just as soon as you know that a ship is coming. I don't want to have to send out messengers to fetch each of you once the *Elizabeth Ella* is already here. I want you to be ready to get the vessel unloaded and then loaded up again as soon as possible. We have another shipment coming in right behind the one from Liverpool, and we may not have much time to rest in between. I certainly don't want to deal with the possibility of the two shipments overlapping because some of you are too slow to get here and get the job done. Is that understood?"

The men all nodded and said that they did before they all went in their separate directions.

As the coopers followed Emmanuel back into the

warehouse, Martin put his arm around Adam's shoulder and said, "So what'd you think of that, my friend?"

"That was incredible! I've never been part of anything like that before."

"I figured you'd be impressed," said Martin. "I've been working here since I was not much older than you, and I remember my first time helping out with a voyage. I'll tell you what, it's still as exciting today as it was the first time. And there ain't too many things in life you can say that about, is there?" He chuckled as he elbowed Adam's side.

Adam smiled and laughed along with him, although he really didn't understand what Martin was talking about.

Everyone was in a good mood, but quite unexpectedly Boaz soon put a damper on the excitement.

"Hey, Fletcher! You do know if you run into your old buddy Rasquelle, this is none of his business, right?"

Adam rushed across the work area to where Boaz stood. "What's your problem? Do you think I'm a fool?"

"I thought we'd already established that you were after what you did on Saturday," said Boaz. He laughed at his own comment.

Adam shoved him. Boaz shoved him back, but his force was so hard, Adam landed flat on his back.

Emmanuel quickly went over and got between them. He reached down to help Adam back to his feet, then turned to face Boaz. "I'll have none of this. You just leave the boy alone and don't provoke him. He's here because I want him here, whether you like it or not."

Then Emmanuel turned his attention to Adam. "And don't you forget that Boaz is your superior on this floor. You will show him respect whether you like what he says to you or not.

And fighting will not be tolerated in this company. I won't fire you, but I'll make your life miserable if you try to bring that here. Boaz could easily tear you limb from limb. You just consider yourself lucky that he only pushed you to the floor rather than knocking you in the head."

Emmanuel looked over at Martin and motioned for him to see the boy out of the warehouse. Adam sighed and went willingly. He understood that Emmanuel just wanted everybody to cool down, and that wouldn't likely happen with him and Boaz stuck together in the same room.

Chapter Fourteen

ADAM LET MARTIN convince him to take him to the Topsail to have breakfast. Martin had told him that he hoped by the time they had full bellies, both Adam and Boaz would have cooled down enough to work together in the warehouse again.

"Adam! What are you doing here this morning?"

"Good morning, Mama." Adam leaned over and kissed Mary on the cheek, then introduced his coworker. "This is Martin Smith. He's a cooper over at the warehouse."

"Nice to meet you, Mr. Smith," said Mary.

"Oh, the pleasure is all mine," cooed Martin. "Adam never mentioned his mother was such a lovely woman."

Adam swiftly elbowed Martin in the ribs. "We just got done seeing off Mr. Rogers's ship. We've already been up for a few hours. Figured we'd come by and fill up on one of Aunt Franny's delicious breakfasts."

"Well, you boys go on and find yourselves a table. I'll go let her know you're here so she can whip up something you'll like. Mr. Smith, what will you have?"

Martin smiled, "Hmm . . . Surprise me." He winked at Mary.

Mary wrinkled her eyebrows—Adam could see she was unsure of how to take his flirtatious friend—then disappeared into the kitchen.

"Martin," said Adam, "you're a nice fellow, and I'm glad we're friends, but that was my mother. You are not allowed to flirt with my mother. Ever."

"Why is that? Because she's your mother, or because it's complicated?" Martin grinned, then leaned back in his chair and rested his elbow on the windowsill.

"Because she's my mother. And there are a dozen other reasons. But mostly because she's my mother."

"Fair enough," said Martin. "But she's still a beauty."

Adam rolled his eyes.

Martin changed the subject. "Boy, you've really got Bo hoppin mad."

"Yeah. Let's talk about that. What in the world were you thinking telling them about that whole mess with Richard Rasquelle? I told you I was going to talk to Valentine. I thought you and I agreed we'd talk about it when I got back."

"You sprang all that on me right before we got to the warehouse," said Martin. "What was I gonna say? I didn't think you understood the danger of the situation, and I wanted to give them notice in case you decided to do something stupid."

"Like what?"

"Well, like telling Bo first, for instance. I made sure to tell them both at the same time. If you'd have just told Bo—well, he'd might've tore your head off."

"Yeah, I guess. I don't think I'd have said anything to him first, though. He doesn't like me very much. Never has."

"Eh, I wouldn't say that," said Martin. "I think he's just a bit jealous."

"Jealous? What for?"

"Well, just think about it. Emmanuel ain't taken on an apprentice since he brought Bo in when he was even younger than you. Bo's like his son. I reckon him taking you on as an apprentice, too, took him by surprise. And it's not just that. He's real protective of Emmanuel. Matter of fact, he once killed a man who was stealin from Emmanuel."

"He did what?"

"Yep. I reckon you hadn't heard about none of that then, have you?"

Adam shook his head. "Boaz killing a man? No! I'd have sure remembered if I'd heard anything about that. What happened?"

"Well, it was all just awful. Before I came to work there. In fact, it was before I was even born—you, too."

Just then Mary came over to the table with a pot of coffee and two mugs. "Here you go, boys. Your breakfast'll be here directly."

Adam smiled up at her. "Thanks."

She disappeared again to wait on other tables.

"Alright, so tell me what happened. Who was the man?" asked Adam.

"I don't remember his full name. I just know his name was Freddy something or other. He was the brother of a girl that Bo was sweet on. In fact, Bo was planning to marry her. The brother was working at the warehouse as a cooper back then—the only person Emmanuel ever had in his shop who wasn't connected to him by family or old friends."

"Bo killed the brother of the girl he planned to marry?"

Martin nodded. "Yep—well, something like that. Turns out the brother and sister had cooked something up. Back in those days, Emmanuel used to be away from the warehouse a lot more than he is now. Those two—Freddy and his sister; her name was Josephine—apparently had been planning the whole mess for a long time. They had this whole complicated scheme where Josephine would work her feminine charms on Bo. Freddy used to tell Bo to go on and spend time with her, that he'd cover for him with Emmanuel. Everything seemed to be going along fine. Bo would go see the girl every Saturday and she'd fix him a meal. Well, one Saturday apparently the plan was for the girl to entice Bo with something more than a meal—something that would keep him away for a while longer. Meanwhile, her brother had his eye on a lot of the antiques in Emmanuel's apartment. He planned to load up, and by the time Bo got back that day, he'd have moved all of the loot to some secret location and would be back at work like nothing ever happened."

Adam's mouth was agape. He couldn't believe all this really happened—and right there in tiny Port Beaufort.

Mary soon appeared at the table again with a huge tray full of food. She served Adam first and then Martin. Then she placed a basket of hot bread in the center of the table, along with a jar of strawberry preserves and another of butter.

"How's this, boys?"

Adam and Martin both smiled and assured her that everything looked great.

"Alright then. Y'all enjoy."

Adam and Martin bowed their heads to give thanks before digging in. Right away Martin commented on the difference between the food on their plates. They both had several strips of thick bacon, eggs that had been scrambled in grease, buttery grits, and each of them had a thick link of rope sausage, but on Adam's plate a couple of the strips of bacon had already been torn up into pieces and stirred into his grits.

"Aww. How sweet!" Martin teased. "That cook must really know you, huh?"

Adam just rolled his eyes and shook his head. His mouth was too full of food to answer right away.

"I mean, I haven't had anyone fix my grits like that for me since I was a tiny thing," said Martin.

Adam nodded and swallowed, then chuckled. "Yeah, well, Aunt Franny has been the cook here since before even my mama came to this tavern. She helped look after me when I was a baby and knows the way I like to eat everything."

"Must be nice," said Martin. "Maybe I should meet her," he joked.

Adam laughed. "Well, you'd never go hungry." He grabbed a piece of bread from the basket and smeared on some butter and preserves, then took a bite. "So tell me the rest of that story," he said through a mouthful of bread.

"Oh, right. Where were we?"

"Something about that man was planning to use his sister to distract Boaz while he stole from Emmanuel."

"Oh, that's right. So what do you think happened?"

Adam just shrugged.

"Well, it turned out Bo was chivalrous. He wanted to preserve the girl's virtue, so he wouldn't give in to her advances. The whole plan of Freddy and Josephine kind of fell apart right there.

Once Bo realized she was trying to seduce him, he left and told her they'd be married soon, that they ought to wait. He went right back to the warehouse and noticed Freddy wasn't there working. He heard noises upstairs and figured Emmanuel might be there, so he went up to the living quarters and there was Freddy, filling a sack full of all kinds of things."

"You're joking!" Adam exclaimed.

"I'm not. Well, you can imagine Bo was mad as fire. He confronted Freddy about what he was doing—told him to put everything back, that he was going to turn him in to the authorities. But Freddy wasn't gonna let him do that. He tried to push past Bo to leave the apartment. Bo tackled him and they ended up fighting. Somehow in the middle of it all, Freddy had a knife. Bo tried to wrestle it away from him, but Freddy wasn't giving up. Somehow Freddy ended up with the knife in his gut, and that was the end of him."

"That's awful! But it doesn't sound like Boaz actually killed him. Sounds like the man fell on his own knife."

"Well, I reckon it was sort of like that, but it wouldn't have happened if Bo had just let him go and then reported him to the authorities."

"So what happened with the girl? Josephine?"

Martin grinned, excited to be able to recount such a shocking tale. "You'll never believe it."

"What?"

"Turns out Josephine wasn't really Freddy's sister. She was his wife. They had done robberies like this in other towns before but had just never gotten caught. Well, this time they did."

"Oh, man! I reckon Boaz was torn up about it."

"He was, and after that he swore off women. That was his first and only sweetheart, and for him to find out she was another man's wife and how she had just used him so her husband could rob Emmanuel—well, it was all too much for him to take."

"That's incredible," said Adam. "I had no idea anything so exciting ever happened at the warehouse. I'll never look at Mr. Rogers's sitting room, or Boaz, without thinking about that now."

Martin nodded.

The two quickly gobbled up the rest of their food. As they did, Adam had more questions for Martin.

"I keep hearing about how Mr. Rogers never brings in anybody new. And I hear about how everybody who works for him is connected to him somehow. What's the story with your family? How'd you end up working for him?"

"I already told you my daddy was a cooper. Well, my mama, she's Laney's aunt, like I told you. She and her brother William had other brothers and sisters, too. Well, their daddy—my granddaddy—was good friends with Emmanuel back when they were young. They sailed together."

"Oh, really?" said Adam. "Was that before Emmanuel came to North Carolina or after he was already living here?"

What Adam really wanted to ask was if Martin's grandfather had also sailed with Blackbeard, but he didn't think it would be a good idea.

"Oh, well, my granddaddy and Emmanuel became good friends before Emmanuel ever came to North Carolina. In fact, he was one of a crowd of 'em from Bath who met Emmanuel after he lost his sloop down in the Caribbean. He ever tell you about that?"

"He sure did," said Adam. "He told me a lot of exciting things about when he was younger."

"I'll bet. Did he tell you who used to be his captain?"

Adam hesitated. He didn't know if he should answer, then

he decided he would, but without saying too much. "I believe he did."

"Come on now! You believe he did? You'd know for sure if he'd have told you."

Adam started to grin and looked away. "Yeah, well, I know what he told me. I just don't know what you were told."

"Blackbeard, damnit!" Martin exclaimed under his breath.

Adam nodded. "Yep. So your grandfather sailed with him, too?"

Martin nodded. "Uh-huh. My granddaddy was one of his friends in Bath. You should know there ain't nobody working for Emmanuel today who ain't connected to those days somehow. Everybody in his company knows about it. And that's why he don't bring in nobody else. So you know what that means, don't you?"

Adam shook his head. "No. What?"

"It means you must have some kind of connection to those days, too. You just don't know it."

"What? Me? To Blackbeard?"

Martin nodded. "Yeah, but don't act so surprised. You wouldn't ever believe how many folks got family members who sailed with him once upon a time. Here, over in New Bern, and in Beaufort County on the Bay River—all over the place."

"Eh, I don't know. Why is this the first I'm hearing about it, then?"

"Don't know. Prob'ly cause a lot of folks ain't proud of having pirates in the old family tree. It ain't really like having a duke or a duchess, now is it?"

Adam laughed. "No, I don't reckon it is."

"Prob'ly the main difference is in those of us who descend from pirates. The ones who just have men in their families who were pirates, like uncles or cousins, they prob'ly don't know the truth and all the stories. They just know what they read in the papers or in books. What was that one by Captain Johnson, or something or other?"

"I read that book. Always figured it was all true," said Adam.

"Yeah. Everyone does. Let 'em. I wouldn't want there to be some book out there with a real history of my family, would you?"

Adam chuckled. "No, I don't guess I would. So you're saying that I must have some sort of connection to Emmanuel's days of piracy? When were those days over?"

"Hmm . . . seems like it was round about 1718, something like that."

"Huh." Adam was trying to calculate dates in his head. "Couldn't have had anything to do with my mother or father's generation, then. My mama's barely thirty-five. I don't know my father, but I do know he wasn't much older than her. That means they weren't even born by the time Mr. Rogers was already done with piracy."

"Maybe one of your grandfathers, then," Martin suggested.

"Maybe." Adam's eyes grew wide. "Or maybe even Valentine's father."

"Maybe so," said Martin. "You oughta ask him."

"Right. I'm just supposed to go up to Valentine and ask him if his daddy sailed with Blackbeard. Just like that, huh?"

Martin laughed. "I don't know. You'll figure it out."

"Yeah, I reckon. Eventually. For right now, maybe we ought to get on back. I want to try to make peace with Boaz."

After he and Martin left the tavern, they returned to the

warehouse, where they found a much calmer Boaz. Emmanuel was back upstairs in the living quarters going over the different orders for the pending arrival of the *Elizabeth Ella*.

Adam wasted no time apologizing for how he'd acted earlier. He explained that he understood why Boaz might have said what he did, but he assured him that he didn't need to worry about him doing anything to betray Emmanuel. By the end of the conversation, the two of them shook hands and agreed to be at peace with one another.

Chapter Fifteen

ADAM AND BOAZ avoided any more confrontations for the rest of the day Monday and all day Tuesday. It was a relief to all of Emmanuel's crew, who had to work later than usual readying the warehouse for the pending shipments.

As soon as the day was done, Adam joined Emmanuel and Boaz for supper at the warehouse. Afterwards, he journeyed back to the tavern to visit for a little while. He enjoyed a brief chat with his mother in between her waiting tables and talked with Valentine while they closed up the tavern for the night.

Just as he was about to bid them farewell, Aunt Franny's son, Tim, appeared at the doorway from the kitchen. "I'm sorry to interrupt y'all, but there's a man here to see you, Mr. Adam."

Adam glanced quickly at Valentine and Mary before Valentine said to Tim, "Who is it? We ain't expectin anyone."

"He didn't say nothin 'bout who he is, 'cept that Mr.

Adam was expecting him for a meetin."

"Thank you, Tim," said Adam. "Send him in, please." He quickly motioned for his mother to go on upstairs out of sight.

Just as she had gotten out of view, Richard Rasquelle entered the tavern from the kitchen—an unsettling sight for both Valentine and Adam.

"What are you doing coming into my tavern after-hours?" demanded Valentine.

"What coarse manners, Mr. Hodges!" said Rasquelle. "Surely our boy here has told you about our arrangement." He looked over at Adam with a saccharine smile.

"Actually, I haven't told him anything specific, Mr. Rasquelle. You had told me to keep everything in confidence. And anyway, I wasn't sure when you would want to meet."

"Meet about what?" said Valentine. He was quite convincing at feigning ignorance about the situation.

"Young Mr. Fletcher and I have some business we need to discuss, but we'll require a private room. Where might you be able to accommodate us?" Rasquelle turned his focus back to Adam. "Perhaps your mother's quarters."

"No, sir. I'm sorry," said Valentine. "No one enters the living quarters here unless they're renting a room or they live here. Well, you don't live here, and you can't rent a room, because we don't have any available right now."

"Mr. Hodges," said Rasquelle, "Mr. Fletcher here assured me that you'd—"

"How about in here, sir?" Adam offered. "The tavern is closed now, and Valentine is just about to retire for the night. We can talk in private right here."

Rasquelle was hesitant.

"Sir, I'm sure you understand that I'm uncomfortable

with bringing a gentleman up to my mother's quarters. I wouldn't want to do anything that might provoke gossip. I'm sure you understand."

Rasquelle reluctantly conceded to Adam's request.

"Very well then. We'll meet in here, but Mr. Hodges, we do require privacy, so if you wouldn't mind."

The tavern keeper glared at Rasquelle and grumbled under his breath as he dried his hands on the towel he'd been using to wipe down the counter. Just before he exited through the kitchen, he turned to Adam and said, "You be sure and lock up before you leave."

Adam nodded. "I will."

Rasquelle waited until Valentine disappeared into the kitchen before he began his inquisition.

He turned his attention to Adam. "So tell me. What information do you have to report?"

Adam shrugged. "What kind of information would you like to know, sir?"

"Several days have passed since we met in my office. I'd like you to start with Saturday and work forward to today and tell me everything that's happened."

"Alright, sir." Adam gave the man a confused look, then thought for a moment before he began. "Well, as you said, we met on Saturday. Let me see . . ."

He acted as if he was searching his memory for every detail. He even sat down at a bar stool, rested his elbow on the bar, and rubbed his forehead.

"Hmm . . . After I left your office, I went back to the warehouse, but Boaz, my boss, said we were already done for the day, so he gave us the afternoon off. I ended up spending the rest of the day hanging around with a friend of mine."

Rasquelle narrowed his eyes with skepticism.

Adam continued: "The next day . . . Let's see . . . Since it was Sunday, there was no work. I went to church, then went straight home because I needed to wash my clothes so I'd have clean ones for this week. You know, I don't have as many clothes as you, sir. Then, let's see. I reckon I spent the rest of the day fishing, resting, visiting with friends and family, that sort of thing."

Rasquelle let out an exasperated sigh. "I don't care about how you spent your Sunday, boy. Just tell me about everything related to the workweek."

"Yes, sir." Adam paused and thought for a moment or two before he began to recount the details of Monday.

"Monday I woke up real early. I mean, real, real early. Mr. Rogers's sloop set sail that day. After that I—"

"Wait a minute," said Rasquelle. "Rogers's sloop left on Monday. Where to? What was her destination? What all did she carry?"

"Oh, I don't know the answers to all that. I mean, I just helped load up what was in the casks—I think some of them were full of pitch or something or other. And I had to make sure that the livestock on board were fed and watered. Then I came here and had breakfast."

"What about today?" Rasquelle asked. "Tell me what you did today."

"Oh, you know, just worked on making more casks. And I have to tell you, sir, I had no idea cooper's work was so hard."

He could tell Rasquelle's patience was growing thin. "Listen, boy—"

"But you know, I have to tell you there was this one thing that kind of surprised me."

Rasquelle raised his eyebrows in anticipation. "Well . . .

What is it?"

"Did you know you have to use white oak for the casks that hold liquid but different kinds of wood, like pine or spruce, for the ones that hold dry things?"

Rasquelle gave him a blank stare.

"Aw, what am I thinking?" said Adam. "Of course you'd know all about that, but I didn't. Just shows how much I have to learn about this business."

Rasquelle opted for a more direct approach. "Have you heard any talk about any shipments coming in or anything going out?"

"I don't know how to tell you this, sir," said Adam, "but the one thing I've learned since I was brought on at Emmanuel Rogers is this . . ."

"What?" Rasquelle said in a sharp tone.

"He never brings anyone new into his warehouse. You already know that. You told me that the other day. Well, do you really think that they would take time to talk to me about things coming in or going out at that warehouse? They've moved me from staves to hoops, and that's near about all the action I've seen these last couple of weeks."

"So you've told me everything you have to report. Am I to understand you correctly?"

"Yes, sir," said Adam. "It has only been a few days, after all."

"You're certain?"

Adam nodded.

"Well, maybe I can jostle your memory. I received word that you and one of Rogers's men were seen going out to Lennox-ville Point, to the Martin estate, right after you left my warehouse on Saturday. Would you like to tell me about that?"

Adam was caught off guard. Who could have told Rasquelle that? Who could have seen them? Rasquelle must have more spies working for him, he reckoned.

Adam thought quick and concocted a story to explain what Rasquelle's spy had seen.

"Oh, that? Well, I told you I spent the day on Saturday after I left your warehouse hanging around with a friend. It was Martin Smith. He works for Mr. Rogers, and he's the cousin of the lady of the house, Miss Laney Martin. You may not know this, but Laney's father is deceased and has left her in the care of a gentleman called Mr. Reading. Well, unfortunately Mr. Reading has been away on some business, so he had asked Martin to come by to check on Miss Laney, and since we were done with work anyway, Mr. Rogers gave us leave to go over there. When we got there, turned out there were a couple of things she needed done around the place, so we were happy to oblige."

"I see," said Rasquelle. He paced across the room and then walked back. "Explain this to me, then: Why did this Mr. Smith need to take you with him to check on his cousin?"

Adam smiled. "Well, uh, you see, this is a little embarrassing, but I asked Martin if I could come along so I could see the girl—his cousin. Lovely girl. But then again you've met her, haven't you, sir?"

Rasquelle was dismissive. "No, I haven't had the pleasure."

"Oh, really? I figured you must have. You know, since I actually first met her at your house, sir."

Rasquelle wrinkled his brow and cocked his head. "My house? When were you ever at my house?"

"Your party, sir."

"The party," he said. "Oh! I see. You met her at my party."

"Yes, sir. Wonderful party, too."

Rasquelle and Adam just stared at each other for a few seconds.

"Is there anything else you'd like to know, sir?" said Adam.

Rasquelle shook his head. Adam could detect the man's frustration when he began speaking to him in the kind of voice one would use when talking to a small child. "No. Perhaps you've not been there long enough to know what sort of information would be desirable to me. We'll not meet again this month, but I should think by next month you will have a better grasp of things, and perhaps you'll be able to learn more that will be of use to me and to the cause of fair trade practices."

"I should hope I will have learned a great deal more by then, sir," said Adam. "When should I expect to meet with you again?"

"Let's just plan to meet back here this same day, same time next month, shall we?"

Adam nodded. "Yes, sir. I'll be here."

"Oh, and Adam, you wouldn't think of concealing information from me, would you?"

Adam wrinkled his brow. "Of course not, sir."

"I certainly hope not."

Adam smiled.

Rasquelle looked like he was exerting quite a bit of effort for him to remain calm.

"I want to make myself clear, Mr. Fletcher. If I ever find for any reason that I cannot trust you, you will find yourself in terrible trouble, and there will be no one who can help you."

Was that a threat? It took Adam a moment to register what the man was saying. Just when he was about to respond, Rasquelle continued.

"And if you're not around, Mr. Fletcher, who will be there

to look after your mother?"

The boy resisted every temptation to lunge for Rasquelle. Instead, he opted for strategy. "Sir, please let me assure you—and I told you this once before—that my word is as good as yours. And I can trust you, right, sir?"

Rasquelle smiled. "Of course." He nodded and excused himself, leaving the way he came through the kitchen. When Adam heard the door slam on the back side of the tavern, he knew the man was gone.

After running upstairs to say good night to his mother, Adam came back downstairs and crept through the kitchen and looked out the small window beside the rear door. He wanted to be sure Rasquelle couldn't be seen loitering around the building outside.

When he felt sure the area was clear, he crossed the small kitchen garden behind the tavern to the tiny house where Valentine lived. He rapped on the front door in a special rhythm that he had always used as a little boy to let Valentine know it was him. He didn't wait for the front door to be opened, though. He knew to run around to the back of the cottage, because that was the door where Valentine would expect him. It was a fun game they used to play. Adam would do his special knock on the front door, then mischievously run around to the back, only so that when Valentine would answer the front door, Adam could call to him from the back of the house. It didn't take long for Valentine to catch on to what little Adam was doing, so he just started opening the back door when he heard the special knock. Sure enough, Adam would be there, quick and quiet. When he was a child, he would go into fits of giggles when Valentine opened the door to him.

On this night there was nothing to laugh about, but Adam

was thankful to have that system with Valentine. He didn't want Rasquelle or one of his spies to possibly see him standing on the porch waiting for the door to open. Rasquelle would immediately suspect Adam was disclosing the details of their conversation.

Valentine didn't let the boy down. He still remembered that knock, and he knew to open the back door.

"Rasquelle's gone," said Adam. "That man is dangerous, though. I think he's worse than we could have ever imagined."

"Really? What did he say?"

Adam told Valentine about Rasquelle's threats.

"What! He said all that?"

Adam nodded. "Yes. I want you to look after my mother. I can take care of myself. Just please keep her safe, Valentine."

"Of course," he replied. "I told you, I always have, I always will."

"I know, but this man, he's evil. I really think he could be capable of anything."

"Well, he is up to something," said Valentine. "Just keep your eyes open and be careful."

"I will. I've gotta get back to the warehouse and let Mr. Rogers and Boaz know what happened."

Chapter Sixteen

"WE NEED TO talk," said Adam as he burst into the warehouse living quarters. Emmanuel and Boaz, who were seated at the chess table intensely concentrating on a game of chess, both looked up.

"What is it, boy?" said Emmanuel.

"Rasquelle showed up at the tavern tonight. They were closing up, and he came in through the kitchen—Tim let him in."

"Who's Tim?" said Boaz.

"He works at the tavern. He belongs to Valentine."

"He's a slave?" said Emmanuel.

Adam nodded.

"Why on earth did he let Rasquelle in through the kitchen?" Emmanuel asked.

"Rasquelle told him that I was expecting to see him there.

Tim didn't know any better."

"What happened?" said Boaz.

Adam crossed the room, pulled up a chair to the table, and proceeded to tell them as much as he could remember from the conversation with Rasquelle.

"Did you tell him about the shipments coming in? The second dock?" said Emmanuel.

"No!" said Adam. "But I did mention that your sloop left on Monday. I didn't figure that would hurt anything."

"You didn't tell him where it was headed, did you?" said Boaz.

"No, of course not. I told him that nobody tells me much, and that I don't ask questions."

Emmanuel and Boaz both nodded. To Adam they looked relieved.

"He accepted my responses—this time. But he seemed suspicious and told me that he'd expect better information next time we meet."

"Next time? When will that be?" said Boaz.

"He told me that in a month's time I should be better acquainted with the goings-on at this place, and so he'd expect me to be able to provide him with better information."

"Did you agree to meet with him again?" said Emmanuel.

Adam shrugged. "Well, I didn't tell him no—of course I told him I'd meet with him next month. What could I say?"

"Good boy," said Emmanuel. "He might be a little suspicious of your loyalty to him, but at least you weren't foolish enough to do or say anything confrontational."

"There is something that you need to know. It's important," said Adam. "He said someone told him they saw Martin and me over at the estate on Saturday."

At first no one said anything in response, but Adam could tell by the expressions on their faces that Boaz and Emmanuel were obviously disturbed at the news.

"He knows about the dock there? The basement?" said Boaz.

Adam shook his head. "I don't think so. He asked me why we had been there. I just told him that Martin was Miss Laney's cousin and that he had gone by to check on her while her guardian was away. I also said that there were some things she needed help with at her house. I told him we tended to them before we left."

"Do you think he believed you?" said Emmanuel.

"I do. At least he didn't give me any reason to think otherwise."

"We need to warn Miss Laney that she's being watched," said Boaz.

Emmanuel nodded. "I think you're right."

"You don't think he'd have a spy just watching that place, do you?" said Adam. "I mean, I told him we were only paying a family visit."

"Did he ask you about why you had accompanied Martin on a family visit?" said Boaz. "Because I sure would have."

Adam nodded. "Yes he did."

"And what did you tell him?" said Emmanuel.

"I told him that I had met Miss Laney once before. I told him I had begged Martin to take me along so I could see her, and that you were gracious enough to let me go."

"Either he believed you and your clever responses have saved you, or he found your narrative questionable and will now ensure that he keeps someone posted outside the Martin estate to watch for anything suspect," said Emmanuel.

"Why would he find my story questionable?" said Adam.

"You said Martin not only went by to check on her while her guardian was away but also to take care of some things around the place, right?" Boaz asked.

"Yep. That's exactly what I told him."

"Well," said Boaz, "Laney Martin has enough servants to take care of any manual labor around the house. There'd be no need for Martin to have to do anything."

Emmanuel nodded. "That's true. The only thing logical would have been a family matter, or perhaps an issue with the servants, but if you spent much time outside the property and Rasquelle's spy spotted you there, then he'll know your story isn't the full truth of the matter."

Adam dropped his head onto his arms folded in front of him at the table. "Ugggh!" he groaned. "Why didn't I think of that?" he said, his voice muffled by his arms.

"It doesn't matter now," said Emmanuel. "We do need to inform Miss Martin that there may be someone watching the estate. She must be cautious. Boaz, have Martin go there first thing in the morning to warn her."

Boaz shook his head. "I don't think that's a good idea."

"Why not?" said Emmanuel.

"Martin was just there Saturday. Rasquelle knows that. What reason would he have to go right back again tomorrow. Rasquelle would immediately suspect that he's just going to warn her about all of this." Boaz thought for a moment as he stroked his stubbly chin.

"You go," he said to Adam.

Adam raised his eyebrows in surprise. "Me?"

"That's a very good idea, Boaz," said Emmanuel.

"Why me? I mean, I'd be happy to, but why me?" Adam

asked.

"Don't you see?" said Boaz. "You told Rasquelle you had begged Martin to go over there with him so that you could see his cousin. Let's let Rasquelle think you really are sweet on her."

Adam grinned.

Emmanuel chuckled. "I don't think that should be too much of a stretch."

"Maybe pick her some flowers on the way over," said Boaz. "That way if anybody sees you they'll figure you're going over there to try to charm her."

"Alright," said Adam, "but I don't think I should go first thing in the morning. That would look suspicious. Why would you let me off from work to go take flowers to a girl?"

"Fair point," said Emmanuel. "Go in the afternoon, then. We risk her not knowing during the first few hours tomorrow, but I don't imagine she'll do anything that would give anything away."

"I doubt she would," said Adam. "I'll just plan to go at noon, if you let me take my break then."

Emmanuel nodded. "That'll be fine. And you can even take my horse."

"Alright, so now we need to figure out what we're going to do about the two shipments coming in." Boaz looked to Emmanuel for a response.

"I don't foresee any problems with the *Elizabeth Ella*. She's an English ship after all, so that would be of little interest to Richard Rasquelle."

"But what about the *Dama*?" said Boaz. "She's from Cuba. Shouldn't we try to keep her away from the Martin estate. Is there someplace else we can direct her when she arrives?"

"Hmm . . ." Emmanuel rested his chin on his hand and

thought for a moment. "You know what? I'm afraid there is no way we can reroute the *Dama*, but I think it will be alright, anyway. We can have our own men posted keeping watch for Rasquelle's spies. The captain of the *Dama* is an old friend of mine, so if his ship is spotted docked at the Martin estate, we can just explain that he had come to town for a visit. No one even needs to know that he is making a delivery or picking up cargo. We'll just need to get that bit of business done quickly and without being noticed."

Boaz was skeptical. "That won't be easy."

"No, of course it won't," Emmanuel agreed, "but what do you think I should do? Sit here and fret about what might happen? There's nothing we can do except try to keep an eye on Rasquelle's spies, warn Miss Rocksolanah, and move the cargo off and on the *Dama* as quickly and quietly as possible."

Once the matter was settled, Adam stood and was about to excuse himself to go to bed. Just before he got to the door to the sleeping quarters, he decided to tell them about Rasquelle's threat.

"What do you think he meant by that?" asked Adam.

"I don't know, son," said Emmanuel. "And let's not try to find out."

Chapter Seventeen

THE RIDE OVER to Laney Martin's estate was a pleasant one in spite of the fact that Adam took the shorter route that cut through the woods to get there rather than riding along the water's edge. That is, it was pleasant until he got about a mile from her house. Suddenly, he saw a fancy horse cart coming down the little lane in his direction. His heart sank when he realized who it was—Francis Smythe. *Don't tell me he was just at the Martin estate*, Adam thought. *But who else would he be going to visit so far from town?*

Apparently, Smythe must've seen him, too, because he gave Adam his typical smarmy grin as his horse trotted past. He couldn't let that bother him too much right now. He was going to Laney's house to take care of business, not on a social call. Suddenly, he wondered if Francis Smythe might have been Richard Rasquelle's spy. He was at Rasquelle's party, too, after all. His father was also the local customs agent. As Adam began trying to put the puzzle pieces together in his mind, he snapped the reins on the horse to encourage it to go faster.

Once he finally arrived, Adam ran his fingers through his hair and took a deep breath before he pulled the cord by the door. If the circumstances were different, he'd have been excited about standing there on the big front porch with flowers waiting to see Laney Martin, but right now he was only focused on the task at hand.

He winced as he looked down and noticed the spindly daisies and dainty purple and pink phlox he had picked on the way over had begun to wilt in the grasp of his calloused hand. He realized that if Smythe had seen the pitiful bouquet, he was likely laughing all the way back to town. There was no time to worry about that now, though.

Within seconds Charles appeared at the door. "Mr. Fletcher," he said. "Good day, sir. How may I help you?"

"Good day," said Adam. "I'm here to see Miss Laney. Is she here?"

Charles nodded. "Wait here please," he said, before disappearing into the house.

Laney soon appeared at the door. "Mr. Fletcher, what a surprise," she said.

She was wearing a simple pale blue calico dress, but to Adam the girl was so beautiful he had nearly forgotten what had brought him there in the first place.

He didn't speak right away, so Laney said, "What are you doing here?"

"Miss Laney," he finally sputtered, "I apologize for the intrusion, but we need to talk."

She gave him a puzzled look. He had hoped she'd invite

him inside, but when she didn't, Adam realized he'd have to be more direct.

"Look, please don't misunderstand me, but I think we should speak inside." He thrust out his arm and presented her with the flowers he had been squeezing in his left hand.

She raised a skeptical eyebrow at him but saw he was insistent that she take them, so she did and then motioned for him to come inside. He nearly pushed past her, and then as soon as they were safely in the house with the heavy oak door closed behind them, Adam crisscrossed the room and looked out the windows to see if he spotted anyone who might be watching the house. He realized at the very least that it was possible Smythe had followed him back to the house and could be watching them at that very moment. Even if he wasn't Rasquelle's spy, it would be just like Francis Smythe to try to pry in a situation like this just so he could use it to mock Adam later.

As she watched him dart from here to there, she asked, "What on earth are you doing?"

"Ma'am, I do apologize for all of this—sorry about the flowers, by the way—but I came to warn you that we think this estate's being watched."

"What?" she exclaimed. "Who is we? And who would be watching this place? And why?"

Adam indicated that she should follow him into the parlor.

"Come in here. Let's sit down," he said, and motioned to the settee.

"What is all this?"

She wasn't cooperating. She wasn't going to sit next to him on the settee, and for that matter she hadn't invited him into the parlor to begin with.

"Please, there might be a man out there in the woods," he said, tipping his head toward the window. "He could be watching us. Trust me on this. Just sit down with me."

"Where?" Laney tried to get a look out the window without looking too obvious.

Adam was growing impatient. "Please, just sit down!"

After giving him a stern look, she eventually sat right down beside him. The settee was situated in the center of the room and was clearly visible from windows on the north and east sides of the house. If anyone was watching from outside, they might not be able to see much detail inside the house, but Adam wasn't going to take any more chances.

If he had gone over there in an attempt to charm Laney Martin—and at least that's what Adam hoped any spy would believe—he knew it wouldn't be effective if she stiffly stood there talking to him in the grand home's foyer. She needed to at least appear gracious.

Adam was beginning to see things more like Boaz and Emmanuel, thinking two or three steps ahead.

"Smile at me," said Adam. "Act friendly." Now he was just milking the situation, and he knew it.

"Excuse me?" said Laney.

"Just do it."

Laney smiled. Through her grinning teeth, she said, "Fine. I'm smiling. What is it?"

"Richard Rasquelle is Mr. Rogers's primary competitor in this town. You know that."

Laney nodded. "I do," she said, still smiling. "Can I stop smiling now?"

"If you want—but it'd be a shame. You have a beautiful smile."

She made a face at him.

"Would you just listen? Richard Rasquelle is intent on spying on Mr. Rogers's business until he has evidence that he can take to the customs officials."

"Evidence of what?" she asked.

"Smuggling."

"Oh!"

"He came to the tavern last night and told me that one of his men saw me and Martin come here on Saturday."

"Wait," she said. "Why would you have been talking to Richard Rasquelle?"

"That's a long story, ma'am, and Emmanuel knows all about it, but I've only come over here today to warn you. You need to be careful that no one sees you do anything that would draw attention to the dock or the ramp leading down to the basement. Also, I just want you to keep your eyes open. Don't go out alone. Strange men lurking around could be dangerous, even if they aren't spying."

"I never go down to the ramp or out on the dock, so you needn't be concerned about that. I also have several servants who can protect me, so I'll be fine—no need to worry about me either."

"What about visitors? Have you received any visitors today?"

"What?" she asked, apparently caught off guard.

"I passed someone on the way here. I wasn't sure if he was your visitor."

"Mr. Fletcher, I'm afraid I fail to understand how it's any of your business if visitors come to this estate, or with whom they were visiting. Don't forget I'm not the only person who lives here. So does my guardian, Mr. Reading, as well as the staff."

Adam took a deep breath. He thought for a moment before he spoke, certain that if he didn't he'd be less gracious than he should.

"Miss Martin, I apologize if this is . . . well . . . out of line, but I just passed Francis Smythe about a mile from this place. Now I don't know if he was here to visit you, but I do know that I saw you talking to him at Richard Rasquelle's party. I also know that his father is the Crown's handpicked customs agent for Port Beaufort, so you're playing a dangerous game if you're intimate in any way with that cad."

She gasped. "Mr. Fletcher!"

Adam couldn't tell from the look of shock on her face if she was more surprised at what he had said or at the idea she could be having any sort of personal relationship with Francis Smythe.

"This isn't a game, Miss Martin. There is a lot at stake here—not the least of which is the future of Rogers's Shipping Company, as well as the personal freedom of everyone and everything who has ever been involved with his clandestine operations. That includes you and this estate."

"Mr. Fletcher," she said, "I am well aware of what's at stake. I inherited this *business*, shall we say, when my father died. I don't need some bumbling apprentice coming here telling me to watch my step. I always tread carefully and would never do anything to jeopardize the relationships that have been so dear to my family since before I was even born."

"Fine, but what about Francis—?"

"And let me tell you about Francis Smythe," she angrily interrupted. "First of all, it is none of your business with whom I have relationships of any kind, but be that as it may, I was raised to be a lady and as such I try to be gracious with visitors—even if one is not an ally, per se. I would think it would raise far more suspicions if I suddenly began treating coldly someone to whom I have heretofore been kind. And *since* Francis Smythe's father is who he is, you can be certain that I've always tried to be gracious to him, as well as to his father—as my father did before he died."

"Fair enough," said Adam. He was pacified with her answer.

Laney, on the other hand, still appeared to be angry. "I still want to know why Richard Rasquelle would have been talking to you at all—or the better question might be, why were you talking to him?"

Adam smiled, then glanced out the window to see if anyone was watching them. "Well, that's a long story, but since you asked, I'd like to know why *you* were at Richard Rasquelle's party a couple of weeks ago."

"The whole town was invited to that party. I thought it would be a clever charade—showing up and offering my support for his business success. Emmanuel knows I'm loyal to him to the end."

"And what about your guardian? Did he know you attended Rasquelle's party?"

"Mr. Reading? Oh, heavens no. He was out of town. He'd have never allowed me to go if he was here."

"Did you talk to Rasquelle while you were at his party?"

"Why do you persist in this interrogation? I think I've answered enough of your questions," said Laney. "Yet you still haven't answered mine. Why were you talking to Richard Rasquelle in the first place?"

"I told you. It's a long story. Let's just save it for another time," Adam replied. "The only thing you need to know is that Emmanuel knows all about it. You just need to be cautious. Keep your eyes open."

Laney stood up quickly. "Very well, Mr. Fletcher." Her tone was curt.

Adam stood and smiled. "Good. And if you notice anything or anyone strange—well, stranger than Francis Smythe—just send one of your servants to let us know."

"Fine," she said, rolling her eyes. Then she walked him towards the front door.

"I do have one question for you," she said. "Why did you bring flowers?"

"It was—what was that phrase you just said?—a 'clever charade.' If Rasquelle does have spies watching the place, it might make them think I fancy you." He looked down and noticed she was caressing the stems of the flowers in her fingers, and he smiled at her.

When she appeared to realize what he was looking at, she stiffened and opened the front door. "Good day, sir."

He tipped his hat with a smile and winked at her before he left.

Chapter Eighteen

Emmanuel's warehouse looked much emptier without all of the casks that the men had been making. The first batch went on the *Carolina Gypsy*. The rest had been picked up and taken to fill with naval stores at pine forests owned by several families on the northern edge of town.

As soon as the *Elizabeth Ella* arrived from Liverpool, Emmanuel's men would help bring in the imported kegs, barrels, and butts from the ship to the warehouse, then quickly load the locally filled casks from the warehouse onto the vessel for export.

Emmanuel had a time-tested system in place that left little room for error. Although the warehouse ordinarily seemed spacious, it filled up quickly when shipments arrived. If the available dock workers didn't know where all of the incoming cargo was to line up, chaos would ensue, and the cargo wouldn't be shifted with efficiency.

Although Adam had helped in preparations for the departure of the *Gypsy*, this would be his first time off-loading an import shipment and then loading the ship up again with local goods for export. He went through several trial runs with a couple of Emmanuel's dock workers so that he could learn how the cargo got handled for both incoming and outgoing orders.

When Emmanuel had told Adam on his first night at the warehouse that he could eventually learn everything, Adam had no idea it would happen so quickly. He was beginning to understand that the shipping merchant's business involved many skills. Anyone could approach a single trade and learn to practice it well, but a shipping merchant—an efficient one—should be a master of many trades.

He had to understand every aspect of the industry, from knowing the shipping routes and how they are affected by ocean currents and wind patterns, to knowing the right people in the right ports for conducting business via correspondence. He needed to be familiar with the commodities that could be sold for profit abroad, but he also had to know how to help facilitate getting those goods to customers.

One key tenet of Emmanuel Rogers's business philosophy was to make every effort to remove any obstacle to fair and reasonable trade. In fact, that philosophy was one of Emmanuel's greatest advantages when he had first arrived in Beaufort decades earlier. He approached the smaller farmers with vast tracts of forestland and arranged with them agreements whereby he would find buyers for the naval stores they produced—the tar, pitch, turpentine, rosin, and such—in return for their commitment to sell their materials only to him. He sweetened the deal by offering his own staff of coopers to make and deliver the barrels for their wares—a great benefit to the new or small farmers, who were not yet able to hire their own coopers full-time.

Emmanuel forged many strong relationships very early on that had continued right up through the time when Adam came on board. It was for this reason that the old man seemed so elusive to those who had moved into the area in recent years—and Beaufort did have quite a transient population with the seafaring business.

It wasn't necessary for Emmanuel to go out and sell his services to the people. That groundwork had been done early on, and any subsequent business came to him by word of mouth from trusted clients. In this way he was able to have his finger on the pulse of the town, and he knew what they needed to live and thrive in their otherwise inconsequential port village.

As the time drew near for that first ship's arrival—at least it would be Adam's first import vessel—he stood and marveled at the company of which he now considered himself proud to be a part. Excitement was in the air. The men in the warehouse all stood a bit taller, laughed a bit louder, and worked a bit harder.

Adam thought again about the contrast between Mr. Rogers's warehouse and what he'd seen at Rasquelle's operation, and it humbled him to remember how at one time he had wanted to work there. He considered how different things would be for him had that actually come to pass. Adam was astonished at how much his view had changed of the man in a period of just a few weeks. He had gone from admiring and even envying Richard Rasquelle, to feeling disgust and pity.

THURSDAY AFTERNOON, EVERYONE FINISHED readying Emmanuel's warehouse for the arrival of the *Elizabeth Ella*. Adam headed back to the tavern to eat. The men hadn't taken a break since they started working before seven, and it was nearly three o'clock. As he made it into the center of town, he noticed a lot of activity over near Richard Rasquelle's warehouse.

It was an outdoor sale. Adam had seen it advertised in the paper, but he had forgotten it was today. Apparently, it was a joint venture on the part of Rasquelle and Everett Bell, the man who had introduced him at the party. Bell had his own mercantile store, and it was in direct competition with Moore's Mercantile, a shop that was one of Emmanuel's best customers. There was quite a crowd gathered over there, rummaging through crates and casks full of all sorts of items—calico cloth, lace, brass ink bottles, tea-kettles, socks, tools, just about anything the townspeople could want.

Before he had gone to work for Emmanuel, there was no way Adam would have passed up an opportunity to browse through the wares at a sale like that, but he wouldn't give Rasquelle one pence now. Nevertheless, he still couldn't help but look over in that direction to see if he recognized anybody.

He did recognize somebody. But it was the last person Adam would've expected to see.

It was Laney Martin and Aunt Celie.

And was that Richard Rasquelle walking over in her direction? It sure was.

As Celie pulled out different bolts of fabric to examine them, Richard Rasquelle had approached Laney and was talking with her as if they had some familiarity with one another. It looked like they might have been sharing a joke.

She can't be actually smiling at that man, Adam thought. He couldn't believe what he was seeing. *What's wrong with that girl? First Smythe and now this. Being gracious is one thing, but this is a bit much.* When he first met Laney Martin, he had poured on the charm—merciless charm that would make most of the girls in Beaufort blush—but Laney never smiled like that at him. Granted, Richard Rasquelle was a handsome fellow and ridiculously wealthy, but still, he was the undisputed enemy. Why on earth would she be standing there talking to him and smiling?

Adam decided he better not stand around to find out. He was getting angry. If he didn't just walk away fast, he knew that he'd end up going over there and doing something rash. Still, there was no way he could forget what he had seen. He wondered if he should tell Martin.

Nah, he decided. Martin probably wouldn't believe him, and even if he did he'd probably just make excuses for his cousin. He decided he would mention it to Emmanuel, though. The old man might want to know that the mistress of the property he was using for his second dock was fraternizing with his adversary.

◊◊◊

WHEN ADAM GOT BACK to the warehouse, Boaz had already gone to bed. That wasn't unusual for him. He typically fell asleep shortly after the sun went down. Adam was relieved this night was no exception. He knew it would be easier to talk to Emmanuel if he didn't have to contend with Boaz's added commentary.

Adam saw Emmanuel sitting in his armchair, struggling to study his Bible by the flickering light of his lantern. He knew what his master was reading without even having to see the cover, because the small text of the scriptures was more difficult for the old man to read than the larger text in his other books.

"Mr. Rogers, I'm sorry to interrupt you, but do you have a minute?"

Emmanuel looked up from the book and smiled at Adam. "Yes, of course, son. Come sit down."

Adam took a seat on the settee next to Emmanuel's chair.

"What's on your mind?" Emmanuel asked.

He wondered how he would tell his master what he had seen. Finally, he spoke. "Mr. Rogers, I don't know how to tell you this, but . . ."

Emmanuel closed the Bible and put it on the table beside him. "Yes? What is it?"

"I saw something today—something that I thought you should know about."

"Yes?"

"Well, there was an outdoor sale at Richard Rasquelle's place. And Laney Martin, she was there."

"Yes?"

"And she was talking to Mr. Rasquelle."

"Is she alright?" asked Emmanuel. "Did anything happen?"

Adam furrowed his brow. "Well, no, but—wait, you're not bothered that she was there? That she was talking to him?"

Emmanuel wrinkled his brow. "My gracious, no," said Emmanuel. "Why would I be? I've known Miss Rocksolanah since she was born. I would never question her loyalties."

"But Richard Rasquelle—he's a problem for us."

"I agree with that," said Emmanuel, "but nevertheless, he is still free to sell merchandise, and Miss Rocksolanah is free to buy from him. I'd never have any problems with her patronizing one of his sales. I know her loyalty to me, to this company, and to the friendship her father and I had is unwavering."

"She was smiling at him, though," said Adam.

Emmanuel chuckled. "I see. Well, that's the real problem, isn't it? If she had made an ugly face at him, you'd probably not be worried enough to bring this matter to my attention."

Adam thought about what his master had said. "Maybe you're right, but still, I was surprised she looked so friendly with him. And there's another thing."

"What's that?"

"I think she may have had a visit from Francis Smythe the other day. He may very well be Rasquelle's spy."

"I very seriously doubt that," said Emmanuel. "And I'm not surprised to hear that the young Mr. Smythe went to call on her. She's a lovely girl, and he knows she's single and close to his own financial stature. There aren't many girls here in Beaufort who would measure up to the necessary qualifications for someone like him. And regardless, I'm sure she was only being gracious if she received him as a visitor."

"But his father," said Adam.

"Quite right," said Emmanuel. "If he did have an interest in Miss Rocksolanah, I would think the smartest thing she could do is follow the expected social graces. Furthermore, in spite of what you might think, Ellison Smythe is a good man. He's not our adversary, son."

"But he's the customs agent."

"Indeed he is. And he's just doing his job. I've never given him any cause for suspicion since he's been appointed, and he's not been unfair or harsh in his dealings with me."

"I see," said Adam. "Still, I just think it's strange that Richard Rasquelle must've gotten the word from someone that Martin and I were out at her estate the other day. Rasquelle's claiming to want to find evidence against you for smuggling. Then I see Francis Smythe out by her place yesterday. And then I see her in town talking to—and even smiling at—Richard Rasquelle at his outdoor sale today. Far too many coincidences, I think."

Emmanuel nodded. "I understand, but let me ask you

something. What would it have been like if Miss Rocksolanah had been rude to Mr. Rasquelle? What if she had refused to smile and instead behaved rudely towards him? She doesn't come into town often, but when she does she's always a perfect lady. She was brought up well, you know."

Adam looked away, unsure of how to respond.

"Adam, I think she is a clever girl. Richard Rasquelle would never even imagine that she could be involved with helping my company in the way that she does. She has always treated him and his business like she would anyone else in the town. The same is true for Francis Smythe, I would imagine. I think that's a fine way to keep suspicion at bay, don't you?"

"I reckon it is," he conceded.

When Adam finally went to bed, he lay there unable to sleep. He turned and faced the slightly opened window and listened as a few heavy drops of rain began to beat against the glass. Before long there was a steady shower, punctuated by low rumbles of thunder. Usually it would be ideal sleeping weather, but as things were, his growing suspicion about Laney Martin and her troubling associations both worried and unsettled him.

Was Mr. Rogers blinded by his long-standing relationship with her family? He said he had known her since she was born, after all. Maybe it was impossible for him to conceive of her ever doing anything to betray him. But then again, he thought, why would she? It was her property that he used as a second dock. She had been seeing him receive clandestine shipments there her whole life. Why would she turn on him now?

While he thought it was unlikely that Laney could be even remotely attracted to pale, gangly Francis Smythe, in spite of his money, he could see how she might be romantically interested in Richard Rasquelle, handsome devil that he was. Adam figured that if Rasquelle had told her what he initially tried to tell him—about how the town could suffer if King George saw it as a haven for smugglers—she might have been naïve enough to believe him. That might have caused her to have second thoughts about allowing the continued use of her property for those purposes. But then again she didn't really seem like the naïve type. Although physical attraction can make a person do stupid things, so anything was possible.

Adam acknowledged to himself that Richard Rasquelle, in spite of his questionable character, was a handsome, successful, and ridiculously wealthy man. And he might be just the kind of person who would make Laney willing to give up her inheritance—at least if it came down to that.

Maybe she'd calculated all that. If the property was lost as Emmanuel's second dock, her guardian, Absalom Reading, might be implicated. After all, she was underage and had been in his care since her father died. That could free her from the conditions in her father's will about whom she could marry. Then her only obstacle would be her brother, and he'd be unlikely to stand in the way of her happiness—at least that's what Martin had said.

The more Adam thought about all of the what-ifs, the more his mind began to run very quickly through possible scenarios. He thought, for instance, about how Rasquelle clearly had an ax to grind with Emmanuel and wanted to see him go out of business. Maybe Laney knew that and was feeding him information in an effort to win his favor. That could be how Rasquelle knew about Adam and Martin going to her estate that day. Maybe she was colluding with Rasquelle to put an end to Emmanuel's use of her property—and if she believed Rasquelle was connected with government officials, she might believe that could exempt her from any sort of punishment and win her the approval of the Crown.

But if she was doing that, why wouldn't she just come out and tell the authorities everything she knew about Emmanuel's past operations and get it over with? Why the charade? Well, she even said herself that pretending to be friendly with Rasquelle was just a "clever charade," so as troubling as it was to consider, it could be a double deception.

But why? And why now?

Maybe Rasquelle had told her that Emmanuel needed to be caught in the act. That would mean Rasquelle enlisting Adam to spy on Emmanuel might have just been a ruse. Adam wouldn't put it past Rasquelle to use him to take the fall so that Emmanuel wouldn't suspect Laney if and when he was reported to the authorities.

In his gut Adam just couldn't believe—or maybe he just didn't want to believe—that Laney could be guilty of such a betrayal. But now that his mind had ventured down this rabbit trail, he'd have a hard time forgetting about what he'd seen and the possibilities he'd imagined.

Chapter Nineteen

"This may serve to inform the publick, especially the traders to North Carolina, that the Hornet sloop-of-war lies in Cape Lookout Bay, has two tenders, one a Virginia-built pilot boat with two swivel guns forward, the other a small schooner, with six swivels, which strictly examine all vessels they meet bound to North Carolina; some have been seized."

So READ THE announcement in *The Gazette*. It sent shock waves through Emmanuel Rogers's company. The news couldn't have come at a worse time.

Operations were already moving slowly and with extreme caution, thanks to the constant threat Rasquelle's spies posed to conducting business as usual. The pending arrival of *La Dama del Caribe*, out of Cuba, which was due to come on the heels of Liverpool's *Elizabeth Ella*, only made things worse—especially since the *Elizabeth Ella*'s arrival was already a few days behind schedule.

Emmanuel and his crew knew the worst possible scenario would be if both ships arrived at the same time, in which case there would be no way to cover both transfers. Now, however, Emmanuel was beginning to wonder if one or both of the shipments might be lost to the customs inspectors offshore.

When the *Elizabeth Ella* finally did arrive, on Friday morning, everyone in the company seemed to let out a collective sigh of relief. Emmanuel and his crew learned in full detail of the vessel's experience at the customs checkpoint. It was a rigorous inspection that had forced many vessels to wait in queue before passing through to their destinations.

The *Elizabeth Ella* had stopped at a few other ports en route to Beaufort, some of which were restricted trade partners. Fortunately, by intermingling contraband with legitimate cargo throughout the cargo hold, the crew managed to trick the inspection team and were free to go.

Within just a few short hours, the crew of the *Elizabeth Ella* were arriving at a rainy Port Beaufort, where they docked right in front of Emmanuel's warehouse. In spite of the stormy weather, not only were they able to off-load the vessel in record time, they were able to load her up without a hitch and get Ellison Smythe to sign off on everything. The ship's captain having documents in hand with the customs agency's certification would make it easier for the *Elizabeth Ella* to return through the customs checkpoint at Cape Lookout before moving on to its next port stop, farther north.

Just before the *Elizabeth Ella* left Emmanuel Rogers's dock, word arrived via a couple of local sailors that there was a ship sinking off of Cape Lookout. The customs sloop *Hornet* was assisting, but more help was needed to try and salvage the cargo, as well as help the poor souls on board.

Emmanuel didn't know if it was one of his shipments, or another, but unfortunately he was not equipped to do anything about it at present. He had only his periauger. It was a small craft, not nearly large enough to conduct the rescue of a large merchant vessel. He had to make a difficult decision that might cost him, but he knew people's lives, as well as their livelihoods, were at stake.

Richard Rasquelle's *Fortuna* was the largest cargo vessel presently in port at Beaufort. There were other ships in port, of course, but Rogers knew that his competitor's ship would be the most efficient means of saving whoever and whatever might be on board.

Without hesitation he went to Rasquelle's warehouse.

After Emmanuel had explained what he had heard about the sinking vessel, Rasquelle wasted no time offering to go assist with the shipment.

"I think you have done a great service today by coming to me about this, Mr. Rogers," said Rasquelle. "It's humble of you to be willing to come to your competition for help."

"Mr. Rasquelle, this isn't about business or competition. This is about a ship full of God only knows how many poor souls, who are in trouble. Unfortunately, with my largest vessel out on delivery at this time, there's little I can do to help. I know you're more equipped to go to their aid, and so I implore you to do so."

Rasquelle nodded. "And I most certainly will, sir. Don't you worry. I'll have my men ready the sloop right now. We'll be under way very shortly. And rest assured we'll do everything we can to save both the passengers and the merchandise on board."

Emmanuel bowed his head and said, "Thank you, sir. I pray you have a safe, speedy journey—that you can get there in time to be of help."

"Fear not, sir," said Rasquelle. "We will handle everything."

As soon as Emmanuel was on his way, Rasquelle went to his floor supervisor and said, "Ready the men. A merchant vessel is in trouble near our coast—a few miles out. We need to send out a ship and offer our assistance."

The merchant's men worked in unison like the gears in a clock. There was no talking, no bravado, just moving in concert to accomplish the task of getting the ship out of the harbor, then beyond the inlet at the eastern end of Taylor Creek.

Soon they were in the open sea approaching the sailing vessel offshore. They all knew what to do. After all, this wasn't the first time they'd come to the aid of a ship in distress. Indeed, Rasquelle's business boomed after *The Gazette*, the region's most popular newspaper, ran a feature celebrating his heroic rescue of the *Sea Sprite* two years earlier. The misfortune of the *Sea Sprite* turned out to be an incredible stroke of good luck for the young merchant. When he first arrived in town, Richard Rasquelle struggled to line up enough shipping customers in Beaufort to make it worth his while to set up shop there. Most folks were either well established with their longtime friend and neighbor Emmanuel Rogers or traded with another merchant, named Faulkner Baldwin.

Unfortunately for Baldwin, Rasquelle's business was built by picking off his customers. When Rasquelle's arrival in town was punctuated by the newspaper article celebrating him as a hero, Baldwin's customers started flocking to his young, new competitor. Baldwin's customers hadn't been with him as long as Emmanuel Rogers's clientele, nor did they have the same loyalty to him. As a result, within eight months of Rasquelle's arrival, Baldwin was forced to close up shop. Word had it that he had planned to move to South Carolina, but no one ever heard from him again after he left town.

On this day, however, things were different than they were during the sinking of the *Sea Sprite*. British customs officials nearby at Cape Lookout were also assisting the sinking vessel.

Rasquelle's men already had a plan in place. They sent word to the customs sloop that if they rescued the passengers, the *Fortuna* would try to salvage the cargo, as their ship was equipped for just such a situation.

Together, the two vessels were able to save all of the people on board the sinking ship, as well as much of the cargo. The passengers went on the *Hornet*, and the cargo on the *Fortuna*.

Chapter Twenty

EARLY ON SATURDAY, *La Dama del Caribe* arrived at Port Beaufort. Rather than coming directly into Topsail Inlet, she first sent one of her tenders, a small and swift cutter, into Taylor Creek to notify Emmanuel Rogers of the ship's arrival.

The timing of *La Dama's* approach was serendipitous. The inspections sloop that had been stationed at Cape Lookout was busy bringing back the passengers of the sunken vessel, and Rasquelle's crew were tied up transporting the cargo back to town.

When Adam and the rest of Emmanuel's men received word that *La Dama* had arrived, they wasted no time traveling over to the Martin estate. The gate at the entrance of the estate was secured, and they all took their positions on the dock, the ramp, and in the basement and awaited *La Dama's* arrival.

Adam wondered what would be on board the foreign ship. He knew whatever contents it carried would have been perfectly legal had the vessel been English, but since it came from Cuba, it was all contraband.

Emmanuel refused to pay an additional tax to receive shipments from the captain of *La Dama*, who was an old friend, simply because his point of origin was a Spanish port. It was the principle of the thing that so frustrated Emmanuel. Why should he be browbeaten into limiting his trade with only English vessels? Merchants the world over had been trading with one another since time immemorial. It was too late for King George to put that genie back in the bottle.

La Dama del Caribe was piloted by a Spaniard named Santiago Velasquez de Leon. He had been sailing between his home port in Havana and destinations up and down the eastern seaboard for nearly two decades, but it had been a long while since he had come to Beaufort, and he dealt more frequently with merchants in Charleston and Providence, Rhode Island.

As soon as the ship docked at the Martin estate, the men of both crews moved swiftly to shift the cargo from the ship to the dock, then down the ramp and into a holding area in the basement. Just as swiftly they rolled several barrels of various naval stores onto the brig and moved some pigs and sheep on board from the Martin farm, which would provide food for the Cuban crew on the long journey back to Havana.

Once the cargo transport was done, Captain Velasquez invited Rogers's crew on board to browse through some limited stores of exotic items he had obtained in trade from various ports and ships with whom he had done business. The merchandise didn't amount to enough to justify wholesale transactions. They were typically slightly damaged goods that weren't acceptable to merchants, but Velasquez had discovered that people everywhere enjoyed his diverse wares. There were vanilla beans and chocolate from Mexico, dominoes from Italy, and various games and toys, including dolls from France and pan flutes from Colombia. Then there were fireworks from China and all sorts of other knickknacks.

All of Rogers's men bought gifts for their families or themselves except Adam, who didn't bring any money to spend on trinkets.

Captain Velasquez noticed him watching the other men browse through his wares and asked him in Spanish, "*¿No quieres comprar nada?*"

Adam gave him a puzzled look. "Huh?"

"You don't want to buy anything?"

He shook his head. "Oh, no thank you." Adam was too embarrassed to admit he didn't have any money.

The captain grabbed a small, crudely sewn cloth sack—the same kind Rogers's men were filling with their desired goodies—and grabbed some Mexican chocolate, some Chinese fireworks, and a handful of candies, and tossed them into the bag and handed it to Adam.

"*Toma esto*," said the captain. "I think you will like these."

"Oh, no thank you," said Adam. "I really don't need anything."

The captain smiled at him. "*No te preocupes. No te cobro nada.* You can have them. You worked very hard today. Everyone should go away with something."

Adam smiled and held out his hand to take the sack from the captain. "Thank you, sir."

"*De nada*," said Velasquez. He smiled at Adam, "*¡Disfrutalos!*"

Adam looked the captain, puzzled.

"I said, 'You are welcome. Enjoy them!'"

Adam couldn't believe how quickly the whole transfer took with *La Dama del Caribe* in comparison to the *Elizabeth Ella*. Then again, the English ship had much more cargo and was also receiving much more in the way of naval stores to be taken back to England. In addition, *La Dama* needed to move out quickly after their transactions were complete. Neither Emmanuel Rogers nor Captain Velasquez wanted to be caught by British customs authorities, nor Rasquelle's spies.

Once *La Dama* was gone and the day was done, Emmanuel Rogers's crew quickly dispersed. There was a great sense of relief that, at least for the time being, they had successfully eluded discovery.

BACK AT THE WAREHOUSE apartment, Adam, Boaz, and Emmanuel sat around the kitchen table.

"Boy, I'm glad that's done," said Boaz. "I didn't know how we were going to pull that one off with that inspections sloop sitting offshore."

"Same here," said Adam. "And I was worried about Rasquelle catching us."

Emmanuel nodded in agreement. "We were indeed quite fortunate today. Things could have gone very differently. So tell me, you lads get anything from the captain's treasure shop?" said Emmanuel.

"I did," said Boaz. "Bought a game from Italy called dominoes. Can't read the instructions, though. They're in Italian. Also got some of those sweets he had."

"I wasn't going to buy anything," said Adam. "Didn't have any money, but the captain gave me this."

He pulled the cloth sack out of his pocket and dropped it on the table in front of him.

"What do you have there?" said Emmanuel, smiling.

Adam dumped out the bag's contents. "Let's see . . . looks like some chocolates—I don't know where they're from, but they've got Spanish writing on them, I think—some firecrackers—what are they? Chinese?—and a bunch of other sweets, but I don't know what they are."

Boaz picked out a piece of the chocolate. "I'll bet this is from Mexico. Be careful with that." Boaz chuckled as he held up a block of the sweet stuff and said, "They put spices in it—cinnamon, peppers. It can set your mouth on fire."

"Peppers? Really? In chocolate? Well, what I can't wait to try out are some of these." Adam fingered through the bundle and picked out some of the brightly wrapped fireworks. "Never had these before. Seen some, but never been able to try them out for myself."

"You'll want to be careful with those, too," said Emmanuel. "They are explosives, you know."

"I know, but they're *fun* explosives."

He stood and said, "In fact, I think I want to try a couple out right now." He grabbed the ember bowl and tongs from the sideboard.

As he darted out the door and down the stairs, Emmanuel called out after him, "Don't set them off in the warehouse! For goodness' sake! You'll blow us all up!"

"I know!" the boy could be heard calling back from downstairs, his voice trailing as he got farther away.

Chapter Twenty-One

THE DAY AFTER the arrival of *La Dama del Caribe*, Adam went to church with Emmanuel and the rest of the men in the company, along with their families, if they had them. The old merchant expected all of his employees to attend church—regardless of their feelings about the local congregation. "Don't ask the Lord to do anything for you if you refuse to do anything for him," he'd often say.

Emmanuel had one time explained to Adam that while he was no theologian, he believed the Lord had saved him from a life of reckless living, so he committed to trying to live a "right and obedient" life, the chief exception being his refusal to follow what he believed were immoral laws imposed by Parliament relating to trade practices.

After the service on Sunday, Adam went to the tavern to visit his mother and Valentine. He had gone to church only infrequently when he lived at the tavern, but since being apprenticed to Emmanuel, he'd gone every Sunday. When he took his regular seat at the bar, everyone was talking about the ship rescue that had taken place earlier that weekend. Adam couldn't help but overhear several conversations going on nearby.

"I can't believe he's done it again," said one man.

"We oughtn't be surprised," said another. "He done it before."

"That Richard Rasquelle's a real hero, he is," declared a particularly loud fellow.

Although Adam was happy to hear the rescue of the sinking ship had been another success, he was annoyed to hear talk of Rasquelle as a hero. He had once thought the same way, but now things were different.

"I'm happy to see you, sweetheart," said Mary as she took a break from waiting tables to give her son a half hug and a kiss on the cheek. "You go to church again this morning?"

Adam nodded. "Yeah. Just got out."

"I'll bet they made a big to-do over Richard Rasquelle today, didn't they?" said Valentine.

"No," said Adam. "Actually, he wasn't even there."

Mary wrinkled her brow. "He wasn't?"

"I was sure he'd have been there," said Valentine.

"He wasn't," said Adam.

"Maybe he's home resting," said Mary.

"Maybe so," said Adam. "I don't care, though. I'm just glad I didn't have to see him."

"I'll go fix you a plate," Mary said as she darted back into the kitchen.

"What have you been busy with this weekend?" said Valentine. "We ain't seen you since last week. Everything alright?"

Adam nodded. "Yeah. Everything's been fine. We've just been busy. That's all."

"Too bad Emmanuel's sloop wasn't here to go help those poor people on Friday. Then he'd be the one getting called a hero."

"I don't think Emmanuel cares a whole lot about that," countered Adam. "He's the one who told Richard Rasquelle that that ship needed help, you know."

"No," said Valentine. "Hadn't heard that."

"Well, I haven't heard much about the rescue, we've been so busy," said Adam. "What ended up happening?"

"Well, turns out apart from the ship's crew, there were sixty passengers on board—mostly women and children. They were coming from England to meet their husbands and fathers here in the colonies. There was also right much cargo on board."

"Sounds like they rescued all the passengers. Did they lose any cargo?"

"Unfortunately," said Valentine, "I think it's a lot like it was that last time. They were able to save right much of it, but apparently some of it was lost to the tides."

"At least they were able to help the passengers. That's the most important thing, anyway."

Mary returned to the bar with Adam's lunch, a plate piled high with roasted chicken and gravy, mashed potatoes, green beans, and pickled beets. Adam gobbled his food up so quickly it prompted Mary to ask him if he was being fed well at Emmanuel Rogers's warehouse. Adam said that he was but the food was no match for Aunt Franny's cooking.

He didn't talk about either of the two recent shipments. Adam figured it was safer if they didn't know too much about Emmanuel's business. The less they knew, the less of a chance they might inadvertently slip something to one of Rasquelle's spies.

Adam was now conscious of the fact that anywhere he went, Rasquelle could have people following him. The town was so small, it was inevitable to see some of the same faces throughout the day. Now he had to wonder if any of them were on Rasquelle's payroll—that is, if Laney Martin wasn't the one feeding him information.

After a long, relaxing visit at the tavern until curfew, Adam returned to the warehouse for a good night's sleep before the start of another workweek.

Chapter Twenty-Two

"I DIDN'T GET a chance to ask you yesterday, Fletcher. How were those firecrackers the other night?" asked Boaz. "You didn't blow a finger off, did you?" He mashed his piece of bread in the runny eggs on his plate and sopped up the yolks.

"Oh, don't even ask," said Adam. He looked in the cupboard for a coffee mug.

"What happened?"

Adam poured himself some coffee and tipped the sugar bowl over his cup to shake in what was left.

"They didn't even go off," he said before grabbing a spoon and scraping out the last bit of sugar from the bowl into his cup. "I only lit a couple, because the smoke was so awful."

Boaz gave a laugh. "Yep. They can do that, alright. Sounds like you got a bunch of duds. Moisture might've got to 'em."

Adam nodded and tore off bread from the loaf and moved

a couple eggs and a few strips of bacon onto his plate from the platter in the center of the table. "I had really hoped to see some lights fly up into the sky. Wonder what they would've thought in town."

"If you had gotten any to take off, you'd have drawn a crowd, I reckon," said Boaz. "So maybe it's just as well they didn't fire."

"You're probably right."

Just then Boaz stood up from his chair and put his plate in the dish tub on the counter. "You better eat fast, boy. We've got a big day ahead of us."

"Be right down," said Adam.

He ate fast, then joined his coworkers on the warehouse floor.

"So what are we working on?" he asked.

"Right now we're just waiting," said Boaz. "Emmanuel and Martin will be back in a minute. We've got to start moving the cargo today from *La Dama*."

Suddenly the voice of a man called into the warehouse from near the street-side cargo doors.

"Good morning, gentlemen. Is Mr. Emmanuel Rogers here?"

Boaz and Adam turned to see who it was. The silhouettes of five men stood near the entrance. Their faces couldn't be seen because of the light pouring in behind them, but Boaz and Adam could tell the voice belonged to the man in front.

"Beg your pardon, sir. Who might you be?" said Boaz as he approached the men.

Adam stayed near the work area but could clearly hear the introductions.

The men stepped farther into the warehouse. The man in

front was dressed in the finery indicative of a royal official, and he was accompanied by a man who appeared to be his assistant, and three men in uniforms of the Royal Navy.

"I'm Edward Sheffield," said the man in fancy dress, "Chief Inspector in service of His Majesty's Revenue Office, stationed on board HMS *Hornet*."

Boaz extended his hand to shake each of the men's hands.

"This is my assistant, Percy," said Sheffield, motioning to a diminutive man standing beside him.

He then motioned to the soldiers standing behind him. "And these men are from the *Hornet*'s Customs Enforcement Regiment."

"How can I help you?" asked Boaz.

"Is Mr. Emmanuel Rogers here?"

"No, sir. I'm afraid he won't be back for a little while yet, but I'd be happy to pass a message along to him."

"That won't be necessary, sir," said Sheffield. "We'll just wait here. In fact, while we wait, I think it might be most efficient if our men here inspect the facility—get that bit out of the way."

"I don't think you will, sir," said Boaz. "What reason do you have? Did you bring a warrant?"

"By writ of assistance, my position is the only warrant I need." The inspector snapped his fingers and motioned for the soldiers to begin their search.

Adam quickly crossed over to where Boaz was standing. "What is all of this about?" he whispered.

Boaz wouldn't answer him. He only shook his head and shot the boy a stern look to silence him.

Sheffield instructed the men to begin examining the cargo nearest the dock entrance.

"I think we at least have the right as subjects of the Crown to know why this building is being inspected," shouted Boaz as the men began their search.

"Because . . ." The inspector broke away from the group and crossed the warehouse again to approach Boaz. "I'm sorry, I didn't get your name."

"Boaz Brooks, sir," he said.

"Well, Mr. Brooks, we are here because we have received a tip from an informant that this company is guilty of trade violations, sir, specifically in regards to the proprietor, Mr. Rogers's, infringements of the Sugar Act—including, but not limited to, the export of prohibited materials to foreign agents, as well as the import of molasses, sugar, and sundry other commodities from those same foreign agents—and that he has committed such practices with regularity for years , which would have placed him in violation of the earlier Molasses Act. Furthermore, it has come to our attention that a shipment was received here not more than two days ago—a vessel from Liverpool, I believe, called the *Elizabeth Ella*—for which no customs agent was physically present to inspect the shipping manifest when she was off-loaded, nor the items loaded onto the vessel from this port."

"Sir," said Boaz, "our local customs agent, Mr. Smythe, knew the *Elizabeth Ella* had passed through your own checkpoint at Cape Lookout before she ever arrived here. And we made sure her cockets were in order before she ever left this port."

The inspector gave Boaz a weak smile. "That may be true, but nevertheless it was this company's responsibility to ensure that Mr. Smythe came by personally to inspect and sign off on the cargo that was received to verify the ship's manifest was in line with what was off-loaded, as well as the cargo that was loaded onto the ship before she ever left your dock. Most regrettably for this company, Mr. Brooks, His Majesty cannot deviate on acceptable standards for shipping practices. There are laws, and they are meant to be followed to the letter. Anyone found guilty of not following the laws that are in place is at odds with His Majesty's government and, by extension, His Majesty."

Just then Emmanuel and Martin entered the warehouse. "Alright, lads. Are we ready?" Emmanuel called out, before he noticed the strange men in his building.

"Mr. Emmanuel Rogers, I presume?" said Sheffield.

Emmanuel walked slowly over to the inspector.

"I am, sir. And you are?"

"Edward Sheffield, sir, Chief Inspector aboard the HMS *Hornet*, of the Royal Customs Service."

"Oh, what a surprise. Well, I'm very pleased to meet you, sir," said Emmanuel. He was surprisingly calm and cordial considering the inevitable meaning of the man's visit.

"Likewise, sir," said Mr. Sheffield.

"What can we help you with?" said Emmanuel.

"Ah, yes. I was just explaining to your worker here—"

"Boaz Brooks is in charge when I'm not present," said Emmanuel. "He is not just a worker."

An annoyed Mr. Sheffield nodded. "Whatever you say. As I was trying to explain to Mr. Brooks, it has been reported to our offices that this company is guilty of various violations of His Majesty's laws relating to trade and commerce. There are several details that we'll need to discuss with you, sir. You do own this company—correct?"

Emmanuel nodded, then looked at Boaz and Adam. His face betrayed his worry, although he tried to appear confident before the inspector.

"Yes, sir. I am the proprietor."

"We will need you to come with us, sir," said Mr.

Sheffield. He snapped his fingers and motioned for Percy to take his place at his side. "I assume we can expect you to come with us voluntarily?"

"Of course I will go with you voluntarily. Why wouldn't I?"

"Very well then," said the inspector.

He called out instructions for the soldiers to complete their inspection, then turned to Emmanuel. "If you would please follow us."

Emmanuel nodded calmly. "Alright, lead the way."

Chapter Twenty-Three

NOT MORE THAN an hour after Emmanuel had left with Mr. Sheffield and his men, Boaz, Adam, Elliot, and Joe were on the dock to see Martin set sail to fetch his cousin William Martin, the attorney, and bring him back for Emmanuel's legal assistance. Austin James, a part-time fisherman who also worked as a pilot, had agreed to take Martin to New Bern on his cutter.

Boaz, Martin, Adam, and Elliot argued about what had happened that morning and what the best course of action was to take.

Meanwhile, Austin waited impatiently on his boat.

"Come on, boy! We got to go!" he urged Martin.

Martin finally climbed into the boat from the dock, then said, "Wait, I might need to get my—"

"If you didn't think of it already, it prob'ly ain't that

important! Just leave it!" Austin demanded. "We ain't never gonna make it to Ocracoke Inlet by nightfall if we don't leave now."

"Why does that matter?" asked Adam.

"They can't cross the inlet from the ocean if it's dark," said Boaz.

His tone reflected his impatience with Adam for asking the question. He turned his attention back to Martin and Austin in the boat.

"We might should just sail up Core Sound, anyway," said Austin. "The sun will set a little after eight o'clock tonight and it's already eight thirty. It takes a good eleven or twelve hours to get to the inlet. If we ain't there before nightfall, we'll be stuck waiting there till the sun comes up. The sailing's a little slower going up the sound side, but at least we won't have to contend with crossing that inlet."

"Fine, let's do that then," said Martin. "We just need to get to New Bern as fast as we can."

"Let's go, then."

Austin waved at the men on the dock with one hand and steered the rudder with his other. Soon they were moving quickly down Taylor Creek, drifting out of sight.

As SOON AS THEY went back into the warehouse, the reality of what had transpired earlier began to set in.

"What in the world even happened this morning?" asked Elliot. "Why would they take Emmanuel?"

Adam looked at Boaz, waiting for him to answer, but he said nothing. Instead, he just clenched his jaw, obviously too angry to speak.

Adam knew that no one saw this coming. Everything had gone so perfectly with the two recent shipments. How could this have happened?

"We have a damned traitor on our hands. That's how," said Boaz.

His voice was calm; he looked squarely at Adam.

Elliot turned and looked at Adam. "You responsible for this, Fletcher?"

Adam's heart was pounding. He couldn't believe Boaz was accusing him.

"*What?* Are you crazy?" he yelled. "I had nothing to do with this."

Suddenly all eyes were on him. He feared that his suspicions about Laney Martin, about Richard Rasquelle, and about being set up to take the fall as the traitor if she turned on Emmanuel were being proved true.

"I tell you what, boy," said Boaz. He grabbed a hammer from a nearby worktable and slowly walked over to stand right in front of Adam. His bulky frame dwarfed Adam's muscular-but-lean seventeen-year-old build. Boaz pointed the business end of the hammer at Adam's face. "You get the hell out of this warehouse. *Now!* I better not ever see you here again."

"Bo!" said Elliot. He hurried over to where the two were locked in confrontation. "We can't really be sure it was him. Don't you think we should wait and see what comes out over the next couple of days? Maybe once that inspector has a chance to see the paperwork from the *Elizabeth Ella*, he'll let Emmanuel go."

Boaz shot Elliot a venomous look, then pointed the hammer at him. "Listen, Salter, you ain't got to share living quarters with the little bastard. I sure ain't gonna sleep with a traitor in the next room."

"Now listen to me," said Adam. His voice was firm, resolute. "I had absolutely nothing to do with this. Use your head, man! Do you honestly think if I were planning to betray Mr. Rogers I would've told you two all that I have?" He thumped his index finger against the side of his head. "*Think!*"

"You might have if you were trying to trick us into thinking you were loyal," said Boaz.

Adam stepped back. He knew he needed to calm down before the two of them got into a fistfight.

"You know what? I don't really care if you believe me or not. Now you can stand here and bully me out of this warehouse, or we can all put our heads together and try to make sense of how this could have happened."

Boaz looked away. Adam wondered what he was thinking. Did Boaz really believe that he could have done something like this?

"You all put your heads together," said Boaz. "I'm getting out of here for a while."

Boaz threw the hammer he was holding across the warehouse and then left through the street-side cargo doors.

Everyone remained silent for what seemed like an eternity. Finally, Adam spoke to Elliot and Joe.

"I don't know if y'all believe me—that I had nothing to do with this—but the way I see it is this: you can either work with me and try to figure out how this happened, or you can sit back and wait for a vice-admiralty court to decide Mr. Rogers's fate. I for one am not going to sit by and just watch this happen. I'm going to find out who's responsible."

"And then what?" said Elliot. "What'll you do if you can sort out who's to blame?"

"I don't know yet," said Adam. "But I'll figure something out."

ADAM SPENT A COUPLE of hours after he left the warehouse down on the docks. As long as he could remember, it was where he would go when he wanted to pass time or to think, or even hide.

Often, as a young boy, when he'd get into trouble for being mischievous he would disappear down on the docks—usually hiding among the fishermen or near the boatbuilders—in hopes of avoiding a good switching from his mother. His aim in those days was to stay gone long enough that by the time he got back to the tavern she'd have forgotten what he had done and he would escape discipline. When he was older he enjoyed talking to the fishermen as they brought in their catches of the day, and the townsfolk buying fresh seafood for their families.

When he wasn't chatting over barrels of flounder, oysters, shrimp, and clams, he passed the time down at the boatbuilder's shop, marveling at the engineering that unfolded before his eyes. Over the course of several months, he loved to see the impressive oceangoing vessels crafted from the ground up.

On this particular day, however, neither the fishermen nor the boatbuilders had his attention. In fact, mostly he was just grateful that it wasn't raining. He was there, but he could have just as easily been anywhere, considering how oblivious he was to the goings-on around him.

He didn't feel like going back to the tavern—at least not yet. He needed time to think about what had happened with Emmanuel. He also knew he needed to do something—whether it was to help his master or to at least prove his own innocence to Boaz and the other coopers. His brain was a blur. It had only been a couple of weeks since he came into this apprenticeship, and already everything seemed to be falling apart.

Finally, he went back to the tavern just before supper and

stayed there for several hours. He explained to Valentine and his mother what had happened to Emmanuel, but implored them not to say anything about it to anybody else.

"Why don't you just stay here tonight, then?" Mary suggested.

Valentine nodded in agreement. "I think your mama is right. Sounds like Boaz Brooks is hoppin mad with you, boy."

"I don't know," said Adam. "I think if I stay away it will just make him suspect me even more—like I'm running away to safety. No, I need to prove somehow that I had nothing to do with this."

"Why do you care so much about what Boaz thinks?" asked Mary. "Sounds like he's been angry ever since you started working there. This situation is enough of a mess and it isn't your battle, so why don't you just leave things alone for once?"

Adam rolled his eyes. He looked at Valentine, hoping for some sympathy. Valentine shook his head and walked away.

"Mama, you just don't understand. I've got at least three men right now who are wondering if I'm some damned traitor—"

"Adam!" Mary smacked his cheek with her palm. "You watch your mouth, young man!"

"Ow!" He grabbed his face and rubbed at it, pretending her slap hurt worse than it did. "I'm sorry! I forgot I wasn't at the warehouse."

She cut her eyes at him. "I don't want you talking coarse anywhere."

"Alright! Fine, Mama." He sighed. "Listen, like I was saying, those fellas at the warehouse—they're all wondering if I'm a traitor right now. When Emmanuel gets out—if he gets out— they might have him thinking the same thing. I can't have them thinking that about me, because it's not true."

"You are so hardheaded. Do you know that?" said Mary. "Every bit of trouble you've ever gotten in has been because you were worried about what somebody else thought about you— that, and you don't know when to leave things alone."

Adam shrugged. "Maybe so, but would you really have me stay here like some coward and let them keep thinking I'm a traitor? Think about it, Mama. I might have gotten into fights, I might have gotten into trouble over some stupid things, but this is different. I can't just let this go."

"Okay, fine, but just think for a minute. Just think about what happens if he was serious when he told you you better not show your face there again. What happens when you turn up?" she asked.

For a moment Adam remembered how things used to be when he was a little boy and he'd hide down at the docks from his mother until she was calm so he could avoid a spanking. While he knew Boaz wouldn't be there waiting with a switch, he hoped that once the hothead had some time to calm down and think, he might be willing to talk things through rationally.

"I'm not sure," said Adam. "But I'm going to find out."

Chapter Twenty-Four

ONCE ADAM FINALLY left the tavern, he decided it might be better to wait and talk to Boaz about everything in the morning. He loitered by the docks until he thought Boaz would be asleep before he tried to sneak back to the upstairs apartment.

In spite of his best efforts tiptoeing through the warehouse and up to the living quarters, it was of no use when he opened the door. Boaz was in the sitting room in a chair by the window. He was staring out at the water, and there was an empty rum bottle on the floor beside him.

Adam thought for a moment. He wondered if he should say something or walk by and go straight to his room, or maybe he should just turn around and leave. He opted to try and slip through the place unnoticed.

Just when he thought he was in the clear, a very drunk

Boaz called out to him, "Hey, boy. Where do you think you're going?" His speech was slurred.

The boy nonchalantly motioned to his room. "I'm going to bed. And it looks like you might need to get some rest yourself."

Boaz stood clumsily from his chair and took a few steps towards Adam. "I thought I told you earlier to leave. So I think you'll want to leave."

Adam dropped his head. He really didn't want any problems with Boaz. He understood why the man was angry, and he probably would have been, too, if the shoe were on the other foot. Nevertheless, he still wasn't going to be intimidated by Boaz's drunken threats.

"Look, I'm not your enemy, Boaz. I would never betray Mr. Rogers or you."

Boaz stepped close to Adam. Adam stood straight and tall as his body tensed up with adrenaline.

"Get"—Boaz shoved Adam in the chest—"out!" He shoved the boy again.

Adam was determined not to fight with the man, but he stood his ground. He had dealt with drunks before. After all, he was raised in the tavern. He knew that while they might be fearless fighters, they could also be sloppy and easily thrown off balance.

"Please just listen," he said. "I am going to find out who is responsible for reporting Mr. Rogers. I'm going to prove to you that it wasn't me."

"*Get out!*" Boaz bellowed.

He swung at Adam. Adam ducked and slipped past him and ran all the way through Boaz's room into his own.

"I will, Boaz!" he shouted back.

The staggering man tried to regain his balance.

"Just as soon as I get my things from this room," Adam said.

Boaz stumbled through the kitchen and his bedroom and had nearly reached Adam's room when the boy swept past him again. With his things bundled under his arm, he ran out and down the stairs.

Adam didn't stop running until he'd made his way out of the warehouse. He wondered where he'd spend the night. He knew he couldn't go back to the tavern. He could've stayed downstairs in the warehouse, but he knew if Boaz found him there in the morning, things probably wouldn't go well. He decided to sneak down onto Emmanuel's boat, which he kept docked near the warehouse. Maybe he could try to sleep there.

He sat longways on a bench at the stern and rolled up his little bundle of clothes to use as a pillow. After he lay down and tried to get comfortable, he had to sit up again to pull the lumpy sack of items that he'd gotten from the Cuban captain out of his makeshift pillow. He stuffed the bag in his pocket and lay back down.

Grateful for the gentle breeze on the water and the soft glow of the waxing moon in the cloudy night sky, Adam tried to get some sleep. Unfortunately, sleep would not come. He kept going over the last couple of weeks in his head. He knew that somehow Richard Rasquelle had to be involved in reporting Emmanuel Rogers to the authorities. And simple logic told him Laney Martin was probably involved, too. He couldn't decide if Francis Smythe was involved, but at this point nothing would surprise him.

The thing that baffled him was why in spite of a vague mention of dealing with foreign ships in the past, the only tip about a recent transaction that Inspector Sheffield received was about the *Elizabeth Ella* rather than *La Dama*. Laney knew about the Cuban ship, and so presumably Rasquelle would, too. The *Elizabeth Ella* shipment had been a straightforward trade operation with an English ship. That was not the kind of situation that Rasquelle would waste time reporting. There'd be too great a risk of it being a completely aboveboard transaction, leaving Rasquelle at risk of sounding a false alarm.

Adam was only able to come up with one explanation—the conspirators decided to tell the authorities about the *Elizabeth Ella* because it happened in town and anybody could've reported it. Maybe they were hoping the investigation would ultimately lead to the Martin estate and the shipment from *La Dama* without it looking like Laney had betrayed Emmanuel's trust. But Adam wondered how he'd be able to prove any of this. Boaz wouldn't talk to him, he wasn't that close to Elliot or Joe, and Martin had gone to New Bern—and even if he were in town, Laney was Martin's cousin, anyway. He wouldn't want to hear Adam's suspicions about his kin.

This was not good.

AFTER HE LAY THERE for a while, Adam accepted that his efforts to sleep were again futile. He decided to get up and take a walk.

He quietly crawled out of the boat and onto the dock. He left his things on board but figured he better put them under the seat so they'd be out of sight. Although he didn't own a watch, he knew he'd never walked around town at this hour before. The street lanterns were still lit, but otherwise the town was completely asleep. It was an eerie feeling walking along the waterfront without another soul in sight.

Soon Richard Rasquelle's warehouse came into view. The windows around the building were all wide open, except they had bars to prevent break-ins. There was a small, soft glow coming from two of the windows on the eastern end of the building. Who could that be, he wondered, as he got closer? Could someone actually be in there at this hour?

He crept up close to the warehouse and then inched along the side until he reached the window closest to the water's edge. First, he waited and listened. There was no sound except for the water lapping up against the docks as it moved with the wind. He crept closer near the open window and then, moving from below, he slowly straightened himself up until he could peer over the ledge and see inside. There was no one in there—at least not that he could see from where he was standing.

Wait . . . What was that?

Now that he was close to the window, Adam heard muffled voices coming from inside. He'd have to move to another window to get a better look. He tiptoed over to the other window and hunched down so that his head was just below the ledge. There were definitely voices coming from inside. He recognized Rasquelle's distinctive manner of speech, but the other man's voice he did not recognize.

He lifted his head to peer over the ledge. It seemed like Rasquelle was sitting in his office, but he was obscured from view by the other gentleman, who was standing in the open doorway. He looked to be in his early- to mid-forties, probably ten to fifteen years older than Rasquelle.

Adam strained to hear what they were saying, but it was no use. The older gentleman seemed quite animated, but he was only speaking in a tense whisper, so it was impossible to make out what he was saying from the distance of the window. Adam peered around the corner to try to gauge the length of the warehouse. He wondered if he might have an easier time hearing if he went to the other side of the building.

He moved carefully to the south side, which faced the water. He would have to take things slowly here. There were many more open windows, and there was only a small ledge along much of that side of the building, except for where the dock jutted out into the creek. He struggled to stay balanced as he sidled on the ledge along the wall. Some of the mortar between the bricks of the foundation had eroded, and Adam felt the bricks wobble beneath his feet.

When he finally got near the first window on the waterfront, he knew he would be close to where Rasquelle and the mysterious man were speaking. He pulled himself up just enough to see over the ledge of the window without being seen. Unfortunately, he could only see endless rows of stacked barrels. Rasquelle's office must be the next window, he thought. Even though he couldn't see the men, at least he could hear them a little better now.

He considered his options. The window for Rasquelle's office was about twelve feet farther down, but he saw that the dockside doors about thirty feet from where he stood were wide open. Should he try to listen from outside the window, or should he try to make it to the cargo doors and get closer to the men from inside the warehouse? It was an easy choice for Adam. His heart pumped with adrenaline. He might get caught, but he didn't care. All he could think about was clearing his name and trying to help Emmanuel.

He took a deep breath and scrambled from the ledge to the dock. Now he was just a couple of feet from the open cargo doors. He pressed his back against the wall near the entrance. *Oh, Lord, please don't let me get caught!* He mentally kept repeating his silent prayer as he tried to peek in through the cargo doors to see if anyone was posted inside. He was surprised that Rasquelle was careless enough to leave the door wide open, but then again it was a warm night and most people wouldn't have even known, since it was on the waterfront side of the building.

It was dark inside the entrance, but the very dim glow of a lantern could be seen coming from the building's eastern end, to his right. Adam knew that was where the two men were talking. When he finally made it inside, he moved slowly and carefully, crouching behind racks upon racks of stacked barrels. There were far more in the building now than there had been the last time he was there. It was like a maze.

As he worked his way towards the soft glow of the lantern's light, the men's voices became clearer. He tried to keep enough distance to not be seen. He also wanted to be sure he would have ample room to make an escape, if the situation called for it.

Finally, he was within about ten feet of the men. He felt safe in a little alcove formed out of racks of stacked barrels right near Rasquelle's office. He craned his head just around the corner of one of the racks so that he could hear them midconversation.

"That was part of the deal! What are you playing at by not following through?" said the older gentleman.

"I think you're getting too greedy," said Rasquelle. "If you want to speak with the Customs Inspector, you're more than welcome to do so. Then you can tell him whatever you want him to know."

"You know I can't do that. How would you expect me to explain what I knew without implicating myself?" the older man scoffed.

"You have to let me do this my way," said Rasquelle. "I agreed to help you in this matter, but it's only because it will benefit me as well."

"But what were you thinking? That English ship is meaningless! The Spanish ship is the only thing that can turn the heads of the authorities."

They were talking about Mr. Rogers! And this man apparently had something to do with reporting him. But who was he? And did Laney Martin figure in all of this somehow? Adam wanted to jump out and confront the two—let the chips fall where they may—but he remembered the advice Emmanuel had given him once and kept quiet so he could continue listening.

"I'm sure you can think of something clever," said Rasquelle. "After all, I'd say your designs for the coming months took a great deal of clever planning."

The man shot Rasquelle a cold look but said nothing.

"You have to understand, sir, that when the inspector begins questioning Rogers, it'll soon come out from where he's had his help," said Rasquelle.

"You better be right," said the older gentleman, "or our deal is off. And let me remind you I did not do this because of any admiration for you. I did this for one reason and one reason only."

Rasquelle was smug. "I know, and men have done much greater and much worse things for the same purpose. In fact, I would imagine there are few things a man wouldn't do to obtain his trophy."

"I would thank you not to speak of her in that way," said the man.

"How can it possibly bother you that I would call her a trophy when you have no problem whatsoever in bringing such trouble to her door?"

"It's all about strategy, Mr. Rasquelle."

"I still don't see how you'll benefit in all of this. It seems you causing her trouble is the last thing you would want to do."

"No, no, no. You see, her *knowing* that I had some part in causing her trouble would be the last thing I'd want to do. On the other hand, if the poor lass found herself in trouble, about to lose her home and her freedom, what would she think if I were the only one able to rush in to her rescue? It's one of the oldest stories in the world—the princess who needs rescuing. She just doesn't realize that I am her knight in shining armor."

Adam thought he might know who they were talking about, and it caught him off guard. As he shifted his feet beneath him to regain his balance, he caught a glimpse of some writing on one of the barrels. It said "MB." He couldn't see far away, but in the close distance from where he hid, all of the barrels around him bore the same mark.

The men continued their conversation, so Adam craned forward again to listen.

"And what if your scheme doesn't work out the way you had hoped?" said Rasquelle. "What then?"

"I am telling you," said the man, "that one way or another I will have her. Rocksolanah Martin will be mine."

Just then one of the barrels that Adam had been leaning on shifted forward, causing those stacked above it to all begin rolling down.

Crash!

In shock, Rasquelle and the other man fell silent.

"What was that?" said the older gentleman.

"Go look! Somebody's here! We have to find whoever it is!" Rasquelle demanded.

He scrambled from his chair toward the rack of barrels that had collapsed, but he couldn't see past them, much less get past them.

It wouldn't have mattered. Adam had already wended his way through the maze of barrel racks. The place was disorienting from where he stood. He had moved too quickly to think about where he was going, and every rack of barrels looked the same. The farther he moved through the building, the darker the place was. No longer able to move toward the glow of the lantern that had been his beacon when he first entered the building, he was now just moving from dark to darker.

He was able to see the faintest glow just a few feet from where he stood. It was a bowl of embers. They were still hot from use by workers lighting their pipes to smoke earlier in the day.

Adam had an idea. He crouched behind the alcove formed by the racks and dug into his pocket. The bag with the fireworks was still there. But the tongs for picking up an ember to light things were not in the bowl. He felt around the table near the bowl trying to find them, with no luck. Just then he started to take a step back, but something was under his shoe. He reached down. It was the tongs.

He grabbed them and pinched them together to grab an ember from the bowl. He fumbled around in the bag to pull out a firecracker with a fuse long enough to easily light. Just as he was able to get the ember to light the fuse, the fuse fell right out of the firecracker. That must be why it was so long, Adam thought.

He chose another firecracker. *Oh, God, please let this work!* The fuse wasn't lighting. *Are these all duds or what?* He pulled out another firecracker. *Finally!* The ember lit the fuse. It started to burn. He quickly tossed it over racks of barrels to the opposite end of the warehouse.

Even though he didn't know whether it would create a bang or just smoke, he hoped it would be enough of a distraction for him to buy some time to make his way out of the building.

For now Rasquelle and the older gentleman were just as lost and confused as he was, trying to make their way through the maze of barrels.

The tiny firecracker sailed through the air and landed about forty feet away, close to where Adam had been squatting earlier near the men's conversation. *Let's just hope there's no rum in those barrels*, he thought. Adam waited to see if it would explode or just create a column of smoke. Either way, he knew it would send the men scrambling over in its direction and allow him a chance to escape.

There was neither sound nor smoke. The men were now dangerously close to where Adam hid.

Then there sounded a dull pop, like a cork gun. The men stopped where they were to listen.

Adam prayed there would be more sounds, but there were not. Instead, a terrible cloud of smoke began coming up over the racks of barrels from that part of the warehouse.

Good enough, Adam thought. Now the men were rushing back over there, figuring they'd find their culprit. Meanwhile, Adam worked his way through the labyrinth to a door—but it was the wrong one. He was at the western end of the building now, not the southern end on the waterfront. This door was locked.

He heard Rasquelle and the other man yelling as they neared the smoke. He was too worried to pay them much attention. At least he had the glow of the opposite end of the building working in his favor again now. He was more easily able to see the silhouettes of the barrel racks.

He made his way back to the south side of the building, where he quickly sneaked out the door, climbed down the dock, and waited underneath. It didn't take long for Rasquelle and the other man to make their way onto the dock. They stood just above where Adam was hidden.

"We have to find whoever it was!" said the stranger. "He will have heard us talking!"

"What are you waiting for, then?" said Rasquelle. "You go that way, and I'll go this way. Move! We'll go back through the building and leave through the street-side door. He can't have gotten far."

Both men quickly ran back into the building and made their way almost straight through, until they burst through the north-side door. Adam couldn't make out what they were saying, but he could hear them now yelling in the street. He knew it wouldn't be safe to return to the warehouse on the street. Too much of a chance that one of the men would spot him. He opted to enter the creek and try to swim underwater as far as possible.

It was more than a mile back to the dock at Emmanuel Rogers's warehouse—but after he'd only made it about half that distance, he knew he wouldn't have the endurance to swim any farther. He was near another dock, so he waited there for a couple of minutes to see if he could hear or spot anyone. Fortunately, the moon was nearly full, so it illuminated the water's edge enough that Adam could see the coast was clear.

He thought it would be safe for him to come back on dry land now. He pulled himself up onto the dock—although he wasn't sure to whom it belonged—and started running as fast as he could along the water's edge until he finally made it back to Rogers's warehouse.

Adam didn't even bother going out to the boat to grab his dry clothes but instead ran inside and right up the stairs, yelling "Boaz! Boaz!" the whole way.

Boaz met Adam in the living quarters as soon as he came in. "Damnit, boy! What do you want now?"

He stared at the boy.

"Why are you soaking wet?"

Adam was out of breath. "Would you listen to me? Just listen! I've just been to Richard Rasquelle's—"

"You've what?" said Boaz. "Have you lost your mind?"

"Listen!" said Adam. He hunched over in an effort to ease the terrible stitch he had in his side. "I thought Laney Martin might've been the one who betrayed Emmanuel, but I was wrong—and she's in trouble!"

"You're not making any sense."

"I'm telling you I know what happened! At least I think I do."

"What are you talking about, boy?"

"There was a man there . . ." he panted. "And Rasquelle was there."

"At this hour?" said Boaz.

Adam just nodded. "Mm-hm."

"How do you know all this?"

"I snuck in! Aren't you listening?"

Boaz grabbed a blanket that was draped over one of the settees and tossed it to Adam.

"You what?"

He was still panting. He gladly took the blanket and wrapped it around himself and tried to dry off.

"The other man—"

"Did you recognize him?"

"No. I've never seen him before—at least I don't remember seeing him. I don't know him, anyway."

"Well what does any of this have to do with Laney Martin?"

"This man, he said he has this whole plan, and then he

said that one way or another 'she will be mine.'"

"What the hell?" Boaz scratched his head. "What did he look like?"

Adam shivered as he talked. "Ah, forty, forty-five—somewhere in there. Tall, powdered wig, distinguished looking."

"And Rasquelle never called him by name?"

Adam shook his head no.

"So what does any of this have to do with Emmanuel?"

"I couldn't tell exactly, but this older man was upset because I reckon he had given some information to Rasquelle about Emmanuel. He knew about the Spanish ship, but he was angry because Rasquelle had only reported the English one. He said they had some kind of deal but that Rasquelle wasn't living up to his end of it."

"And you say he was in his forties?"

Adam nodded. "Yeah, something like that. I mean, Rasquelle is in his early thirties and this fellow looked about ten or fifteen years older."

He watched as Boaz mulled over what he had told him, anxious to know what he would say.

Finally, Boaz said, "Based on how you're describing him and that he knew about the Spanish ship, for much I'd think it might be . . . Nah, can't be. He's out of town."

"Who?"

"What did his voice sound like?"

"How do you mean?" asked Adam.

"I mean was it deep? Soft? Did he speak any particular way?"

"Hmm . . . not really. Well, I guess his voice was somewhat deep, and very proper. And he moved his hands around a lot."

"Well, it sounded like you were describing Absalom Reading, but that doesn't make sense."

Adam shrugged. "I have no idea. I've never met the man, but whoever he was, he said her name—her full name. He called her Rocksolanah, not Laney. Oh, and Rasquelle told him he could go to the inspector himself, but he said no, because he said it would implicate him as well. So maybe you're right! I mean, who else could that be?"

"That devil!" Boaz shouted. "He was supposed to be traveling!"

Adam was still panting, but he let out a little laugh. "Well, apparently he's not."

"Why in the world would he be involved in something like this?" Boaz paced back and forth.

"I have no idea. Never even met the man," said Adam.

"If it was Reading, then he must be the one who tipped Rasquelle off about the second dock. But why now? He's known about it for years and it's never been a problem."

Boaz sat down and furrowed his brow in contemplation.

"Well, if it was Reading," Adam said, "then it's his plan to see her brought up on charges, along with Mr. Rogers—at least that's what it sounded like. He said something about letting her get into trouble and then rushing to her rescue—something about being a hero."

"He what?"

Adam paused for a few seconds, then said, "Well, her brother, Will, is going to have to deal with Absalom Reading when Martin gets him back to town. For now we need to worry about the customs inspector learning about where the second dock is. Sounds like someone is determined for that to come out, and if the inspector presses Emmanuel hard enough, it just might."

"So you're saying right now the inspector still might not know about it?"

"Maybe not," said Boaz. "Depends how far they got with questioning him today."

"They wouldn't torture him to make him talk, would they?"

Boaz shook his head. "I don't think so, but I imagine they still have ways of extracting information."

"And what about Miss Laney? If it was her guardian that I saw, he's a danger to her. We have to protect her!"

"If it was him, from what you're telling me it sounds like he's trying to trap her into some sort of relationship by forcing her into trouble with the law and then rushing in to save her. I can tell you that right now that girl doesn't care for Absalom Reading one bit, so like I said, I think we can leave it to her brother to take care of that."

"But—"

Boaz continued: "I mean, what are we going to do? We don't even know if he's gone back to the estate. He might not be staying there. But if he is, we can't rush in and accuse him of all of this. What will that accomplish? He'll wonder how you found out, and he'll probably just go to the authorities himself at that point. He'd have nothing to lose."

A shivering Adam nodded. "I guess you're right." He tightened the blanket around himself.

"Don't you have any dry clothes?" Boaz asked.

"Yeah. Out on the boat."

"What in the world are they doing out on the boat?"

"Because you told me to get out! Where else was I going to sleep? The street?"

"Ah, just go on and get your clothes and bring 'em back

up here. I reckon you can stay."

"Then you believe me," said Adam.

"Go get your clothes," Boaz demanded. "I'm tired and ready to go back to bed, and I don't want to have to be woken back up by you jostling your way past my room to get to yours."

"Alright, alright. I'm going!"

Chapter Twenty-Five

THE NEXT MORNING, Boaz and Adam called Elliot and Joe up to the living quarters to discuss the previous night's discoveries. They didn't want to risk talking about everything in the warehouse in case someone showed up and stumbled in on their conversation.

After Adam got Elliot and Joe up to speed on what he had overheard from Rasquelle and the other man the previous night, the four of them tried to decide on what, if anything, they could do next.

"I wonder what Mr. Smythe has had to say about all this. He's the official agent for this port, anyway," said Elliot.

The mention of Ellison Smythe unsettled Adam. Not only was he worried about how to best help Mr. Rogers, he also had to worry about what Mr. Smythe would think about everything that had happened, not to mention what impact, if any, the present circumstances would have on his apprenticeship and, consequently, his punishment for assaulting Smythe's son.

"Hey, Fletcher," said Elliot, "I've never been in Rasquelle's place before. What's it like inside?"

"Eh, it's just a warehouse. But I can tell you it was a lot different last night than it was the day I was there for that meeting. The place is completely packed with cargo. It's like a maze inside there right now."

"Hmph," Boaz grumbled. "Did it look like stuff he'd brought in? Or was it cargo ready to ship out?"

"How should I know?" said Adam. "It all looked the same to me. Just racks and racks of casks stacked all over the place. All different sizes, all stacked three or four rows high."

"You'd know if they were from here, Fletcher. Think!" Boaz smacked his forehead. "They'd have a mark saying who the contents were from, along with a stamp from the port of origin—Beaufort."

"Well, I guess not then," said Adam.

He thought for a moment. "I don't think any of the ones I saw last night had marks from Beaufort. I mean, I can't promise you none of them had Beaufort marks, but I couldn't see most of them—it was too dark. All I know is the ones in the little alcove where I was hiding. They were marked with an MB."

Elliot thought for a moment, then shook his head. "Nope, I don't know anybody with an MB. Do you, Bo?"

"Nope," said Boaz. He hesitated for a moment, then said, "Wait a minute. I bet that's the mark for Milton Blount. He bought that pine woods northeast of town last year. I didn't think he was producing anything there yet—at least we ain't seen nothing from him. Maybe he's got some naval stores lined up for shipment with Rasquelle."

Adam was getting exasperated. "Who cares about what kind of cargo is in Richard Rasquelle's warehouse? Mr. Rogers has been arrested! Laney Martin might be next! There prob'ly ain't a whole lot we can do for Mr. Rogers right now, but we've got to warn Laney."

"Calm down, Fletcher," said Boaz.

"I am calm! But we also need to figure out some way to hide the cargo that's out at her place. If Mr. Rogers doesn't come right out and tell them all about the second dock, we may be able to get rid of everything, in case Inspector Sheffield starts poking around over there."

"Whoa there!" said Boaz. "Back up for a minute. Don't be so quick to say that what Richard Rasquelle has in his warehouse ain't important. If it turns out that no ships have come into the port lately and those casks you saw aren't from Milton Blount, then Rasquelle just might be holding some smuggled goods of his own. Wouldn't that be something?"

"Okay, fine, so what if he is? How would we even figure that out?" asked Adam.

"I can go visit Milton Blount," offered Elliot. "Find out if that MB mark is his."

"And if it's not?" Adam said.

"Then we may have something. But we'll cross that bridge when we get to it," said Boaz.

"Fine. In the meantime, I need to go talk to Laney. Warn her. Can we move the cargo somewhere else?"

"Hang on," said Boaz. "If Absalom Reading is the man you saw last night talking to Rasquelle, then that means he's back in town. He'll probably be at the Martin estate. How is that gonna work if you go over there? I mean, if he's conspiring with Rasquelle, I don't think he's gonna be real happy to see you go over there to warn Laney and start hiding cargo. Anyway, even if we were able to hide the cargo, he'd know about it. He could just tell Rasquelle our new hiding place. Then what?"

"From what I could tell—assuming it was Reading—he wants her to take the fall for helping Emmanuel, but he doesn't want her to know he's had a hand in any of it. We can use that. If I do see him there, I can act glad about it—tell him he has to help us for Laney's sake."

Adam looked at the other three and waited for a response.

"That just might work," said Elliot.

Joe nodded enthusiastically. "Mm-hm. Yep."

"Alright, you do that," said Boaz. "Get on over there if you want to. But *do not* tell her about what you saw last night!"

"Obviously," said Adam. "Well, at least not if Reading is there. If he's not there, though, then I'm going to warn her."

"No!" said Boaz. "Are you crazy? If she knows, you'll just make her nervous. She might end up saying something or start acting differently around him. Then he might suspect she knows, and there's no telling what he might do. Martin will be here with her brother in another day or two, and then we can tell him and let him handle it."

"Good point," said Elliot.

Adam nodded to acknowledge what they had said, but he disagreed. He wasn't going to argue with them about it, though. He didn't like the idea of leaving Laney in the house with a man capable of concocting a scheme like that.

"You know, you can take my horse if you want to," Elliot offered.

ADAM WAS ABOUT TO leave the apartment to go see Laney, but when he went to open the door, it seemed to open on its own. It was Emmanuel.

"Mr. Rogers!" said Adam. "What are you—?"

"Good morning, lads," said a weary Emmanuel. "I am alive, and I'm glad to be home."

Once they got past their initial shock of him being there, the men all greeted him with handshakes and pats on the back, welcoming him home.

"Adam, I noticed you were about to leave. Where were you headed, lad?" asked Emmanuel.

"I was just on my way to the Martin estate. I need to warn Laney Martin," said Adam.

"Wait just a minute if you would," said Emmanuel. "Sit back down. I want to talk to all of you."

Adam, Boaz, Elliot, and Joe all went back over to the sitting area and took seats on the settees. Emmanuel sat in his armchair.

"What happened yesterday? Where did they take you?" said Boaz.

"Well, unfortunately Mr. Smythe was gone yesterday, so Inspector Sheffield held me in custody until Mr. Smythe was able to come by and be made current on the situation this morning."

"So Mr. Smythe just found out about the charges against you today?" said Adam.

"Yes. Inspector Sheffield tried to question me when they first took me into custody, but I told him I thought it would put our local customs agent at a disadvantage, considering he could not be present, particularly since some of his questions related to Mr. Smythe's role in our recent transactions. He conceded that might be wise, so we waited until today to have our discussion."

"Where did they keep you yesterday, then?" asked Adam.

"In the gaol, my boy," said Emmanuel. "They held me

there until Mr. Smythe returned. Thankfully, he got back into town late last night, and I was brought in to speak with him early this morning. It went rather quickly, and then Inspector Sheffield left with the *Hornet*—at least for the time being—to return to their watch point near Cape Lookout."

"And Smythe let you go?" said Elliot. "You're free?"

"Only temporarily. They're charging me with trade violations, so they'll hold a special vice-admiralty-court hearing as soon as my attorney arrives. They apparently have a witness who's come forward claiming to have knowledge about this company's commercial activities."

"They say who this witness was?" asked Boaz.

"No. That information will be presented when the charges are read at the vice-admiralty court. I told them my personal attorney is William Martin of New Bern, so they'll not hold court until he arrives, and then we'll have a day or two to prepare for the preliminary hearing."

"Martin left for New Bern right after they took you yesterday," said Boaz. "I reckon he's getting to New Bern right about now, which means they'll probably be back sometime tomorrow evening or early Thursday."

"Good. I'm glad to hear it," said Emmanuel. "I'll need William's expertise. The vice-admiralty court is nothing like our regular county court, lads. There's no jury, and the judge is an appointee of the Crown."

"You didn't tell them about the second dock, did you?" Adam asked.

"No, son. I most certainly did not."

"So they don't know anything about it, then," said Boaz.

Emmanuel shook his head. "I don't think so. Unless this secret witness they have knows about it and has told them of such."

"Well, I hate to tell you this, but Absalom Reading may be the rat!" said Adam.

Emmanuel looked stunned. "Miss Rocksolanah's guardian?"

Boaz nodded. "Yep. The boy went snooping around Rasquelle's place and overheard him talking with another man. He fits the description of Mr. Reading."

"What's this?" Emmanuel said, aghast. "And you went skulking around Rasquelle's place? Oh, I don't like hearing that! That's dangerous business, boy!"

"I heard Rasquelle and another man, who I'm pretty sure was Reading, and they were talking. I couldn't make out what they were saying at first, so I snuck in to the warehouse and got closer. I heard—"

"I thought Mr. Reading was traveling," interrupted Emmanuel.

"Apparently he came back early," said Elliot.

"I see." Emmanuel waved his hand, urging Adam to continue his story. "I'm sorry, boy, please go on."

"Quite a bit was said, actually, but the important part is that Reading and Rasquelle are involved in some kind of conspiracy. Reading knows about *La Dama*, and it sounded like he has done this deal with Rasquelle to get Miss Laney in trouble on purpose."

"What an imbecile!" exclaimed Emmanuel. "Doesn't he know if it comes out about the Martin estate, he'll go down with the ship?"

"We've already talked about all of that," said Adam. "First of all, Richard Rasquelle didn't tell the authorities where the second dock was, and that's what Absalom Reading was mad about. Rasquelle thought they'd be able to extract that information from you somehow. Secondly, Absalom Reading was out of town when *La Dama* unloaded at the estate. He can plead ignorance to the authorities on what was happening there that day."

"He's ignorant alright," said Emmanuel, "but not about our use of the second dock! He's been there many times to oversee the unloading of cargo there, even when I've been unable to be there myself. What does he think he can gain from such a scheme as this?"

Adam, Boaz, and Elliot brought Emmanuel up to speed on everything they knew. Emmanuel agreed with Boaz that Adam should go try to warn Laney. He also agreed that if Reading was there, Adam should urge him to help conceal the contents of the basement, but that under no circumstances should Adam tell the girl what he had overheard at Rasquelle's.

"It would be enough of a reason for you to go warn her simply based on my arrest," suggested Emmanuel. "That would raise no suspicions on the part of Mr. Reading, nor Mr. Rasquelle."

"By the way," said Boaz, "there's a chance Rasquelle is holding some contraband in his own warehouse right now."

"How's that?" Emmanuel asked.

"Have you seen any ships—merchant-type ships—here on Taylor Creek in the last week? I mean other than the *Elizabeth Ella*?" asked Boaz.

Emmanuel shook his head. "No. I have neither seen nor heard of any other merchant-class vessels in this port in the last two weeks."

"Rasquelle's warehouse was full of cargo last night," said Adam. "It wasn't that way when I was there a week ago. Not even close."

"So?" Emmanuel was dismissive. "It's likely just cargo

ready for shipment."

"We've already thought about that," said Boaz. "It may very well be, but Fletcher said the casks he saw were marked with an MB. Do you know anybody around here with an MB mark?"

"We were wondering if they might belong to Milton Blount, over on the western edge of town," said Elliot.

"Milton Blount isn't producing anything yet," argued Emmanuel. "It wouldn't belong to him. In any case, he's promised to bring his business to me if and when he decides to start harvesting stores from his woods."

The men exchanged puzzled looks.

"Well, then, whose cargo is in Rasquelle's warehouse?" said Boaz. "Where'd it come from?"

"It wouldn't be the cargo from that sunken vessel, would it?" asked Elliot.

"No," said Emmanuel. "No, I'd say not. All the cargo that was recovered from that vessel would have been held at the local customs warehouse. They don't use it often, but it's where any confiscated or rescued cargo is held until it can be either sold at public venue or returned to its rightful owners, whichever is appropriate given the situation."

"I want to know if all the cargo in his warehouse is marked from the same shipment or not," said Boaz.

"And how do you reckon you'll be able to find that out?" said Emmanuel.

"Let me go. I can check on it myself," Adam suggested.

"You're not going to sneak in again. You were lucky you didn't get caught last night," said Boaz.

"I wasn't thinking of sneaking in," said Adam. "I was thinking I could go in the middle of the day—when Rasquelle is there."

"Well, we'll have to discuss that later," said Emmanuel. "I think you'd be wise right now to hurry to the Martin estate to warn Miss Rocksolanah."

"I'm going now," said Adam. He rose from the settee.

As he approached the door to leave the apartment, he turned back to look at Emmanuel. "I'm glad you're back, Mr. Rogers."

"Thank you, my boy. Me too."

Chapter Twenty-Six

ADAM LASHED THE horse he'd borrowed from Elliot to the hitching post in front of Laney Martin's house. He looked all around to see if anyone was watching him or the estate, though he doubted there would be now that Reading was back in town and Emmanuel had already been arrested.

Charles answered the door with his customary formality.

Adam said, "Is Miss Laney here?"

"One moment please," said Charles.

He left Adam standing on the porch, waiting until Laney could come to the door herself.

"Mr. Fletcher, what are you doing here?"

"I need to talk to you."

She slowly stepped back into the house and motioned for him to enter. "Of course. Come right in."

Adam walked right into the foyer and looked from room

to room to see if he could see Reading.

"What's going on this time?" Laney asked. "Are you looking for spies again?"

Adam said nothing until he had peered into all of the downstairs rooms.

"We need to talk. Did you know Emmanuel was arrested?"

Laney's eyes grew wide. "What? When did this happen?"

"Yesterday morning."

"Is he alright? Have you seen him?"

"He's out now. He just came back to the warehouse a little while ago, but I needed to let you know. Even though he hasn't told them about this place, we need to—"

Just then someone appeared over the upstairs balcony and started to walk down the stairs.

"Mr. Reading!" said Laney. "Adam Fletcher, this is my guardian, Mr. Absalom Reading."

Adam turned to see the man who he had just seen a few hours earlier in Richard Rasquelle's warehouse. *So it was him!*

Reading walked across the foyer to greet Adam.

Adam enthusiastically shook his hand. "I'm very pleased to meet you, sir. In fact, I'm glad you're here. I was just telling Miss Laney that my master was arrested yesterday."

"Good heavens!" exclaimed Reading. "Is he alright?"

"Yes," said Adam. "He's fine. They let him go this morning, but he'll have to appear in vice-admiralty court just as soon as Miss Laney's brother gets here from New Bern. Martin went to fetch him yesterday."

"Oh, thank God," said Laney.

"Don't you worry, dear," said Reading. "When the authorities come to talk to you, don't you worry. Let me do all the talking."

Laney looked horrified at the prospect of being caught up in a smuggling investigation.

Adam quickly responded, "Oh no, sir! I don't think we'll need to worry about that! Mr. Rogers didn't tell them anything about this place. The authorities know nothing about it—at least not yet. And they won't, provided we are able to conceal the cargo that's downstairs in the basement."

Reading paused at the revelation, then said, "They don't know about this place?"

Adam shook his head. "No, sir! They sure don't!"

"Oh, thank heavens. Well, we'll just have to figure something out, then, shan't we?"

"Yes," said Adam. "I was thinking perhaps you can arrange another temporary location to store the cargo, sir. Perhaps even a neighbor's barn? If you could arrange that, Mr. Reading, I think that may just save us!"

Adam felt as if he'd just cornered his opponent's king on the chessboard.

Reading nervously scratched at his jaw in contemplation. "Why don't we just move everything to one of the barns here?" countered Reading. "I'd be hesitant to get another party involved. They might not prove trustworthy."

"That's a good point," said Laney.

Adam narrowed his eyes. "You can't keep the cargo here. If inspectors come, you can't really think they'll only search the basement! Don't you have any neighbors you could trust?" He looked desperately at Laney, then Mr. Reading. "You don't have to tell them what the cargo is. You can just tell them some work is being done—maybe tell them your basement is flooded—and ask them to store the cargo for a short time until it's dried out."

"Oh, that's a good idea," said Laney. "We could do that!"

she said to Reading.

Reading thought for a moment and then responded. "No, dear. Won't they just wonder why we didn't move the cargo to one of your barns?"

Laney rolled her eyes and sighed. "Ugh! He's right."

Adam tightened his jaw. "Well, how about the tavern?"

Wait, Adam thought to himself. *Did I just say that?* He couldn't believe his own poor judgment. He wished he could take the words back. There was no way he wanted to involve his family in this mess.

Laney wasn't sure. She looked to her guardian for his opinion.

"I'm not so sure that's such a good idea, either," said Reading. "I'm not sure which tavern you're referring to, but there are none close enough to this estate that we could move so much cargo such a distance without being noticed."

"Hmm . . . You're prob'ly right," Adam conceded.

"So let's just move everything to one of the barns. I can have Charles tell George and Pluto to get started right away," said Laney.

"Yes, we'll get on that right away," said Reading.

"Adam, thank you for coming by to warn us," said Laney.

"Oh, of course, Miss Laney," said Adam. "I'm just glad I was able to make it here and that hopefully they won't ever find out about this place. I'm sure gonna do everything I can to make sure they don't."

"Yes, thank you, Mr.—what was it? Fletcher?" said Reading.

"Oh, don't you worry, sir. I'll do whatever it takes to protect my master *and* Miss Laney."

At that, Adam bade them both farewell and headed back

to town.

As he neared the warehouse, Adam made the decision he'd go ahead and see Mr. Rasquelle before Boaz or Emmanuel could tell him not to. He tied the horse to the hitching post nearest Rasquelle's warehouse and then approached the building from the street-side entrance.

"Is Mr. Rasquelle here?" Adam said to a young slave boy of about twelve or so, sweeping outside the entrance of the warehouse.

The boy didn't say anything. He just motioned inside towards the office. Adam nodded his head and thanked him.

He made his way through the warehouse as though he was really going to the office. He paid special attention to all the casks as he walked by them. It appeared that most of them did have Beaufort marks. That left him curious. He looked over in the direction of where the casks with the MB marks had been the previous night.

They were gone. Rasquelle had moved them.

He thought he knew where they might be, so as he got near Rasquelle's office, he tried to quickly glance inside the room with the heavy wooden door and iron-barred window. There they were! He tried to commit the mark to memory. It was a very fancy design with a mark that said "MB" in the center, but there was no further identifying information.

Just then one of the coopers from the warehouse passed by and said, "Oy! Who are you?"

Adam turned around quickly and said, "I'm looking for Mr. Rasquelle's office."

"It's the next one," said the cooper, pointing at the next door down.

At that point, Adam knew he better go see Richard Rasquelle. He couldn't risk having that worker tell him he'd just seen a kid snooping around in his warehouse. He really hadn't thought much about what he would say, but he knew he wanted to try and find out if Rasquelle would tell him anything that could be useful.

As he approached the office, Rasquelle's door was closed. Adam took a deep breath and gave it a sturdy knock.

"I'm here," said a voice from inside the office. "Come on in."

Adam turned the knob and slowly peered around the door. He knew Rasquelle wasn't expecting him, and he didn't want to startle him by just barging right in.

"Mr. Fletcher! To what do I owe this surprise?"

"Sir, I was wondering if I might come in and have a word." Adam was polite. He even made an effort to sound a bit desperate.

Rasquelle motioned for the boy to enter. "Of course, of course. Come in and have a seat."

Adam slowly and carefully closed the door behind him and sat down in one of the chairs opposite the merchant's desk.

"What can I help you with, young man?" said Rasquelle.

"Sir, have you heard about what happened?" the boy said.

"I'm not sure. To what are you referring?"

"Mr. Rogers. He was arrested."

Rasquelle paused a moment before he answered. "I have heard something about that. It hardly comes as a surprise, though, does it?"

Adam shook his head. "No, sir. I suppose not, especially after what you told me."

"I think it's appropriate, if not unfortunate, that it had to happen," said Rasquelle as he reclined in his chair. "So why does this bring you here today?"

"Sir," said Adam, "Mr. Rogers is my master, and I am counting on my apprenticeship to help me make something of myself. I want to be successful like you, but I don't see how that can happen if I'm employed by a criminal. Furthermore, Mr. Ellison Smythe—well, his son was the one I got into that fight with, and, well, he told me that I better complete my apprenticeship or he'll make sure Mr. Robins brings down the full penalty on me."

Rasquelle folded his hands on his desk in front of him and listened.

Adam continued: "I'm no fool, sir. I know you are a successful and shrewd businessman, which is why I originally had hoped I'd be bound to you as apprentice. I see Mr. Rogers's arrest as my chance to be freed from that bond and to be apprenticed under you, sir, if you'll have me."

The merchant leaned back in his chair and smiled at Adam. "I certainly appreciate your forthrightness, but to be honest, I'm not sure that I have a place for you here now. I have all the help I need."

"Please, sir," said Adam. "I don't know what will happen to me now that Rogers's ship is sinking. I don't want to have to wait for the verdict to be read—we both know how that will turn out. I want to get my situation sorted out now, and I had really hoped you could find a place for me here. I really want to work here. I have no doubt I could learn so much from you. You know the right way to run a shipping company."

Rasquelle offered a reserved smile at Adam. "You are so kind, Mr. Fletcher, and I'm sincerely flattered that you want to work here—and frankly surprised to hear the level of confidence you have placed in my abilities to instruct you in the shipping trade. I certainly didn't get the impression you were very fond of me after our last meeting. I will keep in mind your request, and as soon as I have an opening I will let you know. For now you're probably better off remaining at Rogers's warehouse—at least until the verdict has been read. I would imagine at that time it would be determined who, if anyone, will run Rogers's company once he's received his sentence, and then your position can be better ascertained."

"So there's nothing you can do?" Adam pleaded.

"I'm afraid not." Rasquelle stood and walked around to the front of his desk, then motioned to show Adam out of his office.

Adam stood and shook hands with the merchant. "Thank you for your time, sir."

"Of course," said Rasquelle. "And one other thing," he said. "I trust our previous arrangement will remain confidential."

Adam took a moment before he answered. So many words were running through his head, but he finally said, "What previous arrangement?" He then gave the man a knowing smile.

"Excellent." Rasquelle smiled.

They exited his office. Rasquelle started walking him towards the exit when Adam stopped him.

He pointed to one of the barrels in the room with the barred window. "Sir, I was just curious. Those barrels in there— did they come from Milton Blount?"

The color left Rasquelle's face. "Those? Oh, let's see here." He peered in the window of the room and pretended to inspect the brand on the head of one of the barrels. "Yes, those would be Mr. Blount's. He ships naval stores to a buyer in England. Do you know Mr. Blount?"

Adam shook his head. "No. Not personally, anyway. I was

just wondering if those were his. I had heard he was going to be shipping with Mr. Rogers but that he's not producing anything yet."

He resumed walking towards the exit, the merchant alongside him.

Rasquelle chuckled. "You know, you really are an observant young man."

"Thank you, sir."

"You know what?" said Rasquelle. "A thought just occurred to me."

Adam smiled. "What's that?"

"We may actually have something that you'd be perfect for. A very special position."

Adam's heart raced, but he knew he had to play along. "Really? That would be great!"

The merchant put his arm around Adam's shoulder and said, "Come with me."

Adam smiled and nodded. "Alright, sir."

Rasquelle led Adam outside and to the dock. A couple of fellows who appeared to be dock workers were standing near the cargo doors discussing something when their boss stepped up and interrupted them.

"Gentlemen," he said. "This is Adam Fletcher. He has been working for Emmanuel Rogers, but of course with Mr. Rogers's current circumstances, there may not be a position there for Mr. Fletcher much longer. He came here today looking for a job, and I have found him to be an unusually observant boy. Very bright. Very clever. I think he'd be perfect for a special project."

The two men gave a puzzled look to Rasquelle, who apparently either winked at them or mouthed something, and then they nodded. One of the men said, "Uh, alright. Would you like us to help you with something?"

The merchant had a tense smile. He nodded. "Yes, Lot, I would. I would like you to take Mr. Fletcher here and show him our *other* warehouse."

Adam gave Rasquelle a confused look. "You have another warehouse, sir?"

The workers also looked at Mr. Rasquelle with a confused look.

Rasquelle put his hand on Adam's back and led him down the dock, encouraging the two men to follow. "We certainly do, Mr. Fletcher. And these men will take you there."

Adam wrinkled his brow. "I'd love to go, sir, but I think I may need to report back to Rogers's warehouse to at least let them know I have to take care of something today—so they won't worry."

"Oh, no need for that. No need. If I take you on here, you won't have to report back there again," said Rasquelle.

The men still seemed confused about where they were to take the boy, until Rasquelle turned quickly towards them and mouthed something. Adam couldn't hear it, but they understood.

Chapter Twenty-Seven

"COME ON, BOY," said Lot. Adam struggled to break free from the grip of the two men, but as he did, he suddenly felt something sharp at his side. The other man, who Adam learned was called Ajax, was holding a knife.

Adam wasn't one to cry out for help, but right now he wanted to. But he knew if he did, it would take just one jab from Ajax's knife to give him a fatal gash. He had no choice but to get into the boat with the men.

Not too many minutes passed before they were drifting away from the dock and out into the creek, towards the inlet.

"Where are you taking me?" said Adam.

"You heard Mr. Rasquelle," said Lot. "He told us to show you our other warehouse."

"You don't have another warehouse," said Adam.

The men both laughed.

"Just you keep quiet, boy," said Ajax. "It wouldn't take nothin for me to stick you with this and then dump you right here over the edge. If you keep givin me lip, that's exactly what I'm goin to do."

There was no use fighting. Adam would just have to wait until they got to wherever the men were taking him. He already figured wherever it was, they must not be planning to kill him. They could have already done that if that were the plan. He would just jump out of the boat as soon as it neared the shore and run as fast as he could for help.

But then, when they were far enough away from town, he was blindfolded, and his hands and feet were bound. They sailed for a few hours—but since he couldn't see, Adam had no idea where. He thought they had gone north once they left the inlet, but he couldn't be sure.

Once he realized they were marooning him on an island, he begged them not to leave him there, but the men were unmoved by his pleas, and soon he could hear the men get back into the boat and sail away.

As soon as they were gone, Adam wiggled his face against the ground until he was able to get the blindfold off. Then he worked himself up from the prone position the men had him in to an upright and seated position. He then tried to move onto his knees.

He tried pulling his hands apart and working them out of the cords, but it was no use. *A split oyster might work*, he thought. He started scanning the ground for one of the rough-edged shells. If he could get ahold of one, he could work it against the cord and hopefully cut himself free.

It didn't take long to find one, as the mollusks were abundant along the coast. Adam had to sit on the ground right beside the shell to get it into his hands. He quickly worked the cord against the sharp edge of the shell. It didn't break through the cord entirely, but it wore through enough of the fibers that he was able to yank his hands apart. He untied his feet and then stood and looked around at his location. There was water and shoreline for as far as he could see, and the shoreline did appear to curve. There was a forest behind him, but he didn't know how far it went. He wasn't sure what time it was, so he didn't know how much daylight he had left, and he had no high vantage point, so he couldn't see more than a few miles in any direction.

A wave of panic washed over him when he took stock of his circumstances, but the survival instinct quickly kicked in. He remembered a book he had read many times when he was younger—*Robinson Crusoe*. He didn't know how he'd get out of the situation, but at least he had confidence that if one of his childhood heroes could survive on an island for twenty years, he could hopefully survive until somebody found him or he found his own way home—whichever came first.

Chapter Twenty-Eight

"THIS AIN'T GOOD, boys." Elliot led his horse right onto the work floor of the warehouse.

Emmanuel, Boaz, and Joe had been waiting there, hoping Adam would turn up or that Elliot would return with some news. He'd been to town to ask if Adam had gone by the tavern to see his mother.

Boaz's face fell. "That's your horse."

"It sure is," said Elliot.

"But where's Fletcher?"

"Did they say he'd been by the tavern?" asked Emmanuel.

Elliot shook his head. "Nope. Said they haven't seen him at all today."

"Where did you find the horse?" asked Emmanuel.

Elliot stroked the black mane of the tall, chestnut quarter horse. "Tom Gaskins told me ol' Sampson here has been hitched to a post down on Front Street near 'bout all day."

"So that means the boy must've made it back to town at least," said Emmanuel.

Boaz shook his head. "Uh-uh. Not necessarily. If Reading was there at the Martin estate today and he didn't like what Fletcher was saying, he might've done something with the boy and then left the horse in town to throw us off-track."

A heavy cloud of despair descended upon the men.

Emmanuel nodded with worry. "You're absolutely right. And since Reading doesn't know what we know, he surely would assume we'd never guess he could be involved."

"What if Reading was there and Fletcher confronted him?" asked Elliot. "He can be that way, you know."

Emmanuel's eyes grew wide. "Good Lord! I don't even want to think the boy would've done something so foolish!"

"You might not want to think it," said Boaz, "but it is possible."

"Where did you say the horse was hitched?" asked Emmanuel.

"Right in the middle of town, down on Front Street. Near everything."

The men all exchanged nervous glances. No one wanted to be the first to say what they were all thinking.

"And everything would include Richard Rasquelle's warehouse," Emmanuel finally observed.

"Yes, it would," Elliot agreed.

"And the boy did say he wanted to go there," said Emmanuel.

"And I reckon he's just foolish enough that he might've gone and done it," said Boaz.

"But we told him to wait!" said Emmanuel, exasperated.

"Sure we did," said Boaz, "but Fletcher's seventeen. He thinks he knows everything. You remember how things were at that age."

Emmanuel nodded. "Oh, do I ever. That's what worries me."

"Well, so then what do we do?" said Elliot. "Do we go down there and just ask Rasquelle if he's seen the boy?"

"I think we must," said Emmanuel. "But I also think it would be reasonable to ask everyone there along the waterfront if they've seen the boy. We needn't tell Richard Rasquelle that we suspect the boy might've gone by to see him today. That would surely raise far more questions than are necessary."

"I agree," said Boaz. "We can head down there now. Split up. Ask everyone down on the docks, the shop and business owners, townsfolk, everybody."

"Alright," agreed Elliot, "let's go."

The four men piled into Emmanuel's horse cart and headed into town. Once they got there, they split up three ways. The Salter cousins, Joe and Elliot, went in one direction. Boaz went another. Emmanuel went alone and was the one who went to ask Rasquelle if he'd seen Adam.

After more than an hour, they all met back at the horse cart, but none had information on Adam's whereabouts.

"You know what we have to do now," said Boaz.

Emmanuel took a deep breath, then sighed. "Let's just go back to the warehouse and wait for a couple more hours. If he still doesn't turn up, then we'll go tell his mother."

Chapter Twenty-Nine

WITHIN A SHORT time of being marooned on the island, Adam had walked far enough and studied the horizon long enough to realize he had no idea where he was. For the time being, he decided he should stay close to where Rasquelle's men had left him.

Although he could see another body of land in the distance, it looked like it was miles away, and he knew that he wasn't a strong enough swimmer to make it that far. Furthermore, he had no indication that the land he'd spotted was even inhabited within any reasonable distance. It would be a huge risk to attempt swimming so far without knowing if it would improve his situation.

He wondered if he still had the bag of candy that he'd been given by the Spanish captain. He thrust his hand into his pocket. No luck. He tried his other pocket. Still no bag of candy.

He must've left it back at the warehouse. He was relieved to know he at least had his pocketknife.

He decided to set up shelter along the edge of the line of trees. He'd have enough natural canopy to help protect him from the elements, yet he would still be near enough to the shore that a signal fire could be seen by passing vessels. But first, he knew he better get a fire going before sundown.

There was plenty of dried-out driftwood and brush nearby. He gathered it into a pile, then scooped out a shallow dip in the earth for his fire. After putting some sea grass and shrubbery in place for kindling, he picked out a flat piece of the driftwood to make a makeshift hearth for a bow-drill fire starter. It looked like a piece from an old boat. He used the tip of his knife to twist out a little round groove, then notched out a V-shape coming off of that.

Next he found two sturdy sticks. The first—which was as long as his arm from his shoulder to his wrist—would be his bow, but he'd have to find something to use as the bowstring. At first he thought the cord he normally used to tie back his hair might work, but it wasn't long enough. Finally, he decided to cut a strip from the bottom of his shirt. It was just long enough to bring the two ends of the long stick towards each other to form a bow.

The other stick was shorter—just a little bit longer than his forearm—and it would work nicely as the drill. He whittled it along its sides until it was perfectly straight, then gave rounded points to each end. Next he ran down to the sand and found a cockleshell to hold in his hand to protect his palm.

He took the drill stick and twisted it once in the string of the bow, then inserted the tip of the stick into the round groove he had made on the hearth board. Finally, he put one foot on the board to hold it in place and held the cockleshell in his palm over the other end of the drill stick, then worked the bow back and forth until he began to get some smoke. He kept drilling and drilling back and forth with the bow until he had coal. Once he thought it was hot enough, he tapped the hot tinder through the little V-notch onto the kindling he had gathered in his fire pit. After he gently blew on it, it began to smoke, and then finally it ignited into a beautiful, much-welcome, glowing fire.

Since the only tool he had was his pocketknife, he wanted to preserve that as much as possible. He considered trying to take down some trees for a shelter by burning them around the base the way the Indians used to do, but he thought better of it when it occurred to him that with the amount of undergrowth blanketing the area, that kind of fire might quickly get out of hand and consume everything.

He took some time to study the terrain. He knew that trees never get very tall along the beach, because the strong winds stunt their growth and they branch out sideways more than straight upward like their inland counterparts. Also, he could see a lot of thick, clumpy shrubbery and tall sea grasses among the coastal vegetation. All in all, he would have a good variety of materials from which to construct his shelter.

First, he uprooted two young saplings and set them in the ground about seven feet away from two other young saplings. Then he bent the tops of both pairs of saplings towards each other to form a frame, like a wigwam. He used some of the abundant grapevines growing nearby to tie them together.

He repeated the same process perpendicular to the ones he had already lashed together so that the pairs of saplings crossed one another like one big X. Next he began lashing all kinds of limbs and branches along the outside of his structure using more grapevines, but the weight of all of the covering was getting too heavy for the sapling frame. The whole structure looked like it could collapse, so he stepped back and examined everything again to see what he needed to do differently. He hated to have to undo the work he had just done, but he realized he would need to work in more saplings to sturdy up the frame.

He quickly yanked down all of the branches he'd used as covering and tried to find a few more saplings that were suitable in length and circumference to shore up the structure. After he had done that, he was finally able to add back the branches for covering. He left the opening in the front so he would be able to keep a watch on the water. He wanted to be sure and have a way of seeing any vessels that might happen to pass by.

He had heard the local Indians used to make mats by weaving together tall grasses and cattails. If he ended up being stuck there for more than a couple of days, he decided he would try weaving together whatever he could find to give his new home a more practical, weatherproof covering.

Once he was satisfied with his shelter, he had to think about finding water to drink. He knew an aboveground source was unlikely, so he hunted for as many large shells as he could find—some whelks and some very large cockle and clam shells. Those could be set out to collect rainwater. Although the coast had its share of rain the previous week, unfortunately for Adam the sky was clear and blue without a hint of a storm in sight.

He determined his best option was to take a cue from the banker ponies that inhabited an island not far from Beaufort. The wild creatures were able to sustain themselves with freshwater they dug by stomping the ground with their hooves until the refreshing liquid rose to the surface. Adam thought there was no reason he shouldn't be able to imitate their methods, albeit by digging rather than stomping the ground.

It was similar to what happens when a hole is dug on the beach and it begins filling up with water. The only difference between the method used by the ponies and the one that Adam would employ was that instead of stomping the ground, he would dig a hole at least a hundred feet from the shore so the water wouldn't be saline.

He made his well not far from his shelter but was frustrated when the sand kept falling back into the hole. He ended up using some of the other flat pieces of driftwood he had found on the beach to keep the sides from caving in. As he dug deeper, the sand became a finer texture, then started to look more like mud, and finally water began seeping in from the bottom of the hole. He had to dig just a bit farther, then he'd be able to use his hands—or better yet, some large shells—to scoop off the uppermost layer of water as it filled the hole that he would dig.

Adam used his pocketknife again to fashion a couple of spears for catching fish. A net would be useful, too, he thought. Maybe the next day he would try and tie together some of the younger, more pliable grapevines. He had seen the men making nets down by the docks. How hard could it be?

While shellfish were prolific, oysters were off-limits. It was May, and Adam had always been taught that oysters should only be eaten in months that have the letter r in them. Otherwise, he'd have easily been able to enjoy a feast of the rough-looking shellfish. As it was, Adam figured they might be a last resort.

He dug for clams and trapped several small crabs, so his first meal on the island consisted of those. He would've loved to have speared some flounder to eat, but in spite of using a makeshift torch to go out into the water, there were none that he could find right where he was.

Since he figured his location was such a long distance

from the mainland, he was unsure if there would be any warm-blooded wildlife creeping around—at least he hadn't seen any yet, but he'd know come nightfall if there were raccoons or opossums living nearby. If he was really lucky, there might even be some deer living in the woods.

With no one else to talk to, and especially considering the desperate circumstances of his situation, Adam found himself engaged in a continuous conversation with God. It didn't feel like praying, he thought. After all, he wasn't bowing his head and closing his eyes. And he wasn't particularly worried about what he was saying. He was just talking, as if he had a friend stranded there with him.

His continual dialogue with the Almighty reminded him again of his favorite boyhood book about the brave and tenacious Robinson Crusoe, who found himself entirely dependent on Providence as he worked creatively to survive. Adam could see how you might go crazy in such solitude if you not only felt hopeless but as if you had no one to talk to.

The hardest part of being marooned on that island was thinking about the folks back home in Beaufort. He wondered how his mother was handling him being missing. He knew she'd be heartbroken, but would she blame him for foolishly going to Rasquelle's warehouse that morning?

Then he thought about Laney. She wasn't guilty, after all. But she was in danger, and it gnawed at Adam that he couldn't be there now to make sure she was safe. And Emmanuel. That was a whole different subject. Here Adam had gone and learned that Rasquelle did have some questionable cargo in his warehouse, and yet he could tell no one. But that was Rasquelle's plan, wasn't it? That's why he had told those two oafs to leave Adam on that island.

He tried to be grateful for any positive thing he could think of, like that he was stranded in May rather than December, or that he wasn't seriously injured, or that he knew he was at least somewhere along the North Carolina coast rather than half a world away. It was his intention to constantly keep a signal fire burning. While he had no idea where exactly he'd been marooned, he did know that if he could find a way to survive long enough, eventually someone would spot him. He wondered if Richard Rasquelle had intended for him to die on that island, or was he just trying to get him out of the way until the trial was over?

Regardless, Adam knew he had to survive. He had to get back for the sake of his mother, who he knew had to be worried sick about him, and to help Emmanuel and Laney.

Chapter Thirty

RICHARD RASQUELLE HAD stayed behind after his warehouse closed up for the day. He wanted to wait and see what happened with Lot and Ajax. When his henchmen finally got back around six thirty that evening, their boss rushed to greet them as they docked their boat.

"You're back. I trust everything is taken care of," said Rasquelle.

"Yes, sir, Mr. Rasquelle. I don't reckon the boy will be a problem anymore," said Lot.

Ajax chuckled. "Yeah. I give him three days at most."

"Three days?" asked a bewildered Rasquelle. "You mean you didn't . . . ?" He couldn't, or wouldn't, bring himself to say out loud what his intention had been.

Ajax, on the other hand, had no problem with it. "Now, Mr. Rasquelle. You asked us to get rid of him. You didn't say how.

You didn't say 'Kill him,' so we wasn't gonna do that. You don't pay us enough to do that kind of work."

Lot nodded in agreement with his partner-in-kidnapping. "That's right, sir. It ain't a big deal to just dispose of him somewhere, but we ain't gonna have murder on our hands."

"You idiots!" Rasquelle exclaimed. "You've only been gone about seven hours. You've only stranded him! You can't possibly have taken him so far that he couldn't be rescued or find his way back eventually. What do you think will happen if he shows up back in town?"

Lot and Ajax just exchanged blank stares.

Rasquelle took a deep breath, then lowered his head, closed his eyes, and pressed his fingers against the bridge of his nose, exasperated. Finally, he explained, "If Fletcher finds his way back here, he'll talk. He'll say you two kidnapped him. And he'll implicate me as well. Why did you think I wanted you to get rid of him?"

The goons looked at each other and back at Rasquelle, then shrugged.

"So that would never happen!" Rasquelle shouted. "What part of 'get rid of him' did you not understand?"

"We did get rid of him," said Ajax. "And he won't find his way back. Not where we left him. I also don't think you have to worry about him getting rescued. Not many ships pass by there, and no one lives for several miles around."

"Let me see if I understand what you're telling me. A clever seventeen-year-old boy, healthy as a horse, will die where you left him before there's any chance he is rescued, even though you left him, presumably, somewhere along this very coast."

"It was an island," said Lot.

"Excuse me?" said Rasquelle.

"We left him on an island," Lot explained. "There ain't no freshwater. He ain't got no way to hunt or fish. We left him there blindfolded, with cords tied around his hands and feet. He ain't goin nowhere. It'd take a miracle for him to survive until somebody found him."

Rasquelle thought for a moment, then glared at the two men. "It's not good enough. Tomorrow morning first thing I want you both to go back to where you left him and fix this. I don't want there to be any chance of him ever setting foot back in this town again."

"But Mr. Rasquelle," said Ajax, "we already done told you that you ain't payin us enough for murder. Now, if you want to renegotiate our wages—well, then maybe . . ." He stroked his chin and waited for an answer.

"Fool," Rasquelle responded. "You dare try to press me for more money when the two of you are the ones who kidnapped him from this place, who left him on that island. He gets rescued, and you two will hang. Don't forget that."

"We understand, sir," said Lot. "Right, Ajax?" He elbowed his colleague.

Ajax narrowed his eyes and hesitated before he said, "Right."

"Good," said Rasquelle. "I'm glad we understand one another. First thing in the morning, boys. Handle it."

The two nodded and walked away.

Chapter Thirty-One

EMMANUEL RARELY WENT into town, and he certainly didn't frequent the tavern. He was far too private to enjoy sitting down for meals amongst strangers. So when he and Boaz entered the Topsail Tavern, all heads turned his way.

"Is there somewhere more private we can talk?" Emmanuel asked Valentine Hodges.

Valentine's face fell. He knew the men couldn't be bearers of good news. "Mary's upstairs. Should I go get her?"

"Yes, but perhaps we should talk to you first. Then you can decide the best way for us to proceed."

Valentine nodded, then motioned for them to follow him into the kitchen. Emmanuel and Boaz went right behind him, through the kitchen, the back garden of the tavern and into Valentine's house.

"Take a seat, fellas," said Valentine.

"We'd rather not," said Emmanuel.

He and Boaz briefly explained to Valentine what had happened in the last twenty-four hours and everything they knew so far about Adam's disappearance. Valentine stood with his fist on one hip and his other hand rubbing his forehead. He thought for a moment, unable to respond, then finally said, "I'm gonna go get Mary. She's got to know about this. And y'all are gonna have to be the ones to tell her."

Emmanuel nodded. "Of course."

He and Boaz waited impatiently in the sitting room as Valentine went back into the tavern to get Mary and bring her back downstairs to hear the news.

She was already trembling when Valentine escorted her in. She knew something awful had happened, only she didn't know how bad things were. Emmanuel and Boaz looked at her, then at each other, both wondering who would be the one to break the news.

"Just tell me what happened!" said Mary.

"It's Adam," said Emmanuel. "We don't know where he is."

"What do you mean, you don't know where he is? What happened? When did you see him last?"

"He left this morning," said Boaz. "He was heading over to the Martin estate."

"What for?" Mary demanded.

"You heard about Emmanuel's arrest yesterday?" said Boaz.

She nodded. "Yes. What of it?"

"Your son, he found out some information that he needed to tell the Martin girl—for both her safety as well as to help Emmanuel here in the investigation."

Mary was shaking like a leaf. She was enraged to think someone might have done something to her son.

"Why was he doing your dirty work, old man?" she asked Emmanuel.

"Wait a minute—" said Boaz.

Emmanuel held his hand up. "Hush, son," he said to Boaz. "She has every reason to be angry. I'd be furious if I were her."

She stood and began to pace, tears streaming down her cheeks. "We have to look everywhere. We have to find him. *He's all I have!*"

Valentine went over to her and wrapped his arms around her in a fatherly embrace. He stroked her hair and said, "Shh . . . We'll find him, girl. Don't you worry. We'll find him, and if anyone has hurt him, they'll have hell to pay. I'll see to it."

She sobbed into his shoulder. "I just want my son."

"We will do everything we can to find him. As soon as we leave here, we'll be notifying the constable. But we wanted to let you know about this first," said Emmanuel.

Valentine nodded as he stroked Mary's hair in an effort to comfort her and calm her down.

"I will let you know if we hear anything," said Boaz. "I hope you'll do the same for us."

Valentine nodded again.

Emmanuel and Boaz were about to leave when the old man stopped beside Mary and said, "I can't begin to tell you how sorry I am, love."

She lifted her head from Valentine's shoulder for just a moment and stared at him, before burying her face once again.

As soon as Emmanuel and Boaz left their meeting with Mary and Valentine, they went across town to a different tavern, where one of the local constables spent a lot of his time. Although there were other constables appointed in the county, Constable Lawson Squires had a family connection to Boaz, so they felt comfortable telling him information that they might not want to pass along to less familiar lawmen.

They informed him of Adam's disappearance and told him about why they suspected Richard Rasquelle and Absalom Reading. Constable Squires recommended they let all the local fishermen know as well as submit the information to the local print shop so that signs could be made and posted around town. Emmanuel assured him that those tasks would be first on his list as soon as the morning came.

After a lengthy discussion, they ruled out the likelihood of the boy being held somewhere in town. Beaufort was far too small for anyone to keep that kind of secret for very long. Their limited knowledge of the circumstances surrounding Adam's disappearance fomented a fear that the worse had happened to him. Would someone have actually killed him to keep him quiet? Although Emmanuel and Boaz never trusted Richard Rasquelle, they wouldn't have thought he could kill a man, but if Adam had been foolish enough to confront him with what he knew, Rasquelle might've felt backed into a corner and taken drastic action to save himself.

Constable Squires also reminded them that they shouldn't be so quick to dismiss the notion of the boy running away. He said that if Adam felt he was in immediate danger, he might have taken off and gone into hiding. He told them that if that was the case, Adam might turn up again in a day or two once he figured the coast was clear.

Chapter Thirty-Two

L ATE MORNING ON Wednesday, Ajax and Lot made it back to the island where they had marooned Adam. They went to the very spot, or near about, where they had left him on the beach, but he wasn't there. At least he wasn't there like they expected him to be, which would have been still bound up and blindfolded. What they did find, however, was a smoldering fire, a crudely constructed shelter, and evidence that their kidnap victim had not only managed to free himself but had enjoyed a productive time since they'd abandoned him there. The color completely left their faces when they realized the boy was surviving on the island.

"What do we do, then?" said Lot.

"We gotta find him. That's what," said Ajax.

After the men looked in the shelter to see if Adam was inside, they started walking along the edge of the woods and calling out the boy's name.

"Maybe if we call him he'll come to us. Maybe he'll be happy to see us and think we're here to rescue him," Lot suggested.

"Yeah. Yeah, that's a right good plan. You stay here by the boat in case he comes back to his camp. I'll go search for him."

Lot nodded and did as he was told.

While Ajax began the search, Adam was exploring the island's interior. He was trying to learn more about his new, hopefully temporary home. When he heard someone calling his name, he quickly ran through the woods towards the sound to see who it was. The voice was becoming clearer, and a shiver ran through him when he realized who it was. The ruffian Ajax had a very distinctive manner of speech. His sharp-toned, nasally voice sounded hyper when he spoke.

What are they doing here? Adam wondered if he was being rescued or a more sinister plan was at work. He had to think fast, and logically. Why would they be coming to rescue him? Maybe they were having second thoughts and felt bad about leaving him there.

Nah. That would be ridiculous. They had left him on this spit of land. It was unlikely they were suddenly feeling pangs of guilt about it. No, the more likely explanation was that they were having second thoughts about leaving him there *alive*.

Adam tried to move quietly towards his camp to see if the men had left their boat unattended. If so, he could hop in and try to sail the thing towards civilization. Although sailing was a skill he hadn't yet had the opportunity to learn, he was willing to take his chances if he could get off of the island and out into the shipping lanes.

Unfortunately, Lot's hulking presence keeping watch in the boat dashed that hope. Still, Adam made a mental note to ask

Emmanuel to teach him to sail if he ever made it back to town. He decided his best course of action would be to hide. Just knowing that they had come back for him, Adam calculated that meant they thought there was a reasonable chance he could be rescued, or even find his way back, if he could survive long enough.

He stopped long enough to listen again for Ajax's voice so he could try to position where he was. It wasn't easy, but he determined vaguely what direction he was in, so Adam took off in the opposite direction.

Suddenly he heard Ajax call out, "I hear you runnin, boy, but it sounds like you're goin the wrong way. Follow the sound of my voice. We're here to take you back to town."

Adam wanted to stop again but decided it would probably be best if he kept running without acknowledging the man's voice. Maybe Ajax would think the sound might be a deer.

Meanwhile, Lot suddenly called out to his partner. "Ajax! Get out here!"

He walked back over to where Adam's camp was, and he looked around a bit. He went over to where Ajax had entered the wood and he called for him again.

Finally, Ajax emerged from the trees. "What is it? I still haven't found him."

"I can see that. Listen, I just thought of something."

"What is it?"

"He might've already been rescued. Or maybe something happened to him."

"I just heard somebody runnin in the woods. It had to be him," said Ajax.

"Or it could've been a deer or even a wolf."

"A wolf? Out here?" Ajax was skeptical. He'd seen deer on some of the local islands but never heard of any wolves—at least not since he'd been living in the colony.

"What I'm tryin to tell you is, he might not still be here, or if he is, he might already be dead. If he was still here, don't you think he'd rush right out to us thinkin we can rescue him?"

Lot looked at Ajax and waited for an answer. When Ajax didn't respond, Lot said, "I think we better go."

Ajax wrinkled his forehead and looked at Lot like he thought he was an imbecile.

"You're joking, right? Where do you think he could've gone? And if somethin had happened to him, don't you think his body would be somewhere near his camp?"

"Maybe, maybe not," said Lot. "Could be that he was rescued. And if he has been rescued, we prob'ly ought not be hangin around here. In fact, we prob'ly ought not hang around Beaufort. I think we should go back to town and get our things and hightail it out of here. We can't go back up north, but maybe we can head farther south or out west."

Ajax looked back towards the woods as he contemplated their next move.

"You might be right," he conceded. "But we ain't just gonna leave here. Let's sail around this whole island, see if we can see any evidence of him anywhere. If not, we'll do like you said."

Lot nodded in agreement. "Sounds fair enough."

They got back into their boat and started to sail along the island's perimeter.

Adam had watched their whole exchange from his hiding spot in a tiny clearing in a thicket. He couldn't hear what they were saying, but he knew he wouldn't risk coming back out anytime soon. He figured they probably wouldn't bother hanging around once it got dark. He decided he'd wait until then before returning to his camp.

He ended up falling asleep in his hiding spot.

ADAM DIDN'T WAKE UP again until sunrise the next morning.

His whole body ached from sleeping on lumpy ground and broken branches. It was pure exhaustion that had gotten to him. He'd been on the go almost nonstop since he had been marooned, so when he finally took time for a forced rest, his body had just collapsed for some much-needed sleep.

He made his way back to his campsite. Much to his delight, his fire was still smoldering. He added some more kindling and fanned it to get the flames going again. Once his fire was fed, he went down to the beach to see what he could rustle up to eat.

Summer was still a few weeks away, and the water had a chill. Although he could stand it when the sun was high in the sky, he preferred not to go in so early in the morning. As a result he didn't bother to take his spear and opted instead to dig for clams.

He found a good spot where the muddy sand appeared to be bubbling up, so he dropped down and began to dig.

Ouch! What was that?

The left side of his neck had a little pain every time he exerted himself to dig. At first he thought it might just be a crick in his neck from his awkward sleeping position the night before. He rolled his head around in a circle to try to loosen up the muscles, but it didn't seem to help.

He reached up and touched his neck with his hand. There was a spot that felt tender. *That's strange*, he thought. He wished he had a mirror so he could see what it was. He didn't feel anything on the surface of his skin. He scratched at the area and then looked at his fingers to see if there was any blood. Nope.

Nothing. He pressed on the spot, then moved his head back and forth, wondering if that might get blood flowing to the area and make it feel better. No use. Finally, he decided it was probably some kind of a bite. After all, he had spent the previous night in the woods on a bunch of leaves and dead branches.

In spite of the pain in his neck, he was glad Ajax and Lot were gone. He hoped they wouldn't come back, and he determined that as soon as he had a chance to explore the island he'd start making a plan for how he might be able to get back. He could possibly even build some kind of raft, he thought.

But for now he just needed to find something to eat.

Chapter Thirty-Three

THREE FULL DAYS after Adam's disappearance, Martin Smith returned with his cousin William Martin on Austin James's sloop. Almost immediately the young lawyer met with Emmanuel and company at the warehouse apartment.

"Please, please let's not put the cart before the horse," said William. "We must put the subject of the Fletcher boy aside right now. Idle speculation will do nothing to help him, so at this moment what I need to know is exactly how everything happened up until that day. We have a court day fast approaching, for which we desperately need to prepare. Let's go back to the day you were arrested, Emmanuel."

All of the coopers were there in the warehouse apartment. Boaz, Elliot, and Martin were each trying to interject their version of what had taken place over the last couple of weeks since the arrivals of the *Elizabeth Ella* and *La Dama del Caribe*. Joe just sat silent as always but nodded along with anything he knew to be true or agreed with.

After furiously scribbling notes as each day's events were recounted to him, William began to offer his professional opinion. He was twenty-five years old, which meant he had only been practicing on his own as a lawyer for about four years, but he had been working at the legal profession since he was eleven years old, when his father began training him in his law firm.

"We're in a very fortunate position in that the customs inspector's case is based almost entirely upon Richard Rasquelle's accusations," said William. "It is essentially your word against his—at least right now it is. We need only show him to be an untrustworthy witness. Then the Crown's case will crumble."

"But what about that conversation Fletcher overheard in the warehouse that night between Rasquelle and Absalom Reading?" said Martin.

"Unfortunately, Mr. Fletcher isn't here. I don't think hearsay would go over well in a court such as this. And considering the boy is nowhere to be found, how could you prove that you weren't the one who disposed of him, so that you could concoct this story and try to pass it off to frame Rasquelle?"

Emmanuel lowered his gaze and shook his head. "It sounds absurd, but you're right. And if it turns out they are holding the boy somewhere and he's alive, they might decide to kill him to ensure his silence."

"Damn them to hell!" said Boaz. "This is all just a real fine mess, ain't it? I'm liable to kill Rasquelle and Reading myself before it's all over with."

"Our strategy will be to prepare you as well as possible for any questions that might arise and to ensure that enough doubt is raised about Rasquelle's character that the judge is reluctant to pursue the case any further. I'll have questions prepared to serve just that purpose."

"How do we know he'll be there?" said Boaz.

"He's the Crown's chief witness—even though he doesn't realize we know that. But rest assured he will be there," said William. "He instigated this business, and I have no doubt he'll see it through till he gets what he was after at the start."

"What do you reckon that is?" said Boaz.

"To do away with his competition, of course," said William.

"Of course," said Emmanuel.

"And Absalom Reading?" asked Boaz.

William sighed deeply. "Well, after all you've told me about what the boy heard, I'm furious of course, but I also have no intention of confronting Absalom about it, nor telling Laney right now—"

"You must be out of your damned mind!" shouted Martin.

William raised his hand to gently silence his cousin. "Would you just be quiet? Let me handle things with my sister and Absalom. I'll deal with him, I can assure you." He then turned his attention back to the group. "As I was saying, there will be no confrontation, at least not until this whole mess is behind us. In fact, I will lean more heavily on my sister's guardian now than I ever have before. I intend to pour upon him gratitude and praise for always having my sister's best interests at heart as well as for being a faithful and loyal friend to our father. Indeed, I will remind him that he is the closest thing we have to a father living on this earth. At no point do I intend to make it easy for him to continue carrying out this betrayal. I intend to bathe the wretch in guilt, if it's at all possible to do so."

Emmanuel smiled and nodded. "You, sir, are a wise man

for your young years."

Boaz scoffed. "Alright, so let's get back to what can be done about Fletcher. He's been gone since Monday. We know Rasquelle had to have something to do with it!"

"And we've been through this already. What proof do you have?" said William.

"There ain't no definite proof," said Elliot. "We just have a hunch. I mean, my horse was tied out in the street not far from his warehouse. We knew Fletcher had talked about going there. What more proof do we need?"

"The problem is that Rasquelle has a solid alibi for that day," William argued. "You said it yourself. Constable Squires already questioned him about it."

The men all shook their heads in disbelief that no action could be taken against Rasquelle with what they already knew.

William sensed their frustration. "Please don't misunderstand me. I have no doubt that Richard Rasquelle could have had a hand in this boy's disappearance, but he never left his warehouse—he has witnesses who can place him there the whole day. And so far, no witnesses have come forward to say Adam had even been seen there."

"I think there is a witness who might've seen something," said Emmanuel, "but I very much doubt that he'd come forward."

"Who's that?" Boaz asked.

"Rasquelle's slave—that young lad who's out in front of his building sweeping every day," answered Emmanuel.

"Well, sadly, as far as implicating Rasquelle in any way, the word of a slave cannot be taken as proof of wrongdoing. You know that Negroes cannot legally appear as witnesses against white men in court."

Emmanuel rolled his eyes and grumbled in frustration.

"I wouldn't expect the poor lad to come forward. He's probably frightened of his master, anyway. That despicable man has already shown he possesses no moral compass."

"Are you quite certain the Fletcher boy wouldn't have just run away?" said William.

Emmanuel shook his head. "No, he would not have run away. Even if I didn't suspect him to be a faithful employee, I'd know he wouldn't leave, because of his mother. He loves her and is far too protective of her to just take off."

William nodded. "Very well. Men are already on the lookout for him, correct? Signs have been posted? A reward has been offered for information concerning his whereabouts?"

Everyone nodded.

"Well then," said William, "I'm afraid all we can do at this point is wait and pray the boy turns up. Meanwhile, we need to begin preparations for court, Emmanuel."

"What will that involve?" asked the old man.

"I'm going to ask you several questions as though I wanted to prove your guilt, and it will be your job to answer them in a clear, truthful way that will not call your honesty or integrity into question. Do you understand?"

Emmanuel gave a slow nod.

"Would you please state your full name for the record, sir?"

"Emmanuel Rogers."

"What is your date of birth?"

"I was born on the twenty-seventh of November, 1697."

"For the record, what is your age?"

Emmanuel looked at William as if to say, *Do the math!*

"Please answer the question, sir," said William.

"I'm sixty-seven years old. If the Lord permits me to live

until November 27, I shall be sixty-eight."

"Very good then. At what age did you first begin working in the shipping trade?"

Emmanuel thought for a moment. "I worked some with my father as a lad, but I didn't become a merchant in my own right until about 1725."

"Please, sir," said William, "only answer the questions that have been put to you. You mustn't volunteer information if it is not required of you."

The old man nodded. "Alright then. Get on with it."

"Very well. What was your age when you first established your shipping company?"

"I was about twenty-seven, I think. Or maybe twenty-eight."

William nodded in praise. He could tell Emmanuel was tempted to say more regarding that question, but he restrained himself and only gave his age, as that was all that was asked of him.

Their mock trial continued on for more than an hour, when finally Emmanuel grew tired of it.

"What are your expectations, William?" said a somber Emmanuel.

"My expectations? Regarding what specifically?"

"This trial. These charges."

William looked down at his fingers, which were crossed on the table in front of him. He hesitated before answering. "Emmanuel, I've known you my whole life. My father counted you among his closest friends, so you know that I value your trust in me and would never lie to you or be intentionally dishonest in any way."

"I know these things, William, but what? Just tell me."

"I'm afraid this is a very grim situation. It would take a miracle at this point to see you acquitted, because as soon as Rasquelle realizes that the Crown has no evidence from your own warehouse, he will surely reveal his knowledge about the second dock, and then it will only be a question of whether we will come up with some way to discredit him or conceal the cargo before the inspectors search our family's estate. Considering Absalom Reading's role in this complicates matters a great deal. If we do anything right now to implicate him, he will likely turn quickly and tell everything he knows from decades of covering for your shipping activities at my father's house to the Crown's attorney just to obtain a plea bargain for himself. We still don't know what exactly he hoped to gain from whatever deal he'd concocted with Richard Rasquelle."

"And maybe now that Rasquelle has his information from Reading, he may not even find him so useful anymore," said Boaz. "In fact, I can't really think of any reason why Rasquelle would want to continue to protect Reading."

"Goodness gracious," said Emmanuel. "This is a very grim situation indeed."

Chapter Thirty-Four

THE SYMPTOMS HAD started slowly. First, there was the sore neck early Thursday morning. By the next day it was much more painful. And by Saturday, fever had set in, followed by nausea and vomiting, accompanied by a pounding headache. Adam knew the bite on his neck had to be the cause. By Saturday evening he had lost all energy and was overwhelmed with fatigue.

When he woke up Sunday morning, his muscles felt weak, his joints felt sore, and all he could do was lie still. Occasionally, he was having muscle cramps, which radiated down from his neck into his shoulder and out to his arm, chest, and back. He was dehydrated, so his eyes and mouth felt dry.

I'm dying, he thought.

In fact, he nearly wished for death. He had never felt so awful. He was so thirsty, but he didn't even feel like going over to his beach well to get some water. Instead he remained next to his signal fire and prayed for rain. On this clear morning, he doubted it would come, but at least he had some big shells within arm's reach that he could drink from if it did. *Maybe if I just rest,* he thought, *I can crawl over to the well later and get some water.* But for now he was too tired to think about that. He just needed to rest . . .

Chapter Thirty-Five

WILLIAM MARTIN SPENT the rest of the weekend with Emmanuel, trying to help him prepare for court on Monday. As they continued rehearsing his answers, and as William formulated a line of questioning for Rasquelle, they began to feel the slightest glimmer of hope, though it still seemed a remote chance Emmanuel and his company would come through the situation unscathed.

They rested from trial practice on Sunday. Emmanuel insisted as always that the men in his company attend church. This week would be no exception.

Since the whole town knew by now of Adam Fletcher's disappearance, the Reverend George Miller led his congregation in prayer for the boy's safe return. For at least the short duration of the church service, the tongues of the townspeople who had speculated wildly about what had happened to Adam were silenced. Local gossips had been making every kind of assumption imaginable about what had happened. Some suggested he had run away because of his master's cruelty, which was of course laughable to anyone who actually knew Emmanuel Rogers.

One story floating around insisted that he had gotten drunk in the tavern, then fallen in the creek and drowned. A particularly lurid tale was invented by one of the tavern regulars, who said that since he'd heard Adam's mother was a prostitute, the boy surely must've run off with a band of pirates to escape the shame and embarrassment.

The truth was no one knew where he was, or even if he was still alive. Local sailors and fishermen were encouraged to keep their eyes open in case they spotted Adam anywhere—in a worst-case scenario, floating in the water or washed up on the banks.

Mary couldn't eat. She was sick at the idea of losing her boy. She couldn't, or wouldn't, believe he was dead, though. She knew he was alive, even while she feared the worst.

At first Valentine offered her some time off. Then he decided she was better off working. It helped keep her mind busy, which meant less time to think about all of the awful possibilities of what might have happened to her son.

Chapter Thirty-Six

O N SUNDAY AFTERNOON, Adam was awakened when drops of rain began to fall on his face. His throat burned and his mouth felt rusted shut when he tried to open it in anticipation of some sweet relief. The refreshing rain fell slowly at first and then started pouring down, allowing him to get the first decent bit of water he'd had since he was marooned on the island.

He looked at the shells that were nearby. They were catching some rain but not much. He cupped his hands to catch as much as he could, then weakly pressed his hands to his mouth to drink. Now he had a new problem. His campfire would go out if he didn't think fast. But his brain wasn't working quickly. He felt like he was stuck in a dream. His surroundings seemed unreal, and he was unable to control his limbs very well.

Still, he was able to think through the fact that there was

a little cluster of trees not far from his fire, so he determined he would move it somehow. Adrenaline gave him enough energy to grab the bundle of wood he'd collected to have near his fire and pull it back under the trees. Then, using a long stick and a large shell, he scooped some embers out of the fire and lifted them over to the bundle of dry wood under the trees. He added as much dry seagrass as he could find and blew on it all until he was able to get new flames going. Then he crawled back over to his original fire and tried grabbing the sticks along the edge of the flames with a couple of pieces of green wood, and moved them over to his new small fire in the grove. He continued to do this until he had moved most of the wood surrounding the fire, and the flames began to die down. He then used the bottom of his boot to try and scoot the remaining pieces of wood over to the grove to add to his new fire, but a couple of them were just too hot.

Finally, he abandoned the remnants of his first fire and concentrated his efforts on building up the new fire and keeping it sheltered. He draped his shirt across two sticks he thrust down into the ground to shield his fire from the rain that was being blown into the grove by the wind. Fortunately, the live oak under which he had assembled this new fire provided adequate shelter from the rain that might blow in as the wind shifted.

He looked around him to see how his shells were doing gathering water. When he moved his head from side to side, he felt dizzy. Still, he was able to see that the shells placed out in the open rain were too small to hold water very well. Instead, it splashed out as the heavy raindrops hit the surface. He mustered up enough energy to gather as many conchs and large scallop shells as he could place around him and set them out strategically under tree branches that were dripping water at a steady pace.

Having had several days to accustom himself to the

limited catalog of sounds present on the island, Adam was suddenly startled by a new noise. He had just started to drift off to sleep again by his fire when he heard a shuffling noise some distance away. It seemed to be getting closer, and he soon realized it sounded like footsteps.

Dear God, please don't let that be Rasquelle's men, he silently prayed. He raised himself up to look around to see who or what might be out there. He tried to console himself. *Maybe it's just deer*, he thought. *No, probably not.* He hadn't seen any deer since he'd been on the island. *Alright, then, maybe it's raccoons.*

He thought about it for a moment. *No, it can't be raccoons. Raccoons don't come out in the daytime.* He wondered if he was just imagining things. Then he realized he was too exhausted to care.

He gave up thinking about it and decided to lie back down and sleep. That's all he wanted—sleep. His eyelids felt so, so heavy. And it was so hard trying holding his head up.

At this point, he didn't care what the sound was—even if it was Rasquelle's men. *Worst thing that could happen is they could kill me*, he thought. *But at least then I'd be in heaven, and that's got to be better than this.*

Chapter Thirty-Seven

THERE WAS ONE person in Beaufort who hadn't expected to be as distraught as she was about Adam's disappearance: Laney Martin.

The last time she saw Adam had been on Tuesday morning. That was the last time anybody had seen the boy, but it overwhelmed her with worry to know that she and Mr. Reading were the last two people in town who had acknowledged seeing him alive. She realized that what may have been the last act he committed in his life was one of bravery when he came to warn her about Emmanuel's arrest. And to think she might never even be able to thank him made her feel guilty beyond belief.

Rationally, she knew it wasn't her fault—whatever had happened to him—but still, she wished she had treated him better when she'd seen him. Now she'd have to live with herself knowing she treated him so coldly in spite of her true feelings, which she was only just beginning to realize.

The truth was, she felt attracted to him—she had since the day they met—but she knew that there could never be anything between them. He was not a suitable prospect for her—not by any stretch of the imagination. She feared if she received him warmly, her feelings might become transparent, and Adam might think he had a chance. She didn't want to lead him on, nor did she want to risk allowing her heart to slip into a maelstrom of affection that she knew she wouldn't likely be able to control.

No one was surprised that Adam's mother had been unable to eat since she'd learned of his disappearance, but both Laney's brother, Will, and Absalom Reading were stunned to see Laney displaying similar behaviors. She just stared blankly out the window of the parlor, where she had shared the settee with Adam two weeks earlier.

Will stood in the doorway. "You have to eat something. You look dreadful."

She said nothing.

He continued: "Aunt Celie is worried about you. You know she'll make you whatever you want. Just tell me. She says you won't even take broth."

Laney finally turned and looked at her brother. "You never met him, Will. He was a good boy, you know. I just pray that nothing has happened to him. If only he hadn't come here to warn us . . ." She began to weep.

Will rushed over to comfort his sister. He put his arm around her shoulders and drew her close, planting a kiss on the top of her head. "I don't think it would've made a bit of difference," he said. "All evidence suggests he made it back to town. So whatever happened to him could've just as easily happened without the benefit of him making a trip to this estate."

She wanted to tell her brother how she felt about Adam. And she wanted him to tell her that her feelings were understandable, that they were acceptable, but she knew he would never approve of her interest in a boy like that. So instead she said nothing.

"You know they have to find him," Will said. "We've got every fisherman, every pilot, every man in every boat of every size—they're all looking for him. If he's out there, we'll find him."

"That 'if' is such a big word," said Laney. "If he's out there, fine, but what if he's not? What happened to him? Will we ever even know? If somebody in this town hurt him, are they still out there? And will they ever be punished?"

William leaned back and took his sister's delicate hands into his own. "They will if I have anything to do with it. I'll make sure if—no, when—they find out who did this, he is punished to the fullest extent of the law."

Laney dabbed her eyes with the wrinkled handkerchief she had been clutching in her hand. She was able to muster a weak smile for her brother.

"Would you like to come with us into town when we go to court tomorrow? I can introduce you to the boy's mother. Maybe the two of you can visit with one another for a little while if she's not too busy working. I hear she's understandably very distressed. Perhaps you can find a way to offer her a bit of encouragement and good cheer."

"I'd like that," she said. "Does that mean you'll let me go to the tavern?"

"Not a chance," he responded. "But I'll see if Mr. Hodges will let her have a little bit of time off to visit with you elsewhere. Perhaps a nice walk down by the shore. I've heard he's been very lenient with her schedule of late."

Fine, she thought. *We'll be able to cry on each other's shoulders. I'll be glad to have at least met Adam's mother.* But all she said was, "Sounds lovely."

"Good then," he said. "So will you eat something now?"

She took a deep breath and gave a reluctant nod.

Chapter Thirty-Eight

ADAM'S HEAD WAS still pounding when he woke up to the unmistakable rocking of a ship at sea. His vision was blurred, but he was able to adjust his eyes enough to look around and observe the men at work around him. He recognized their uniforms and quickly realized he was on board one of His Majesty's vessels. He didn't remain conscious for long at first. His pulse had become so weak that at one point the ship's physician feared he might not survive.

Not long after he'd been brought on board the vessel, one of the officials came down to see their latest rescue. He immediately recognized the boy, although he had never actually met him. He instructed the physician that under no circumstances was he to tell the boy where exactly, he was. In fact, if the boy came to, the physician was instructed only to tell him that he was on a naval vessel on a special task for the Crown, and to urge him to explain how he'd come to be stranded. The official feared that if the boy saw him or knew the vessel he was on, he might not be forthcoming, for fear of repercussions.

Around four in the afternoon, Adam was awakened by loud cracks of thunder and what sounded like a torrential downpour.

"Where am I?" asked Adam, his voice weak.

"You are aboard one of His Majesty's ships in service to the Royal Navy."

Adam nodded. He felt a little dizzy, but at least he didn't feel as sick to his stomach. He told the physician he'd been stranded for a week. When the physician asked him when he began to feel unwell, Adam told him about falling asleep on the ground in the forest and being bitten by something.

"Yes, I figured as much," said the physician. "I noticed these marks on your neck." The physician leaned forward and gently touched Adam near the place where his bite wound was. "I believe you've had a spider bite. A very serious one, in fact. You didn't see it?"

Adam shook his head. "No, sir. It must've bit me while I was sleeping."

He then explained about how he'd been getting his food and water, but that he had not really been able to eat or drink anything for a couple of days because he'd been sick.

The physician replied, "Worry not, dear boy. I have been treating you with paregoric elixir. Now we just need to get some fluids in you and something to eat. Are you well enough to speak with me for a little while?"

"Yes, sir. I reckon so."

"Very good," said the physician. "If at any time you feel unwell, like you can't bear to talk anymore and you need to rest, simply say so, alright? I've sent for someone to bring you some sustenance."

The boy nodded.

"Well, as you might imagine, young man, you caused us quite a scare. We certainly didn't anticipate finding one of His Majesty's subjects marooned on an island on the Carolina coast. We do have a few questions for you, if you don't mind me asking them."

Adam shook his head. "No, that's fine."

"First thing we'd like to know is your name and age, as well as where you are from, so we can get you home."

"My name is Adam Fletcher, sir. I'm seventeen years old and I'm from Port Beaufort in Carteret County."

"Very well. And how is it you came to be stranded on that island?"

"It's a long story, sir, but I'll try to tell you," said Adam.

He proceeded to tell the doctor about everything, from how he came to be marooned all the way up through to the present day. It was a struggle for him to talk because his throat was so sore, but the doctor listened most intently, taking copious notes as quickly as he could write them down as the boy made his account.

When they were done talking, the physician stood beside Adam's bed and said, "I think you will be alright, Mr. Fletcher. You just rest here. I'm not sure if the weather will allow us to make it back to town tonight, but I'll go and speak with someone about that right now."

Adam nodded. Just then one of the men who worked in the galley brought him a tray with some food and drink. The physician excused himself and said he'd be back to check on him again shortly. He went to the quarters of the official who'd requested the interrogation and he reported all that Adam had told him. The official immediately sent instructions to the captain to get them back to Beaufort. He urged the captain and his crew to make haste. Nightfall would soon be upon them and what he had to do couldn't wait until morning.

The captain said he was skeptical they'd make it back that night. The storm would make for tricky sailing in the treacherous shoals along the Beaufort coast.

Chapter Thirty-Nine

B RIGHT AND EARLY Monday morning, Will and Laney arrived in town. It was Will's intention to stop by the Topsail Tavern briefly before he met Emmanuel and company over at the courthouse.

"You just wait here," said Will. His sister smiled and nodded as he climbed out of the carriage and informed the coachman he'd be back momentarily.

Laney was wearing a lovely, but simple, pale peach gown. The color was brighter than her mood, but she had thought it looked like an optimistic color, and she hoped it might be more pleasant for Miss Fletcher than if she had chosen to wear a darker dress. As she sat and waited, she began to feel silly, wondering if Adam's mother would even want to meet her, much less spend a few hours with her.

Within a few moments, Will came back out to the carriage.

He climbed inside and told his sister, "Miss Fletcher would like to meet you—said she would enjoy the company—but, sadly, she's not up for leaving the tavern. You know I would never want you to hang around a place like this. However, given the circumstances, I think it would be a kind act of Christian charity if you felt comfortable enough to go inside and visit with Miss Fletcher up in her quarters. Would you find that acceptable?"

Laney nodded. "Of course. I'd be happy to."

William smiled and exited the carriage. He helped his sister step out and then led her into the tavern. Even though it was only seven thirty, the place was packed with its breakfast regulars—mostly men who worked down at the boatbuilding shop or in the businesses nearby.

"Miss Fletcher, I'd like to introduce you to my sister, Rocksolanah."

Mary smiled and gave a little curtsy. "How do you do, miss?"

"Rocksolanah, this is Miss Fletcher, Adam's mother."

"I'm so very pleased to meet you, ma'am," said Laney with a nod.

"Well, ladies, I'll leave you two to visit for a while. Laney, I will come and collect you directly after court."

Laney nodded.

"Good luck," said Mary.

"Thank you, ma'am." He smiled and gave a nod before he left the tavern.

"Well, Miss Rocksolanah—"

"Please, ma'am, call me Laney. All of my friends and family do."

Mary smiled and nodded in deference to her request. "Alright, Miss Laney. How about I prepare a pot of tea for us and we can take it to my quarters?"

Laney nodded. "Yes, ma'am. I'd like that."

"Would you like to wait here, or would you rather wait upstairs?" Mary asked.

Laney knew her brother would insist she go on upstairs to wait. He wouldn't want her sitting in a tavern full of men. It wouldn't look appropriate, he'd say. But she didn't care. "I'll wait right here," she said as she took a seat on one of the bar stools.

Valentine looked at Laney and reflexively was about to ask her if he could get her anything when he thought better of it. He just gave her an awkward smile. She smiled back.

This feels strange, she thought, *sitting here waiting at a bar. What will people say?*

Just then there came sounds of a flurry of activity in the kitchen. Laney thought she heard Mary cry out. Valentine darted from behind the bar through the kitchen door to see what was happening. Laney wanted to follow but feared it would be improper behavior. *What is happening back there?* she wondered.

Within a couple of moments, Valentine came back out of the kitchen and said to Laney, "Miss, you need to get on upstairs. Go on. It's the first door at the top of the stairs."

Laney gave him a worried look.

"It's alright," he said. "Don't worry. Just get on up there. Miss Fletcher's up there. She went up the back stairs from the kitchen."

Laney hopped down from the bar stool and ran up the stairs, still unsure of what was going on.

◊◊◊

THE PORT BEAUFORT VICE-ADMIRALTY Court didn't convene

regularly, but when it did the whole town knew about it.

Emmanuel and his contingent arrived early. Ordinarily, Emmanuel always liked being prompt, but on this day, anxiety was working on him as he watched the various officials of the court scurrying around making preparations for the trial to begin.

Suddenly a man entered the doors to the courtroom where the trial was about to take place and raised his hand in order to catch the attention of the court officer. The officer motioned for him to come forward. The man swiftly walked down the aisle and began speaking in a hushed voice to the officer.

All participants were already in their seats and ready for proceedings to begin. William Martin and his client, Emmanuel, wondered if the man who'd just darted in was working for the Crown. The barrister for the prosecution, Alistair Bird, wondered if he was working for the defense. To both parties' surprise, the man was quickly ushered into the judge's chambers. After a few moments, the man scurried back out.

The marshall then took his place near the bench. A hush fell over the courtroom. He called out, "God save the King and his honorable court!"

Everyone responded in unison, "God save the King!"

At that moment, the vice-admiralty-court justice exited his chambers and appeared in the courtroom.

"All rise," said the marshall.

Everyone stood and watched as the judge stepped up to his place on the bench.

The marshall continued: "The Honorable Justice of the Court of Vice-Admiralty of Great Britain. Oyez! Oyez! Oyez! All persons having business before the Honorable Court of Vice-Admiralty of Great Britain at Port Beaufort, Justice James B. Simpkins presiding, are admonished to draw near and give their attention, for the court is now in session."

Justice Simpkins said, "Please be seated."

Afterward, more procedural instructions were given, and the attorneys for both the Crown and the defense were introduced. The charges were read against Emmanuel, and then the first witness was called to the bench.

Alistair Bird began his side of the proceedings by questioning the Crown's only witness.

"Would you please state your full name for the court?"

"Richard Rasquelle."

"And would you tell us your age?"

"I'm thirty-two years old."

"What business are you in, Mr. Rasquelle?"

"I'm a shipping merchant."

"How long have you been in that business, sir?"

"In Beaufort? About two years."

"Two years. So that means you came here in spring of 1763?"

"Yes, sir," Rasquelle answered.

Just then a representative from Ellison Smythe's office passed a note to Mr. Bird. As Mr. Bird read the note, he wrinkled his brow and appeared to whisper something to the man who had handed him the note. "This is a bit unorthodox, don't you think?" he was overheard saying.

The other man just nodded and encouraged Mr. Bird to proceed with the questions on the paper.

"Mr. Rasquelle, this might seem out of place in this particular trial, but I'd like to ask you for a moment about a few things, if that's alright."

Rasquelle crossed one leg over another and rested his hands on his knees as he nodded. "Of course."

"Very well. You're thought of as a bit of a hero in this town, is that right?"

William Martin was incensed. "Objection! This line of questioning is irrelevant."

"Overruled. Please continue," said Justice Simpkins.

William's eyes grew wide and he turned back and looked at Emmanuel. He shrugged his shoulders to emphasize the fact that this was highly unusual for these sorts of proceedings.

Mr. Bird continued with his questioning.

"Would you tell us a little bit about how it came to be that you earned that reputation—of being a hero, that is—in this town?"

"Oh, I'm not sure that the defense team wants to hear about that," said Rasquelle, feigning modesty.

"Please indulge the court, sir," said Mr. Bird.

Rasquelle took a deep breath and then said, "Well, since you asked . . . Shortly after I first arrived in this town, I assisted with the rescue of a vessel that was sinking just a few miles off-shore. Nothing special really. Anyone with an ounce of decency would've done the same."

"My, that certainly is heroic," said Mr. Bird. "And what was the name of that vessel, sir? Do you recall?"

Rasquelle nodded. "Of course I do. How could I forget something like that? It was called the *Sea Sprite*."

"Indeed," said Mr. Bird. "And it just so happens that you've recently had occasion to assist another vessel in distress. Is that right?"

"Yes, sir," said Rasquelle. "Just a little over a week ago, in fact."

"That's wonderful to hear. Were you able to help with the rescue of the passengers on board? I heard there were mostly women and children."

Rasquelle smiled. "Actually, sir, we assisted with attempting to salvage the cargo so that the customs sloop could facilitate the rescue of the passengers."

"I see," said Mr. Bird. "So the passengers were assisted by HMS *Hornet*, and your men helped with salvaging the cargo that would've surely been lost at sea had you not been able to come to the aid of this sinking vessel. Is that right?"

"I'm afraid so," said Rasquelle.

"And when these rescues happen, sir, where do your men take the salvaged cargo?"

"We take it straightaway to the storage warehouse owned by the local customs office."

"Very good. And this is standard procedure. There are never any reasons to deviate from this practice, correct?"

Rasquelle furrowed his brow, unsure of where this line of questioning was headed. "I would say that is standard procedure, sir. But if you don't mind, sir, we're here today to discuss the case of Emmanuel Rogers. If I won't be needed in that capacity, I really have a great deal of work to do."

Mr. Bird nodded. "Certainly, Mr. Rasquelle. I understand. Not to worry. I only have a couple more questions here, and I assure you that will be the last of this particular series of questions. At that point we'll get right to the Crown's case against Mr. Emmanuel Rogers."

Rasquelle nodded and impatiently waited for the last questions.

"Mr. Rasquelle, would you tell the court the name of the vessel you recently assisted?"

"I believe she was called the *Mary Belle*."

"And do you recall the mark on the cargo that your men

salvaged from the *Mary Belle*?"

The color quickly left Rasquelle's face, just as it had on the day Adam asked him about the barrels in his high-security storage room at the warehouse.

"Mr. Rasquelle, let me ask you again. Do you recall the mark on the cargo that your men salvaged from the *Mary Belle*?"

"Ah, no, sir. I'm afraid I don't recall the mark on that particular cargo. We work with so much cargo every day—it's hard to remember what's what."

"Certainly, I understand," said Mr. Bird. "Perhaps we can make this a bit easier."

Just then several men from the Royal Navy rolled into the courtroom three barrels and set them up in front of the bench.

"Mr. Rasquelle," said Mr. Bird. "Would you say the mark on the cargo of the *Mary Belle* looked anything like the marks found on these casks here?"

Richard Rasquelle peered over the box and looked at the barrels lined up in front of him on the floor.

"Yes, sir. Yes, I believe those casks must be from the *Mary Belle*. That mark does look familiar now that I see it in front of me."

"Do you know anything about these casks, Mr. Rasquelle?" asked Mr. Bird.

Richard Rasquelle shook his head. "I don't recall, sir, but they're clearly from the cargo of the *Mary Belle*. I'm assuming these are from the storage facility where all the cargo was stored after the rescue."

"Thank you, Mr. Rasquelle. I have no further questions."

"Permission to approach the bench, Your Honor," said William Martin.

"Permission granted," said Justice Simpkins. "Mr. Bird,

I'd also like you to approach the bench."

"Yes, Your Honor," said Mr. Bird.

Another anxious moment or two passed while the judge arranged some documents on his desk, then motioned for an assistant to approach the bench, to whom he whispered some brief conversation.

After the assistant left the bench and made his way out of the courtroom, Alistair Bird said, "Your Honor, I apologize, but I was handed a note just before I began my questioning and I had not had the opportunity to review it."

"I'd like to know the meaning of all of this, Your Honor," said William Martin. "I don't have much experience in vice-admiralty court, I'll admit, but I've never seen anything like what just happened."

"Gentlemen," said the justice, "just moments before this trial began I received word that earlier this very day a sloop arrived in Beaufort carrying His Majesty's Customs Inspector Edward Sheffield, and he has uncovered some troubling information. It appears that the *Hornet* recently discovered a young man who had been marooned on an island not too many miles from here. He was abandoned there on the orders of Mr. Bird's witness, Richard Rasquelle."

Alistair Bird and William Martin were stunned.

"Is it Adam Fletcher, Your Honor?" said William.

"The name of the young man was not given," said the justice, "but we do know that he provided detailed information about Mr. Rasquelle, and it was brought to our attention that his warehouse has been housing a portion of cargo from the recently unfortunate vessel, the *Mary Belle*, which was said to have been lost at sea. A fact which Inspector Sheffield and his team have recently verified."

"So why are we continuing this trial, Your Honor?" asked Mr. Bird. "Are we going to arrest Mr. Rasquelle?"

"I believe an arrest is forthcoming," said Justice Simpkins. "He was allowed to take the stand today to see if he'd acknowledge a particular case of wrongdoing on his part, and unfortunately he failed and has, in turn, perjured himself."

Both Mr. Bird and Mr. Martin gave the judge a puzzled look.

The justice explained: "Mr. Rasquelle sent crew out with his company's sloop to help the rescue effort when the *Mary Belle* was taking water. Apparently, on Rasquelle's instructions, his men offered to help recover as much of the cargo as possible while the customs ship assisted the passengers on board. When all were brought back to this port, Mr. Rasquelle's men claimed a substantial quantity of cargo was lost to the tides, but apparently that was untrue. The casks were, in fact, recovered by Rasquelle's crew and simply stored in a separate compartment of the vessel. Now there is some suspicion he may have used this same tactic with the *Sea Sprite*—the rescue he performed a couple of years ago."

"You know what this means, don't you, Mr. Bird?" said William.

Bird grimaced. He knew, but William was going to tell him, anyway.

"Your chief witness—your only witness—has just been thoroughly discredited. I think the only reasonable action to take at this point is to dismiss the charges against my client and focus on your own client, who we now know is as guilty as sin."

Bird nodded. "I agree with him, Your Honor. The charges against Emmanuel Rogers were based wholly on the sworn testimony of Richard Rasquelle. If he has now been discredited as a witness, we have no case."

The two attorneys were instructed to return to their seats.

The judge tapped his gavel against the bench. "In light of evidence that has been brought to the court this morning, the Crown's charges against Emmanuel Rogers are now dismissed. I'd like Mr. Richard Rasquelle to report to the marshall's office, where, I believe, Inspector Edward Sheffield is awaiting a meeting."

Emmanuel's eyes grew wide and his mouth dropped open. No one could believe what had just happened, but William patted Emmanuel on the back and said, "I think your boy Fletcher may have saved the day."

Chapter Forty

INSPECTOR SHEFFIELD WAS awaiting Richard Rasquelle in the marshall's office of the vice-admiralty court, along with Port Beaufort customs agent Ellison Smythe.

As soon as Rasquelle entered the room, Sheffield nodded at Smythe, who then unfolded a document which had been in his pocket and began to read aloud. "Richard Rasquelle, you are hereby under arrest for conspiring to deceive His Majesty's appointed representatives serving in the British Customs Agency, as well as the captain and crew of the *Mary Belle*."

"What's the meaning of this?" asked the young merchant. He quickly looked back over each shoulder as two guards seized him and placed him in irons.

"I have done nothing wrong," Rasquelle insisted. "What do you say is my crime? Give me an opportunity to address your accusations. I'm sure there is a reasonable explanation."

"Of that I have no doubt," said Smythe. "And you will have your opportunity to provide your explanations—any that you are able to concoct—when you appear before the vice-admiralty-court judge."

"I still have a right to know the charges I am facing," Rasquelle demanded.

"Theft of cargo belonging to the *Mary Belle*, perjury, and then there is your role as conspirator to kidnapping—just for a start. Shall I continue?"

Rasquelle's face twisted up. "You can't prove I have done any of those things. Who has accused me of committing such abhorrent acts?"

"*I* am accusing you," said Sheffield. "You know a young man who lives in this town called Adam Fletcher, of course."

Rasquelle's face fell.

"Some of our men ran into him yesterday," said Sheffield.

Rasquelle swallowed hard. "Is that so?"

Sheffield nodded. "Indeed it is."

"Don't know the boy very well, but it seems I heard he was missing. How's he doing?" said Rasquelle.

"Funny you should ask such a question," said Smythe. "Other than resting and attempting to recover from having been dumped on an island and left to defend against the elements for nearly a week without food or water, I'd say he's doing quite well."

"I have no idea what you're talking about."

"I think we all know that you know exactly what I'm talking about. As our men were bringing him into town, he explained everything that had happened, as well as what we'd find if we came and searched your warehouse."

"You're free to search my warehouse now," said Rasquelle. "Have a look."

"Ah," said Smythe, "I thank you for your willingness to expedite the delivery of justice. However, late last night Mr. Sheffield and I, along with several members of the Royal Navy, entered your warehouse by Writ of Assistance and found everything we were looking for. In fact, where do you think we got those casks that were rolled into the courtroom a few minutes ago?"

"You came into my warehouse last night?" Rasquelle was incensed. "You broke in?"

"Call it what you like, Mr. Rasquelle," said Smythe. "You are finished in this town."

"You don't understand," said Rasquelle. "I can explain everything."

"Fine," said Smythe. "And like I said, you'll get your chance in court. Meanwhile, it's the gaol for you."

Smythe nodded at the guards and signaled them to take Rasquelle into custody.

Chapter Forty-One

A S SOON AS court was dismissed, Emmanuel and company made a beeline for the Topsail Tavern. They knew if Adam really was back in town, he'd be there.

Sure enough, as soon as they set foot in the place, Valentine welcomed the men. "Congratulations, fellas. I reckon this means your troubles are behind you."

Emmanuel nodded. "By God's grace, yes they seem to be—for now, anyway. But more importantly, tell me something. Is the boy here?"

Valentine nodded. "He is. He was brought in by some men from the *Hornet* this morning. Poor boy had been marooned on an island a right good ways south of here by orders of Richard Rasquelle."

"Good Lord!" said Emmanuel. "Is he alright?"

"Apparently he got bit by something—they think it was

prob'ly a spider—a few days ago. Made him deathly sick—fever, dizziness, vomiting, all of it."

"How on earth did they find him?" said Boaz.

"They said they spotted a dark column of smoke coming from the island when they were patrolling the area. There wasn't any boat or ship docked nearby, so they figured they better check things out. They found him passed out there in a grove of trees near the shore, and so they placed him in care of the ship's physician until they were able to get him back to town. The doctor says he'll be checking back in on him before they set sail again, and then he'll turn him over to our town doc."

"Can we see him?" Emmanuel asked.

"I think maybe it's best if just one or two of you go up. He's real weak."

Emmanuel and Boaz knocked on the door of Mary's apartment.

"Come in," whispered Mary.

Adam was sleeping on his old bed in the corner of the little room. Laney and Mary had moved the chairs that were usually at the dining table over near Adam's bed and they were sitting there watching over him and visiting with one another.

"How is he?" said Emmanuel.

"Thank God he's going to be alright, I think," said Mary.

"Oh, Mary, I'm so sorry to have gotten him into this mess," said Emmanuel.

She nodded. "It's alright. My boy is home now. The doctor said it might be a couple of weeks before he's well—says it's a miracle he's not worse off, all things considered. I'm going to take care of him, get him healthy again, and that's all I care about."

"I understand completely. He's a hero, you know," said

the old man. "Your boy saved me. He saved a lot of people with his bravery."

Mary smiled.

"And you, Miss Rocksolanah, I reckon you've had a bit of an exciting morning with all that's gone on here, haven't you?"

Laney smiled and nodded. "I'm just thankful he's here and he's going to be fine. I never got a chance to tell him how much I appreciated his warnings—until today."

"Well, your brother will be here to take you home soon," said Emmanuel. "He's back at the courthouse right now taking care of some business."

Laney nodded. "That's fine. I'm just enjoying visiting with Miss Fletcher and Adam right now."

Emmanuel came over and stood near where Mary and Laney sat by Adam's bed. He put his hand on Mary's shoulder. "He's obviously been raised by a fine, virtuous woman. You have much to be proud of."

"Thank you," said Mary, "but I'm afraid I can't take credit for Adam's courage. If it would have been up to me, I'd have tried to talk him out of getting involved like he did. I reckon Providence had other plans, though."

Emmanuel nodded. "Well, I'm glad to hear he's doing alright. We'll leave him here to rest. Just let him know—"

Just then Adam lifted his head from the pillow on his bed. "Mr. Rogers?"

Emmanuel's face lit up. He looked at Mary for permission to speak to the boy. She nodded. The old man grabbed a chair that was nearby and brought it over next to the bed to sit down and talk to the patient.

"My dear boy! You're alright," he said.

Adam nodded. "I'm alright. My throat's sore, though," he

said in a gravelly whisper. "It got so dry."

"No need for you to speak," said Emmanuel. "I just want to tell you that I think your deeds were heroic, and I am forever indebted to you for your courage in trying to help me in my circumstances."

"Did everything turn out alright?" asked Adam.

Emmanuel nodded. "Indeed it did. The charges were all dismissed. And it appears that Richard Rasquelle has just been arrested."

"What about Reading?" Adam asked.

Laney's eyes grew wide. "Absalom? What about him?"

Emmanuel looked at Adam.

Adam said, "Will you tell her? I don't know that I can talk that much right now."

Emmanuel nodded. "Certainly."

He proceeded to explain what had happened with Adam sneaking into Rasquelle's warehouse and overhearing his conversation with Reading. He told her that Adam knew about Reading's part in the conspiracy to see Emmanuel arrested. He also explained that everyone had told Adam not to dare let Laney know that Absalom was involved.

"Why wouldn't you have wanted him to tell me?" asked Laney.

"I wanted to," said Adam, "but they were afraid you wouldn't be safe if you knew."

"We understood as long as Mr. Reading didn't realize we were aware of his involvement he'd just continue on with his guardianship duties as he always has in the past," said Emmanuel. "We were concerned that if he found out that you knew his plan, he might do something desperate."

"His plan? But what was his plan?" she asked.

"I think it's probably best if your brother discusses that with you," said Emmanuel.

Adam wasn't going to miss his chance to tell her what he'd heard.

"No, I'll tell you. I had wanted to tell you that morning, but . . ." He struggled to speak.

"Oh, Adam," said Laney, "it's alright. You don't have to."

"I do!" he strained. "Reading wanted you to take the fall for Mr. Roger's use of your estate as the second dock. He wanted you to face charges so he could rush in and rescue you. He thought he could position himself as your hero, and that he would somehow win your affection that way."

Emmanuel took a deep breath and shook his head. He wouldn't have advised Adam to tell Laney something so shocking, but the cat was out of the bag now.

Laney looked at Emmanuel to see if he'd verify what she'd just heard.

He looked at Adam, then back at her, then nodded his head. "I'm afraid it's all true, dear."

Laney sat in stunned silence.

"But please remember, dear," said Emmanuel, "you don't have to worry about that anymore. We know about his plot, and your brother won't let him do anything to harm you."

She considered all of the implications of what she had just learned. Finally, she said, "Adam Fletcher, if you hadn't been so brave, if you hadn't risked your life to go into Rasquelle's warehouse, you'd have never even overheard their conversation. We might still not know of Absalom's involvement with this plot. He would still be free to control my future. Adam, that means if anyone is my hero, you are."

Adam didn't know what to say. He hadn't meant to be

anyone's hero. He was just trying to do the right thing.

"So what happens to him now? Do we go to the authorities? Does my brother know about all of this?" said Laney.

"Yes, from what your brother has told us, Mr. Reading's involvement in this whole plot should lead to his arrest as well, as an accomplice to Richard Rasquelle. And you'll be happy to know that William has already drawn up papers to have Absalom Reading disqualified as your guardian, Miss Rocksolanah."

Adam smiled and lowered his head back onto the pillow.

"You rest now," said Emmanuel. "I want you to get well quickly. I have something I want to give you as a thank-you once you're all better."

"Alright." Adam smiled weakly. "Mr. Rogers, when I get back, will you teach me how to sail?"

"Ah, my boy, I have many great plans for you, many things I'd like to teach you."

Emmanuel smiled at Adam, then turned back to smile at Mary. "So long as your mother agrees, that is."

Mary nodded. "I'll send him by to see you as soon as his strength returns," she said.

"Miss Rocksolanah, we'll be happy to accompany you back over to the courthouse, if you'd like to meet your brother there," offered Boaz.

"No, thank you, Mr. Brooks. I think I'd like to stay here with Adam and his mother until my brother comes for me."

At that, Emmanuel and Boaz bade Adam, Mary, and Laney farewell.

Chapter Forty-Two

"WELCOME BACK, FLETCHER!" Everyone on the shipping floor cheered as the boy finally returned to the warehouse two weeks after the court victory.

Adam had a huge grin on his face at the warm welcome. "I reckon I ought to get kidnapped more often if it'll get me a welcome like this!"

"My boy!" exclaimed Emmanuel. "We're so happy you're back."

He approached Adam and gave him a big hug.

"Me too," said Adam. "Wasn't sure I would be back. Things were kind of rough there on that island for a while. Never thought I'd be happy to see a customs ship until I realized I'd been rescued by one."

"We all agree you're a hero, Fletcher," said Boaz, "but don't let it go to your head."

He laughed. The other men chuckled, too.

"Don't worry," said Adam. "I figure if I start to get too cocky, I can count on you to take me down a peg."

Boaz smiled and nodded.

"I have something for you, boy," said Emmanuel. He went over to a shelf in the warehouse, where he grabbed two packages. "Two things, actually," he said.

Adam raised his eyebrows. "What are these?"

"Open them," said Emmanuel. "You'll see."

Adam took the two objects over to the workbench and placed one on the benchtop while he opened the first—the smaller of the two objects. It was a gold pocket watch. Adam's jaw dropped. "Oh, Mr. Rogers. This is . . . Well, this is incredible. It looks so expensive . . . I can't take this."

"You can," said Emmanuel, "and you will. To start, it will ensure you will always know the correct time, so you have no excuse to be late for work."

Adam grinned, admiring the shiny gift. It wasn't brand-new. It was quite old, actually. Weathered and worn with a few scratches, but still in very good condition.

"Go on," said Emmanuel. "Open the other one."

Adam tore open the other piece of paper. There was a box inside with a small compass and a spyglass.

"This is too much," said Adam.

"Nonsense," said Emmanuel. "I'd have likely lost every-thing, not the least of which is my dignity, and a place of employment for all these men had it not been for your tenacity. I wanted to give you these items, which belonged to me when I was not much older than you, so you can always find your way and see clearly where you're headed."

"These are all wonderful, Mr. Rogers. Thank you so

much."

"Now," said Emmanuel, "I think one thing we've all seen is that you are surely capable of much more than just warehouse work. Not to mention you're a young man. Young men crave adventure, and if that desire is not honed and aimed in a right direction, it can lead a man astray."

"I don't understand, sir," said Adam.

Emmanuel smiled. "If you recall, I told you I had great plans for you."

Adam nodded.

"Well, sometime in the near future I'm going to want you to put to work these gifts I've given you. There is a voyage that my sloop will be making several months from now. Would you like to go?"

"Are you serious? You mean this winter?" said Adam. He was thrilled at the prospect.

The old man nodded. "I am. But it will take some intensive training between now and then to get you ready to go on a trip of that duration. Do you think you're up for it?"

"Yes, sir! I'd be grateful for the opportunity," said Adam.

"Good, then! So it's settled. You'll leave with the sloop just after it returns at summer's end."

"Great! Where will I be going? Charleston? Salem? Providence?"

"No," said Emmanuel. "You'll be going to Havana."

Chapter Forty-Three

"SOUNDS LIKE YOU got the hero's welcome today," said Mary. She smiled, grateful to have her son back and proud of what his courage achieved.

Adam smiled sheepishly. "I don't know about that, but everyone does seem pretty happy about how everything turned out."

"I'm still upset you got involved in all of it, but I have to admit I'm proud of you, to know that had it not been for what you did, and the information you were able to provide about Richard Rasquelle, he'd still be free to deceive everybody. And then poor Laney Martin—to hear about the plans her guardian had for her!"

"I know! It's all terrible. And to think I actually wanted to work for Richard Rasquelle," Adam exclaimed. "It's a good thing Mr. Robins put me with Mr. Rogers instead. By the way, you know what he told me today?"

Mary shook her head. "Who? Emmanuel? No, what did he say?"

"He's said he's going to be sending me out on his sloop in a few months!"

Mary's face fell. "He is? Already?"

"That's great news!" said Valentine, who had just returned from the kitchen to the bar. "Where'd he say he's sending you?"

"Havana! Can you believe it?" Adam beamed. "I'm going to the Caribbean!"

Mary and Valentine looked at each other with astonishment.

"Havana?" said Mary. "You can't go to Havana! It's out of the question!"

"Don't worry! I'll be fine. I'm really excited about this. It'll be a great adventure!"

Mary shot a look at Valentine. He just shrugged his shoulders and then set to work cleaning up the bar.

"When did you say this is supposed to happen?" she asked.

"Emmanuel says we'll be leaving not long after the *Gypsy* gets back," said Adam. "We're just waiting for it to arrive so we can off-load everything, then get the ship ready to load up again with local cargo for the West Indies. That, and he wants to get me trained up on some things before we set sail."

"And how long will you be gone?"

"I'm not sure exactly," said Adam, "but it will be a few months."

"Is Emmanuel going?"

"No, at least I doubt he'd be going. I'd be sailing under Captain Phillips—but Martin, he'll be going.

"I don't know about this," said Mary. "I don't want you to go. That's too far, and it could be dangerous. I just about lost you once already. And now you're telling me this?" She threw up her hands, exasperated. "I can't take thinking about this right now."

"This is a great chance for me. It'll help me start learning a whole new side of the shipping business—far more than I could ever learn just staying at the warehouse here in Beaufort."

"There are other places you can go. You don't need to go all the way to Havana. You haven't even been outside of this colony, for goodness sake!"

"I know you want me to stay close, but this is just part of the industry. This can be a really big chance for me. I don't want to be at sea all the time, but I do need to learn about it if I'm training as a merchant."

As he observed Mary's reaction to the news, he recognized the telltale signs of her trying to restrain her emotions.

"Listen, I know you'll miss me," he said, attempting to calm her fears, "but I'll be back. I promise! And when I am, I'll bring you the most wonderful gifts."

Mary suddenly burst into tears. She shot a desperate look at Valentine, then took off up the stairs.

"What in the world was that about?" Adam asked Valentine.

The tavern keeper stopped wiping the counter and looked at Adam. He started to say something but stopped short.

"What is it?" said Adam. "I know she's my mother. I know she'll miss me, but you know how it is. We're men. We have to do these things."

"Son," said Valentine. He took a deep breath and braced himself on the counter before speaking. "It ain't just that your mama's gonna miss you. She will miss you, but that ain't what this is about."

"What is it, then?"

"She remembers somebody else who once left for Havana and promised to come back, but never did."

Adam furrowed his brow. "Who?"

"Your father."

<<<<>>>>

Acknowledgements

FIRST AND FOREMOST, *I give thanks to God.* I know that it's only by His grace that I was able to write and publish this novel. To Mama— Thank you for believing in me. I am blessed to have been raised up under your covering of prayers, love, and encouragement. You've always made me feel like I could accomplish anything, and for that I am truly grateful. To Daddy—Whether you meant to or not, you have been helping me prepare to be an independent author ever since I was a little girl. The vast array of opportunities and resources you've provided me over the years have helped me learn to handle just about every aspect of this book's production myself. For that, I sincerely thank you. To Terrance—We've been friends now for well over a decade. In that time, I have learned so much from you about what it means to be an author, as well as how the publishing industry works. I want you to know how much I appreciate your advice, your encouragement, *and* your reality checks. To Sam—Anyone who reads this novel owes you a big "thank you." People don't know how utterly awful a first draft can be, and our thorough and candid discussions after you read the earliest version of this novel played a big role in helping me shape several characters and smooth out some sticky plot points. Thank you for never tiring of being one of my key story consultants, especially regarding the legal aspects of colonial-era smuggling. To Rey—I'm grateful to you for your constant encouragement, not just about this novel, but about so many things. I also want to thank you for helping to make sure my Spanish is correct in this story. To Kevin—I appreciate your friendship and your advice. You are a historian and researcher I greatly respect, and I thank you for always being willing to answer my seemingly endless list of questions. You know how getting the historical details right is important to me and your input has helped me achieve that with *The Smuggler's Gambit*. To Marcus Trower—I am grateful that you were my copy editor for this novel. Not only did you help ensure that the manuscript was cleanly edited, but you also offered some brilliant suggestions that helped enrich the story. Thank you. To Kristy Acevedo and my friends and fellow writers in the WritingChallenge.org community—Thank you for being a daily source of motivation and encouragement as I was banging out the first draft of this novel. I also want express my appreciation to historians Victor T. Jones, Alan D. Watson, and Charles L. Paul for researching, documenting, and preserving our regional history, as well as the Kellenberger Room at New Bern-Craven County Public Library, the North Carolina Division of Archives and History, the Carteret County Public Library at Beaufort, and the North Carolina Maritime Museum at Beaufort for making our history easily accessible. And last, but certainly not least, I'd like to express my gratitude to three individuals who were the most enthusiastic and public supporters of this book long before its release: Mike and Sherry Morris and Phil Molloy—Thank you from the bottom of my heart. I hope it was worth the wait.

—S.D.G.—

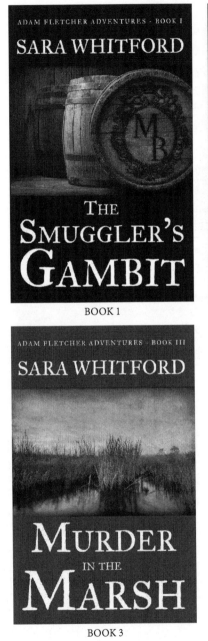